LOVE LIKE POISON

CORSICAN CRIME LORD, BOOK ONE

CHARMAINE PAULS

Published by Charmaine Pauls

Montpellier, 34090, France

www.charmainepauls.com

Published in France

This is a work of fiction. Names, characters, and incidents depicted in this book are products of the author's imagination or are used fictitiously. Any resemblance to actual events, locales, organizations, or persons, living or dead, is entirely coincidental and beyond the intent of the author or the publisher. No part of this book may be reproduced in any form or by any electronic or mechanical means, including photocopying, recording, information storage and retrieval systems, without written permission from the author, except for the use of brief quotations in a book review.

Copyright © 2023 by Charmaine Pauls

All rights reserved.

Cover design by Rachel Christley of The Author Buddy

ISBN: 9782491833244 (Paperback)

ISBN: 9782491833275 (Hardcover)

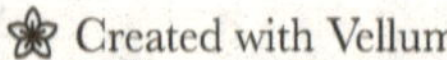 Created with Vellum

With much love to you, my inspiration.

Charmaine Pauls

CHAPTER ONE

Angelo

Most people don't know they're going to get married the first time they meet. Relationships develop over time. Some men and women weigh up the pros and cons to decide if they can live with someone until death do them part. Others follow their heart.

Not me.

In my family, tradition dictates differently. The decision was made for me a long time ago. That's how the business works. Money is power, and power is everything. Power means survival. It's the most fundamental rule of the world.

Only the strongest survive.

That's why I'm here, why we're driving up the road that zigzags to the top of the hill and ends in a cul-de-sac. A mansion peeks from behind high walls. Beyond, the ocean glimmers in the golden dusk. Below, to the right, the lagoon is a flawless mirror surrounding the stilt cabins on the island. The town of Great Brak River lies a kilometer inland on the bank of the river, consisting of a supermarket, a post office, an old as well as a new church, a small police station, an art gallery, a gas station, and a handful of shops and restaurants.

Anticipation tightens my gut. The reaction is involuntary. Far from being pure or innocent, it's born from instinct, from the darker, animalistic side of me that needs to claim and procreate.

Survival.

That's why we came all the way from Corsica to this secluded town in South Africa that's no bigger than the point of a needle on the map.

To meet my bride.

I've known for ten years, but twenty or thirty couldn't be long enough to prepare me for the moment. Whereas most human beings take the freedom of dating whoever they like for granted, I see it for what it is. A chore.

Dating is nothing but a tedious process of selection via elimination. There's a certain calm in knowing one woman is destined to be mine. Our union will serve in fulfilling my duty. There's logic in that. It gives stability to life in a world where little and few can be trusted. It gives meaning to existence. No soul searching or introspection are necessary.

It's been decided.

The outcome has been predetermined.

The timing, however, could've been better. We left my mother and sister alone for New Year, but I understand only too well why my father is eager to see this contract to fruition. The reason for his haste eats at me too.

Instead of flying to the nearest airport, we rented a car in Cape Town and drove the four hundred and twenty-eight kilometers to George. My father wanted to see the

Garden Route and stop on the way to buy wine. We took the scenic road along the coast, passing cliffs that broke off into the stormy sea and bays studded with smooth rocks and penguins. Sea bamboo drifting on the dark waters of small coves marked the whale coast. The rugged shores eventually gave way to dunes covered with Aloe Vera, their red flowers like flaming torches in the clear blue sky, and long stretches of white sand where the air smelled of salt and succulent groundcovers.

After booking into a hotel on the golf estate in the neighboring town of George, my father needed a day to rest and recover his strength. The following day, we did a reconnaissance of the area and paid our business partner —my future father-in-law—an unscheduled visit at his office. My father believes in catching his associates off guard. That way, they don't have time to hide any unorthodox dealings they prefer to keep in the dark. "If you want to know the true nature of a man," my father always says, "catch him with his pants down."

My father stops next to an intercom with a camera and pushes the button. The gates swing open without a squeak. We follow the road to where several cars are parked around a fountain on a circular driveway.

Benjamin Edwards appears on his doorstep before my father has cut the engine. I get out and straighten my jacket, taking stock of the surroundings like a soldier scouts a battlefield.

The house is the most impressive for miles around, built on the highest hill. Edwards stands on the porch like a cock crowing on his dunghill. In this sparsely populated part of South Africa, he may be the wealthiest man living in the biggest house. Compared to our property in Corsica, which is nothing short of a castle, the house that defines Edwards's status is unsubstantial. Inconsequential.

Much good all that money does us. Like Edwards's pretentious residence, our stronghold and landscaped gardens are for show. It's like putting a scumbag in a fancy suit. The centuries-old stigma still clings to our name. We come from a long line of vicious pirates and uneducated scoundrels. We're not welcome in the circles of the refined, religious, and elite.

That will change soon.

Edwards descends the steps to meet us.

"I'm glad you could make it," he says, shaking our hands, but his fake smile says otherwise.

The garden is buzzing with the commotion appropriate for a rich girl's sixteenth birthday party. Staff wearing black uniforms and white aprons are running up and down between the house and a cool truck parked in the far corner of the garden. White and pink flower wreaths decorate the balustrades, and a silver balloon arch frames the doorway. The breeze carries the notes of string music from the front of the house.

Edwards leads us to the lounge, which is similarly decorated with flowers and balloons. Bouquets of lilies and roses perfume the air. A round table in the center of the room is piled high with parcels wrapped in pink with white ribbons and vice versa. Did they specify the color of the wrapping paper like a fucking dress code on the invitation? I won't be surprised if Edwards introduces his daughter by marching her down the stairs in billows of white and pink voile.

What does she look like? I resisted the urge to look her up on social media. A part of me, the darker, more deviant part that can resist neither gamble nor dare, wanted to walk into this unprepared and let the surprise take me wherever it would. Shock me. Please me.

I'm about to find out which.

My father takes the box wrapped in golden paper from his jacket pocket and leaves it with the mountain of packets on the table. He's gone to a great deal of trouble to select a fine piece of craftsmanship from one of the best jewelers in Italy.

The sliding doors are open, revealing the green lawn that sweeps to the edge of the dune and the sea that's visible all the way to the convex curve of the horizon. The party is already in full swing. Guests mingle around cocktail tables, their droning conversations audible above the music. The string quartet is set up under a pine tree, the musicians expertly keeping the volume on a level that allows for chatter.

The women are decked out in their best, some of them sporting hats you'd see at the Derby, and, like my father and Edwards, the men are dressed in tuxedos. Personally, I prefer a style less universal. I opted for a modern European look with a designer jacket, a fitted shirt, and tailored pants.

"Welcome to my humble home," Edwards says, waving a waiter closer. "Can I offer you a glass of champagne?"

"Maybe Scotch first," my father says. "While we talk business."

Edwards glances at the top of the stairs and then at his watch. "It's hardly the moment."

My father's smile is indulgent. "It won't take long."

Our host doesn't have a choice but to comply. Our family is an important *service provider*—for lack of a better word—in his business. Although, from our impromptu visit to his office yesterday, I got the impression he wasn't ecstatic about our presence.

As manners dictate, my father asked about the welfare of his family and specifically about news of his youngest daughter. I could almost see the gears turning in Edwards's head, questioning the unlikely coincidence of our uninvited visit that happened to fall on the date of his daughter's sixteenth birthday. He couldn't do otherwise but to tell us about the party. The town is small. News travels. It would've been rude and politically incorrect not to invite us. We traveled across the whole of Africa after all, going to considerable efforts and expenses to call on him. Of course, my father accepted the invitation gracefully.

Judging by Edwards's reaction yesterday, I won't be surprised if my bride-to-be has no knowledge of my existence. Edwards isn't a good actor. He couldn't hide his aversion. He barely endured shaking my hand. People either fear or despise me. Mostly, they do both.

Too bad.

Benjamin Edwards may think he's better than us where morals are concerned, but we put him on his throne. He may sit there with a lily-white conscience and pretend his empire isn't built on blood, but I'm not scared to face the truth or to roll up my sleeves and get my hands dirty.

Edwards shows us into a study with leather couches facing a coffee table in the center of the floor but indicates the visitors' chairs in front of the desk.

My father shoots me a look as we take our seats. It doesn't take a psychiatrist to understand that Ben Edwards is scavenging whatever power he can, even if said power comes from hiding behind a desk.

Edwards pours Scotch at the wet bar and offers us each a drink, omitting one for himself.

He sits down and folds his hands on the desk. "What can I do for you, Santino?"

My father takes his box of cigarillos from his pocket and holds it out to Ben. Ben shakes his head.

"It's time for Angelo and Sabella to meet," my father says, measuring Edwards.

Edwards keeps a poker face, but he sits up straighter. "Why?"

"Sabella will be eighteen in two years."

The only reaction Edwards shows is the twitch of his eyes. "Indeed. What of it?"

My father rolls a cigarillo between his fingers and puts away the box. "She'll be an adult." When Edwards doesn't comment, he continues, "Of marriageable age."

Edwards spares me no more than a glance, his upper lip curling as if I'm an unpleasant sight. "I don't see what that has to do with Angelo."

"She's been promised to Angelo." My father smiles. "Have you forgotten?"

Edwards's face turns red. "I didn't agree to any such thing."

My anger ignites in a second. I know what he's doing, why he's denying the oath he made. We're good enough to do his dirty work, but we're not good enough for his daughter.

"We shook hands on the deal," my father says.

Edwards no longer makes an effort to disguise his anger. "I didn't consent to what you're implying,"

"Where I come from, a handshake is as good as a signature. Giving your handshake is giving your word." My father looks Edwards straight in the eyes. "Lying about it does not only make you a coward, but it's also a slap in our faces."

Edwards turns from red to purple. "In my country, a handshake holds no hidden meaning. Its only purpose is expressing politeness. We congratulated each other on a successful negotiation, nothing more. You get your fair cut every year."

"You seem to have a short memory, my friend." My father leans forward, bracing his elbow on the desk. "Part of the deal was always that Angelo would enter the business when he graduates from university and that we'd strengthen our mutual interests in blood."

"You're mistaken," Edwards says, his voice rising in volume.

"You act as if being tied to the Russo family is an insult." My father makes that statement like a challenge. "It will only benefit you." He takes a stack of folded papers from his inside jacket pocket and slides it over the desk. "I took the liberty of getting my lawyer to draw up a contract. They'll get married when she turns eighteen, but she can stay with us to acclimatize while Angelo finishes his MBA in Rome. Of course, she'll get a house in her name and a monthly allowance. Provision for the children born from their union, including expenses, education, trust funds, and such, has been stipulated. They won't want for anything. The marriage will be out of community of property, but in the unlikely event that my son decides to leave her, she will retain her property and possessions, and she will receive a handsome compensation." My father relaxes in his seat again. "Take your time to look it over."

Edwards doesn't as much as glance at the contract. "You seem to have it all figured out." He sneers. "What happens if she leaves him?"

"In that case, she gets nothing, but let's not bring them bad luck by focusing on the negative aspects before we've even celebrated their engagement. As you know, divorce is highly unusual in my family."

"Engagement?" Edwards exclaims. "She's sixteen, for crying out loud." He points a finger at me. "You're twenty." Scornfully, he adds, "Correct me if I'm wrong."

"That's right," I drawl. "I'm not asking to marry her straight away. Like my father, I prefer that she finishes school. I believe she's attending an excellent establishment with a prestigious reputation, and a good education is important to me. Four years may seem like a big age difference now, but once she's an adult, the gap won't be significant. Aren't you seven years older than your wife?"

All but choking on his spit, Edwards pushes back his chair.

We didn't come to the birthday party of a sixteen-year-old girl with guns, but maybe we should've.

When I make to get up, my father exchanges a look with me, wordlessly instructing me to let him handle it.

"They should announce their betrothal as soon as possible," he says in a placating tone, "but the actual engagement doesn't have to take place until she's turned of legal age. In the meantime, it'll be wise to let them get to know each other." My father spreads his hands. "The fact that I'm behaving so considerately and in the best interest of your daughter should reassure you."

The laugh Edwards utters is cold. "Reassure me?"

My father waves at the papers on the desk. "If my promise isn't enough, the figures will surely satisfy you."

"Like I said," Edwards says, balling his hands on the desk, "it's not going to happen. My daughter is independent. She has a free will." He slams a fist on his desk. "She will marry when she's ready and who she bloody well wants."

The patience vanishes from my father's features. He stands. His smile is intact, but the quiet authority of his voice as he towers over Edwards leaves no uncertainty as to the outcome of this conversation. "Take some time to share the happy news with her. I can see it won't be today. What's another few months if it'll help her get used to the idea? However, make no mistake. The wedding will happen. You made the bargain, and I'll hold you to it."

Edwards jumps to his feet. He opens his mouth but

wisely thinks the better of whatever he was going to say and shuts it again. He's got money, but we're the ones bargaining with fear. Our threats are never empty.

The door is yanked open, cutting into the tense atmosphere.

A thickset woman with short auburn hair wearing a burgundy silk dress bulldozes into the room. "Sabella hasn't come down yet. I swear—" She stops short when she notices us and quickly schools herself. "Oh. I didn't know you were busy."

Like gentlemen are taught to do when a woman enters a room, I get to my feet. Not that I'm anything of the kind. I just prefer the intimidating advantage of my height.

When she cowers a little, I can't suppress a grin.

My father bows. "We were just done." He takes her hand and kisses her fingers without touching his lips to her skin. "How are you, Margaret?"

"Fine, thank you," she says with a stiff back.

My father extends an arm toward me. "This is my son, Angelo."

I offer her a hand. "It's a pleasure to meet you, Mrs. Edwards."

Her fingers are limp in my mine. She pulls away before we've properly shaken hands, regarding me with a downturned mouth.

An awkward silence follows, which she breaks by asking my father, "How is Teresa?"

"In good health." My father inclines his head. "She asked me to congratulate you on Sabella's birthday. She would've come, but this is a business trip for Angelo and me."

The polite exchange is amusing. It's nothing but role play, a practiced stage act devised by civil society. Yet when cut down to the bone, we're all selfish monsters.

Underneath the pretense, we only care about furthering our own agendas.

Margaret pulls her lips into a pinch. "Maybe next time."

"Maybe." My father shrugs. "Who knows? Next time, we may welcome you in Corsica."

She glances at her husband with a question burning in her eyes.

"We've kept you from your guests," my father says. "We should let you get back to them."

"Yes." Margaret looks both worried and relieved. "We better go outside before our absence appears rude."

Edwards comes around his desk and opens a door that exits onto the veranda. "This way."

We step aside for Margaret to go ahead.

"If you'll excuse us," she says when we're outside. "I need a word with my husband."

"I know how taxing these affairs can be." My father takes a lighter from his pocket. "Don't worry about us. We'll make ourselves at home."

Frowning, she takes her husband's arm and leads him down the veranda and through the sliding doors. Before disappearing into the lounge, she looks over her shoulder with the expression of someone who's just stepped into dog shit.

My father lights his cigarillo, takes a drag, and studies the crowd as he blows out the smoke.

Like mine, his calmness is deceptive. Inside, I'm a fucking stick of dynamite with a burning fuse.

No one promises me something and then takes it away.

No one refuses me what's mine.

It's a tactical mistake.

Denying me only makes me want it twice as much. I'll

not only fight ten times harder to get it but also as dirty as necessary.

I can't say I didn't expect resistance after our cool reception at the office. I bargained on some negotiations and modifications of the terms of our contract. What I didn't foresee was Edwards's blunt refusal to honor an oath he'd made to my father. I remember his promise. I was there.

No one fucks us over, and no one throws our generosity back in our faces. Our surname isn't Russo for nothing.

"That's the oldest sister," my father says, waving his cigarillo toward the people milling on the lawn. "The one with the burgundy dress."

I spot her easily. She's an attractive woman by classical standards. According to rumors, she's the beautiful one. When people talk about the sisters, they refer to Sabella as the *other* one.

"Takes after her mother," he muses. "The man at her side is her fiancé. He's not involved in the business."

Meaning he's no one to be worried about. That's not who I'm interested in. My gaze is drawn to Ryan Edwards, Benjamin's first-born.

Like I weigh him, he measures me from across the distance. We only met yesterday at his father's office, and we're already enemies.

"That's who you have to watch out for," my father says, following my gaze. "He's the sole heir of Edwards's business. He won't be happy when he finds out he'll have to share the power."

I'm not worried about Ryan Edwards. He may be six years older, but he's no match for me. He's soft and impassive, a man who doesn't like to get down and dirty when the work gets gritty.

My dad coughs.

I jut my chin toward the cigarillo. "Should you be doing that?"

"Grant an old man the small pleasures he has left," he says, but he does put the cigarillo out in an ashtray on the garden table. "Want a drink? I need something to ease this scratch in my throat."

Looking at the bar where rosé and champagne are cooling in ice buckets, I shake my head. I haven't touched the Scotch Edwards poured. I'm too fucking livid, and alcohol only makes me more aggressive.

"Suit yourself," he says, making his way to the lawn where the waiters are circulating. "In that case, you're driving."

Brooding, I watch his back. I don't like the way he handled Edwards. He should've been firmer with him.

Years ago, Edwards came to my father and asked him to help remove a few obstacles in his business. As an imports and exports broker, Edwards saw an opportunity to make money by letting illegal shipments enter the country via the port of Cape Town. He had the right connections. He had the capital to buy off the government officials and to pay the controllers to turn a blind eye. Our job was to get rid of the ones who stood in his way, the ones who couldn't be corrupted.

The part we contributed, doing his dirty work for more than a decade, made him one of the big players in the industry. Today, he controls everything that comes and goes through Cape Town by sea. Yes, we get our cut, but we don't need the money. Not anymore. We've made enough. What we need is power. Recognition. An open door into circles where those born with the right surname and status pull their noses up at us. We need to be in on the deals. That has always been the objective.

As Edwards's son-in-law, I'll be rewarded shares and a

position on the board of his company. As per the contract, he'll give me a fancy title and voting rights. Of his three children, Sabella is Edwards's favorite. She's been the apple of his eye since the day she was born. He makes no secret of it. He'll never do anything to jeopardize her future. Marrying her is the only sure way of getting my foot in the door and keeping it there. As soon as my seed is planted in her belly and she gives me an heir, war will no longer be necessary. The Edwards family won't kill their grandchild's father. Correction—they won't hire an assassin to do it.

Owning a stake in the company will give us access to information that will make us more powerful than the governments of the countries involved in Edwards's illegal smuggling. It will open a new avenue for us, giving us direct access to Africa. It will guarantee us unequalled leverage in negotiating terms with the companies that currently pay the government bribes to smuggle their illegal arms via the port of Durban in the Kwazulu-Natal province. We can have the government by the balls and secure kickbacks that will earn us a monopoly in Africa. Governments and arms dealers alike will have no one else to turn to but us. They'll be our puppets. The Russo family will rule. Our name will be revered. The only thing standing between that kind of power and my family is a sixteen-year-old girl.

Edwards walks outside, searches the crowd, and heads toward where my father is standing at the edge of the lawn. Despite his bulk, his stride is lithe. I watch him like a tiger, ready to pounce. Once, my father was invincible. He could hold his own in any fist or gunfight. Now, he's old and growing weaker by the day.

They fall into what looks like a tense discussion, but they're not ripping each other's heads off. How long is the princess going to wait before making her grand entry? As soon as the introductions are out of the way, we can get the fuck out of here. I won't see her for more than a couple of days per year until we move her to Corsica. I'm a devil, but I'm not a creep. I've never been into underaged girls. The getting-to-know-each-other is my father's bright idea. If it was up to me, I'd just go into the whole thing cold turkey.

I plunge a hand into my pocket and fold my fingers around the joint the hotel bellboy slipped me. The over-dressed women with their lace, silk, and ostrich feathers bug me. Margaret's snobbish air of superiority where she's mingling with the guests is as irritating as hell. The pretentiousness of the whole lot gathered on the lawn, smiling and kissing Edwards's ass, grates on my nerves.

Fuck, I need to get away.

Making an impulsive decision, I walk down the length of the veranda and turn the corner.

I need to get stoned before I lose my shit and rip someone to pieces.

CHAPTER
TWO

Sabella

Just one more minute.

I let a little air from my lungs and sink deeper into the cool water. The salt no longer burns my open eyes. A wedge of sun rays pierces the surface and fans out to the bottom. Bubbles catch the light. Like tiny beads of fragile glass, they stick to my arms and legs. Life under the water is muted, the sounds dispersed. The rhythmic ebb and flow of the break is a distant lullaby. The tide gently rocks me to that beat. Forward and backward. Push and pull.

If I could, I'd stay here forever, but I can only hold my breath for so long.

I swim up and gulp in air when I break the surface. Treading water, I catch my breath. It's warmer in the water than outside. The late afternoon sky already glows with a champagne-colored tint. The whining of a violin drifts down from our garden. It must be the string quartet Mom hired for the party.

I'd rather make the most of the last hour of daylight and swim until my muscles cramp than listen to Aunt Judith's critique of the latest performing arts drama or pretend Uncle Fred hasn't told the story about how he walked into a bank robbery for the trillionth time. I'd give all my pocket money to sit on the sand and watch the bioluminescence in the water instead of telling Aunt Mary that no, I'm not too thin, and yes, I'm eating enough. But this is my party, and I'm already in trouble for being late as it is.

Unable to put the inevitable off longer, I swim to the shore and surf the waves to prevent myself from being tumbled and crushed in the roaring mass of foam. Once my feet touch ground, I waddle out of the water. The fine sand is dusted with flecks of gold. The shallow water is like a magnifying glass on the shiny particles that, once upon a time, were majestic shells and pearly abalone.

I dig my toes into the wet sand, enjoying the tickle as the water pulls back and the sand sucks my feet deeper. A breeze picks up from the sea. Goosebumps run over my arms. A woman's shrill laughter pierces the music coming from the hill, reminding me the guests are waiting.

Pulling my feet from the soft suction of the sand with a sigh, I run to the cave at the foot of the cliff where I left my clothes. Hurriedly, I pull my denim cutoffs and shirt on over my bikini. The thin linen doesn't do much to warm me. In the darkness of the cave, the sand is cold, and the musty air is humid. I should've brought a sweater, but I wasn't planning on staying so late.

The tide has come in. The river that feeds the lagoon flows too strongly now to swim across. On the other side of the river, a bridge spans over the lagoon to connect the beach with the island. Another bridge at the back of the island leads to the main road that runs to town. A ninety-degree bend on the right diverts to the beachfront. Our mansion stands on the highest hill at the end of that road, right on the edge, overlooking the massive dunes and a stretch of sand so long you can see Glentana in the north and Mossel Bay in the south.

Instead of going via the road, I climb straight up the steep side of the biggest dune. It's high, and by the time I'm three-quarters up, I'm panting from the exertion. The vegetation that caps the top is dense. I have to crawl down the secret footpath I've walked out over the years. The fynbos forms a tunnel around me until I exit on the other side. From here, I veer left and jog around the edge of the outcrop until I reach the tar road.

Our house can only be accessed from the back of the hill. I circle the hilltop and cut across the neighborhood via a smaller road. As I turn the corner, a sound coming from one of the trashcans on the pavement stops me. Going closer, I pause and listen. There it is again, a faint scratching. My pulse quickens. It can be a snake, but it can also be a hedgehog trapped inside. Carefully, I throw back the lid and peer over the top, my body poised for action, and then my heart melts on the spot.

A small furry face with big yellow eyes and long white whiskers stares up from the trash. His fur is black except for a white patch over his left eye. At the sight of me, the kitten mewls. For such a tiny thing, the cry he pushes from his chest is loud. He tries to claw his way outside only to sink deeper. From the state of the torn bags and the waste spilling out of them, he's been trying to get out for a while.

"You poor thing," I exclaim, reaching inside and carefully lifting him out.

He's so tiny, I can feel his fragile ribs beneath the

softness of his fur. His little heart is pounding between my palms. He mewls even louder, pawing at the air.

"There now." I hug him to my chest and stroke his head. "You're safe."

The kitten settles with a purr that vibrates in his ribcage. He mewls again, hauntingly this time, and instinctively I know the little creature is hungry. He's too small for solid food. He needs milk.

As I huddle the hungry, helpless animal, trying my best to soothe him, anger heats my blood. Who abandons a kitten and throws him away with the trash? I have a good mind to knock on the door of the house and give them a piece of my mind, but anyone could've driven here and left the kitten in the trashcan. Besides, the priority is feeding him. But how do I smuggle him into the house? My mom will have a fit if she finds out.

A few cardboard boxes are stacked next to the trashcan. I go through them until I find one that's clean and empty before lowering my charge inside. He protests loudly at being separated from the heat of my body.

"Don't worry." I stroke his back. "I won't leave you. I promise."

His claws are minuscule but sharp. I earn a scratch on my hand for my efforts. After some petting, the kitten calms again.

"I'll call you Pirate. That's a cool name, right?"

Pirate doesn't like his new prison. He puts his front paws on the side of the box and tries to climb out.

"Don't be scared," I say, closing the flaps. "You just have to stay in there for a little while."

Pirate mewls again when I straighten with the box in my arms. I ignore the little meows of distress, making my way home as fast as I can without jostling him.

The double gates that give access to our property are

closed. The driveway leading up to the house is visible through the bars. The front parking is already packed with luxury cars. After ensuring that no one is hanging around the entrance, I fish my key from my pocket and let myself in through the pedestrian gate before sneaking around the side of the house.

Caterers carry crates of food from a cool truck parked on a strip of paving. On the front lawn, where the guests are mingling, waiters are serving champagne and oysters. Aunt Judith, my late grandmother's sister, stands at the edge of the garden, wearing a powder-blue lace dress and matching hat. She talks animatedly, waving an empty champagne glass to emphasize whatever point she's making.

My sister, Matilde, faces her with a solemn face. Dressed in a mauve silk dress and matching heels with a short string of pearls around her neck, Mattie looks older than her eighteen years. Her fiancé, Jared, stands like a puppet in his tux at her side, offering a stiff smile at anyone who makes eye contact. A man I don't know talks to Dad. Dad slips a finger into his collar and cracks his neck. It looks as if his bowtie is already strangling him.

Great.

How am I going to get through this evening?

Falling into step behind one of the caterers, I manage to arrive at the side door that the staff use to access the kitchen without being spotted by any of the guests. Just as I exhale a sigh of relief, Doris, our housekeeper, waggles through the door. Blotchy patches redden her cheeks, and perspiration shines on her forehead.

She shuffles down the path, waving a dishcloth in the air. "Hey, you. Yes, you with the mustache. Come back here."

I duck, trying to make myself small, but the man I'm

using as a shield steps aside to let her pass and thereby exposes me.

When her gaze falls on me, her eyes bulge. Her face turns pink as she takes in my state.

"It's about time you show your face," she says with a scowl. "You should've been ready two hours ago. What an insolent girl you are." She points toward the kitchen. "Get inside now before I call Mrs. Edwards." Throwing her arms in the air, she hurries on her way. "Hey, you. Are you deaf? I told you to wait. We need more ice."

Holding my breath, I glance at Doris's retreat from over my shoulder. She's in such a flat spin with the party arrangements that she didn't pay attention to the box in my hands.

"Where the hell is your manager?" she asks the poor man she cornered. "You're running late with the starters." Grabbing his arm, she drags him in the direction of the cooler truck. "This won't do. It won't do at all. It's not my job to…"

Her ranting trails off as she and the man disappear around the corner.

"Not in the mood for the party either?" someone with a deep voice and a slight foreign accent asks.

I turn my face toward the voice, and then everything inside me goes still. The guy leaning on the wall next to the door is both the most arresting and scariest male specimen I've seen. With a square jaw and strong nose, his angular face is strikingly handsome. Yet at a certain angle, there's a harshness to those lines. Tall and broad with hair as black as coal and a skin with a Mediterranean coloring, he looks like a character who emerged straight from a fantasy book. From a different world. He can be either a fallen angel or a demon, depending on his mood.

Right now, with the tilt to his lips, he leans toward the

angelic side, but rather an archangel with a sword decapitating dragons than an angel with soft white wings. If he scowls, he'll look more like a demon. He's so beautiful, so utterly perfectly created, that something twists in my stomach. He's dark like the ocean and breathless like water. That's how I'd describe him if I could only use one word.

Water.

However, it's not his external beauty that makes my heart skid to a complete stop before resuming to beat like a drum in my chest. It's the energy surrounding him, a vibe of danger and deadly allure. He looks nineteen or twenty maybe, but there's a worldly air to him that makes him seem older and more experienced. Even as my pulse spikes and awareness contracts my skin, instinct tells me he's the kind of guy I should stay away from. Yet I stand rooted to the spot. What can I say? It's not my fault I'm a Capricorn with a sea-goat star sign who's attracted to water.

With one hand shoved into the pocket of his slacks and his knee bent, his pose is relaxed. It's just acting though. Tension oozes from his pores. I'm good at *feeling* people.

He chuckles at my silence. "I guess not."

Giving myself an internal shake, I try to remember what he asked.

Not in the mood for the party either?

He's not wearing a tux, but his formal slacks and jacket tell me he's a guest. The pang in my belly intensifies. I recognize the sentiment with a start. Regret. Regret that I don't know him. Regret that I won't. Already regretting that I'll listen to my mind even though my heart loves water.

"What are you doing here?" I ask in a hostile tone designed to mask my overwhelming reaction to him. "This entrance is for staff only."

He lifts his free hand, showing me a joint. Beneath the collar of the white shirt that's open to the third button, his chest is visible. Just the glimpse is enough to hint at well-defined pecs. He's inked, the top of the tattoo that's showing jet black. I can make out the decorative curls of a border. I wish I could see the whole picture. Where it ends. His broad shoulders taper to a narrow waist. The tailored pants and the fitted cut of the shirt where his jacket falls open show off his lean shape. He's a good dresser. I know all about understated elegance. Mom drilled it into me.

I drag my gaze back to his face lest I give him the impression that I'm staring. His full lips stretch, revealing straight white teeth set off by the olive tone of his skin. He observes me with eyes blacker than onyx, which are framed by long, dark lashes and thick eyebrows. Running a gaze over me, he weighs me in turn. When he lingers for a couple of seconds on my breasts, my heart does something funny in my chest. My shirt is still wet in patches, particularly where it's plastered to my boobs. The red bikini top is visible underneath, as is the dip of my stomach where he fixes his attention next.

"You don't look old enough to be a waitress," he says, finishing his evaluation by inspecting my legs. "How young are they hiring these days?"

I don't correct him. If he knows how young I really am, he won't give me another ounce of his attention. Although walking away is without a doubt the wiser option, I don't want to turn my back on him. Not just yet.

His lips quirk, amusement sparking in his eyes. "Has the cat got your tongue, *bella*?"

A jolt runs through me. How does he know my name? Only my family and close friends call me Bella. But no. He said it differently. He said it like a term of endearment. I know what *bella* in that context means, and it warms my chest with a pleasant heat.

"You have an accent," I say.

"French-Italian."

"Are you from Italy or France?"

"Corsica."

"You speak English very well."

"My mother insisted that we learn from a young age. It's important to speak it for business."

His cryptic and polite answers are a clear sign that he's getting bored with the conversation. I should go, but I linger, unable to pull myself away. "I wish I could speak a foreign language."

"Shouldn't you be working?" he asks, nodding at the box in my hands.

His animosity gets my hackles up. "Shouldn't you be mingling with the guests?"

He grins. Taking a Zippo lighter from his pocket, he taps the joint against the metal. "Parties are boring, but birthday parties are the worst." He casts another glance at my unsuitable attire. "You obviously agree."

Although I do share his sentiment, I can't help but turn defensive. "Then why did you come?"

Bringing the joint to his mouth, he watches me from the slits of his eyes as he lights it. He inhales and blows out a thin line of smoke. "Business."

The smoke twists into a ribbon before dispersing in the air, leaving the pungent odor of weed behind.

"Business?" Was I wrong about him being a guest? "Are you with the caterers?"

He laughs. "My father and Mr. Edwards are business associates." Studying me through the thick lashes of his hooded eyes as he takes another drag of the joint, he adds after blowing out the smoke, "Of sorts."

"So you're only here for business reasons," I say, my ego unjustifiably bruised.

"That's how it would seem."

I fail to keep the sarcasm from my voice. "I can see how that must suck for you."

He shrugs. "It comes with the territory."

When I don't reply, he holds the joint out to me.

I shake my head. "I don't smoke."

"Do you drink?"

My parents let me have a little wine or champagne on important occasions. "Not often."

His voice drops an octave. "Good."

He carries on smoking while I just stand there, racking my brain for something to say.

Turning his face, he looks at me as if to ask why I'm still there. "You better run inside and get to work."

I don't like the way he speaks to me. I resent how he thinks he can order me around. Most of all, I hate how easily he dismisses me.

When he stubs the joint out on the wall and flicks the butt in the party trash that's piling up next to the door, I know he's going to walk away. And I don't want him to. I stall by using what my feminine intuition tells me will get his attention. Defiance.

"No," I say, lifting my chin.

His eyes flare as if he doesn't hear that word often.

"I won't jump because you told me to," I continue.

He pushes off the wall. "What did you say to me?"

Standing taller, I tap into my confidence that usually comes naturally but for some reason now has failed me. "Why must *I* go? You leave if you don't want me here. You shouldn't have picked this spot if you were hoping to smoke your drugs without being caught. Which is completely not cool. Not smoking in secret but smoking at all. Especially drugs. It makes you totally uncool."

Shit. Can I just shut up now?

His dark eyes widen with humor rather than anger. A smile flirts with his lips.

He's laughing at me. How embarrassing.

I don't wait for his reply. My intention is making a grand exit while I still have some dregs of dignity left to cling to, but just as I turn toward the kitchen, my mom walks through the door.

Double shit.

"Sabella Daphne Edwards." She grabs my arm, her nails cutting into my skin. "Where have you been?" Her face pales as she takes me in. "My goodness. Look at you. This is too much." She gives me a not-too-gentle shake. "I've had it with you."

The stranger slides his gaze toward the lawn where white and pink balloons arch around silver blown-up numbers writing sixteen in the center. His lips curve into a full smile as he no doubt puts two and two together.

I nearly die of humiliation. My mom is really upset with me this time, so much so she doesn't notice the young man standing to the side while catering staff enter and exit the house like a steady file of ants.

"Get inside." She lets go of my arm and grabs the box from my hands. "Now."

"Wait," I cry out, trying to take back the box. "You'll drop it."

My mom holds the box out of reach. "What have you done now?"

"Nothing, I swear."

Pursing her lips, she opens the flap.

"His name is Pirate," I say, talking so fast my tongue trips over the words. "Please, you have to let me keep him."

My mom holds the box at arm's length. "You know I'm allergic to cats."

"Please." I press my palms together in a begging gesture. "It's the only birthday gift I want. I'll never ask you for anything else."

My mom flicks her fingers. Miraculously, a staff member appears at her side.

"Put this in the guest bathroom upstairs." She thrusts the box at the man, who's one of our gardeners. "We'll take it to the SPCA tomorrow."

"No," the stranger says, the word loaded with so much authority that both my mom and the gardener freeze.

I don't know who's more surprised, my mom or me.

My mom spins around and gives a start when her gaze falls on the guy. She looks between us, suspicion tightening her eyes. "What are you doing here at the back of the house?"

He steps up and takes the box from the gardener. "I was just giving Sabella her birthday present."

Reeling, my mother says in a high-pitched voice, "Excuse me?"

Carefully, he hands the box back to me. "If I'd known you were allergic, Mrs. Edwards, I would've included antihistamines with the gift. It's an easy enough problem to solve and a small sacrifice to pay for Sabella's happiness." He adds with a mocking smile, "I'm sure you'll forgive me for the oversight."

My mom's nostrils flare. Her chest rises as she inhales sharply. Seemingly unable to string together words to make a sentence, she flicks her fingers again at which the gardener slips away as fast as he appeared.

"Well," my mom says, giving me a narrow-eyed look. "You better go settle your new pet and get ready. You've kept everyone waiting long enough. I'll tell Mattie to help you get dressed so that your guests don't have to wait another hour."

Turning up her nose, she leaves as regally as her high heels allow.

I'm shocked to a standstill, unable to believe my luck. Gaping at the handsome stranger, I say with all the sincerity I possess, "Thank you."

A hint of warmth softens the harsh blackness of his eyes. "You're welcome, *cara*."

My stomach flutters at yet another term of endearment. "Why did you do it?"

His statement is casual, but the words are loaded. "Because you should get what you want for your birthday."

"Your business must be really important to my dad. My mom never gives in like that."

He shoves a hand in his pocket and glances at the partygoers. "There are only old people here. Don't you have friends?"

"I'm not socially awkward and incapable of making friends, if that's what you're implying," I say with a grin.

"I'd never be so crass," he deadpans. "I'm just wondering why they're not invited."

"Everyone is away for the big summer holiday." I pout. "If it wasn't for this party, I would've been in Plettenberg Bay with them right now."

His expression darkens. "Alone?"

"I wish." I make a face. "My brother and his wife would've gone along to chaperone."

"Ah." Some of his tenseness evaporates. "If it makes you feel better, I could've been skiing in the Alps."

"Really?" That pang of defensiveness hits me again. "You must be very disappointed about missing out on that."

"Not so much now. The view here is very nice."

I laugh. "*Nice?*"

"A lot more than I expected."

My breathing quickens. I'm new at the nuances of our game, but I like playing it with him.

"Can I see?" he asks, motioning at the box.

"Oh." His interest in Pirate makes me happy. Giddily, so. "Of course."

I lift the flap. We both peer into the box, our heads close together. His cologne is a blend of something woodsy and citrusy, a subtle perfume that makes me want to bury my face in his neck and inhale the fragrance of his skin. He tickles Pirate under the chin and chuckles when the kitten purrs, but I'm not focused on the cat. I'm too aware of our proximity and how good he smells.

"He's cute," he says, raising his gaze to mine.

I clear my throat. "He is."

A weird, almost calculated look comes over his face. "Who gave him to you?"

"I found him in a trashcan on my way home."

At that, his features relax. "I'm glad he found a good home."

"I'm sorry about earlier," I say on impulse as a fresh bout of gratitude washes over me. "I was rude."

The smile he offers me is so warm and unguarded it not only makes me feel as if the sun is shining on my face but also that I'm special. To him.

"I'm sorry for mistaking you for a waitress," he says. "I should've asked instead of assumed."

"Quits?"

"Quits," he agrees, his dark gaze piercing mine.

My blood heats under the intensity of his stare. No one has ever looked at me with so much possession. No man has ever smiled at me as if I'm valuable and important.

Slowly, something serious replaces the warmth of his

expression, something predatory and carnal. I know he's aware of how close we're standing, invading each other's personal space. I'm out of my depth, unequipped for what's passing through his eyes, but I can't make myself move.

He acts first, not stepping away but closer still, so close that the box is pressed between us. Raising his arm, he brushes his fingertips over my temple and hooks my hair behind my ear. The touch is so gentle it's barely there, but it jolts me. It ripples over my entire body, covering every inch of my skin in goosebumps.

"Happy birthday, *cara*," he says in that deep, low voice with a hint of an accent.

A beat passes in which I hold my breath, although I'm not sure for what.

And then he backs off, putting space between us.

It physically hurts. Whether it's the distance or his proximity, it aches with the same intensity, leaving a hollow sensation in my stomach and a fluttering in my temples. My heart thumps and my knees are wobbly. It's confusing. I both want to burrow against his chest and run away from the fiercely wonderful and scary feelings.

Worried that he'll notice my weakness, I flee inside the house, miraculously managing an unwavering smile from over my shoulder, but he's already strolling away with his hands shoved in his pockets and his gaze trained on the horizon. Just when my heart is about to sink, he looks back. I'm so ecstatic, I don't care he caught me staring, because I caught him too.

For the first time in my life, I hurry to make myself pretty.

CHAPTER
THREE

Angelo

P ossession flows in my veins when I leave Sabella to dress and walk back to the party. The heady cocktail of ownership and responsibility sends a thrill through my body and rushes like a drug to my brain.

The sentiments are foreign and unexpected. I've taken care of our pets since a young age, but a human has never been dependent on me. Up to yesterday, Sabella Edwards was an abstract concept. I gambled with the element of surprise, and it's not shock that won. Far from it. What I saw pleased me. A lot. Seeing her triggered something in me. Marrying her is no longer a blurry picture with intangible edges. The prospect is real. She's not an image of a person with indistinguishable features. She's a young woman of flesh and blood, and a stunning one at that.

The knowledge that this beautiful girl is mine fills me not only with pride but also with a heavy dose of jealousy.

She's a looker, and she doesn't know it. Not yet. Soon, however, she'll grow aware of her beauty and the power she can hold over men.

Take me, for example. Not even five minutes into meeting her, I've already broken my promise to myself. I've touched her when I knew better. She's an innocent girl with the curves of a woman. Only a dead man wouldn't notice those firm breasts, tight ass, and long legs. Her body is like a succulent fruit on the verge of ripening, soon to be ready for the picking.

The thought alone is enough to make me see green when I think about the distance I'll be putting between us tomorrow and how many horny boys may show up on her doorstep while I'm fighting this war with her father.

I'll have to send a man to keep an eye on her. Our most loyal and trusted man. The decision eases my worry, although only marginally.

Back on the front lawn, I look for my father among the throng of people. Finally, I spot him sitting on a bench in a secluded corner of the veranda. His face is as white as chalk, and he's coughing into his handkerchief.

Alarm triples my pulse. I make it to him in a few long strides and pour a glass of water from the nearest pitcher. Shoving the glass into his hand, I block him from potentially curious spectators with my body.

"Drink," I say, glancing around to gauge if anyone is looking, but no one takes notice.

He manages to swallow a sip, which helps to calm the coughing, and hands the glass back while resting his head on the wall and breathing through his mouth.

"Come." I put the glass on the table and take his arm, helping him to his feet. "Don't let them see you like this."

Unable to speak, he nods his agreement and lets me guide him back to the car. We're barely inside before another bout of coughing wracks his shoulders. I reach in the back for his inhaler, but he shakes his head.

"Leave it. It'll pass."

Stubborn bastard. "You have nothing to prove by refusing your medicine. No one will think you are weak for taking it."

He sucks air through his teeth and forces the words from a wheezy chest. "I just need a moment."

Arguing is fruitless. My father is nothing if not hardheaded and proud. I start the car and drive to the gates. At the intercom on the inside of the garden, I push the button. A beat later, the gates open as someone in the house, presumably one of the staff, lets us out.

Etiquette states leaving without saying goodbye to the host is an unforgivable rudeness, but Edwards declared himself our enemy, tonight, and you never show your enemy your weakness.

Keeping one eye on my father and the other on the road, I take the turn toward George. He winds down the window and takes a few deep breaths of the cool air. By the time the lights of the airport come into view, the attack has passed, and his muscles are slack again.

"You should call your doctor," I say. "You need to see him when we get home."

He dismisses the idea with a flick of his hand. "Nothing but a waste of time." Shooting me a look, he says, "Not a word about this to your mother."

"You shouldn't hide this from her."

"What's the point of making her worry? It's not going to change anything."

I clench the wheel. I both agree and disagree with that statement, but I respect his decision. It's what I would've wanted if I'd been in his position.

"I'm sorry," he says, staring through his window toward the distance where the hills swell in the moonlight.

It's such a rare occurrence for my father to apologize that I'm not sure how to reply. All I can say is, "It's not your fault."

His voice hardens. "I meant that we had to leave before Sabella made her appearance."

"I met her."

He looks at me.

"We ran into each other by accident," I explain. "She tried to slip into the back of the house without being noticed."

The corners of his mouth pull down. "She doesn't seem like a very obedient daughter."

Feeling compelled to defend her, I say, "She was rescuing an abandoned kitten."

He makes a noncommittal sound. "What was your impression?"

I consider my answer. "She likes me." Surprisingly. "I think I can make her fall in love with me. It won't be very difficult."

"Mm." He contemplates my answer, studying the road in the headlights of the car. "That will certainly win you her agreement to marry you, but emotions are fickle. You can't trust love alone to seal such an important deal. From what I've heard, she's close to her father. If he doesn't consent, she may refuse to marry you for not wanting to disappoint him or evoke his disapproval. If Edwards was the only stumbling block, it would've been easy enough to simply get rid of him, but if he dies before you've taken possession of your share of the company, Ryan will inherit everything. No," he muses. "We need Edwards to agree. We need a much stronger incentive than love."

I hit the brakes and slow down to the speed limit as we approach the golf estate. A guard signs us in at the gates.

Drumming my fingers on the wheel, I contemplate our situation. Edwards isn't pulling out of the deal he made only because he doesn't want his princess to marry a lowly, filthy Russo with blood and sins on his hands. Edwards doesn't want to share his power and fortune. He doesn't strike me as a man who'll give in easily. A little arm wrestling won't be enough to sway him. No. Edwards declared war, and war requires a much more radical approach. I won't rest until what's been promised me is mine.

I park in front of the hotel and cut the engine. My voice is flat, my mind made up. "Leave it to me. I'll handle Edwards."

"We have to call a meeting with your uncles. They should be involved."

Turning in my seat, I face my father. "Sabella is my responsibility. It's my problem, not a family matter."

"You're young. There's a lot about the business you've yet to learn. Edwards may look docile, but he's shrewder and more dangerous than you think."

I smile. "Then this is the perfect opportunity to prove my worth. You taught me. Now's a good time to show our family you trust me."

In the moonlight that sifts through the window, the shadows under his eyes are deep. "Fate is forcing you to take on too much, too soon. You shouldn't have to fill my shoes when your life is only starting. Let your uncles help."

"I'll deal with this my way. If it doesn't work out, we'll involve your brothers."

He chuckles and grips my shoulder. "There's no question about it. You're undoubtably my son." His expression sobers. "Don't underestimate Edwards. That will be a mistake."

"Don't worry." I open the door and get out. "I have no intention of making mistakes."

If Edwards thinks he's seen the worse of what and who we are, he's in for an unpleasant surprise. He unleashed the devil in me.

Soon enough, he'll face that monster.

CHAPTER FOUR

Sabella

Mattie's voice pulls me from my revery. "Bella! What are you doing? Why aren't you in the shower? Mom is having a nervous breakdown. And what's in that box you're carrying?" She shudders. "I swear I just heard something scratching inside."

Mechanically, I look at my sister, but my heart stayed behind on the side of the house next to the trashcans. I have a frightful, terrifying feeling that's where it's bound to stay forever.

She frowns. "What's with that look on your face?"

I try to school my features. "What look?"

"That goofy look."

"Nothing."

Narrowing her eyes, she darts to the backdoor and looks around the doorframe. When she pulls back into the scullery, her lips are pursed and her forehead pleated, making her resemble Mom more than ever.

"Come," she says, taking my arm. "Let's get you cleaned up." She pulls up her nose. "At least as best as we can."

For once, I don't argue. I couldn't be bothered about the outfit my mom chose for the party, but now I'm glad the dress makes me look older. It's between burgundy and mauve, like my mom's and Mattie's, but two shades lighter. Delicate lace overlays a silk slip and ties with a sash around my waist. With the heels, I'll be as tall as Mattie.

I follow my sister to my room where I build a bed for Pirate with my softest blanket while she turns the water in the shower on to run warm. Fishing my phone from my pocket, I dial the twenty-four-hour emergency veterinary clinic in George and, after describing my dilemma, order a delivery. George is a big town but still small enough for everyone to know everyone. The receptionist doesn't argue when I tell her who I am and that my dad will settle the bill.

Reassured that milk for Pirate will arrive in twenty minutes, I give him a little water and get ready as fast as I can. My eagerness has nothing to do with the tantrum my mom is going to throw and everything with the guy who gave me the best birthday gift in the world. I want him to see me in my new dress with my hair and make-up done properly. For the first time in my life, I want to look feminine and desirable.

Doris knocks on the door with Pirate's bottle and milk while Mattie is curling my hair. My sister utters a curse when I abandon my post in front of the mirror to mix the milk and give Pirate the bottle. He kneads my wrist with his paws as he greedily gulps down the milk until not a drop is left. The fact that his tummy is full reminds me that he'll need a litter tray, but when I ask Mattie to call the clinic, she says a little sand from the garden in a shoebox will have to suffice because she has better things to do, such as finishing my hair.

By the time Pirate dozes off curled up on the blanket, Mattie has finished my make-up. I study my reflection in the mirror with a critical eye. My hair doesn't have Mattie's auburn tint, but the dark tresses are thick and glossy. The many hours I spent outdoors have darkened my skin. A few white sunspots mark my arms and legs, but my cheeks have a healthy glow, and the color of the dress shows off my tan.

Mattie rolls her eyes when I wipe off the red lipstick and replace it with a dab of gloss. It makes my lips look fuller.

"Ready?" she asks with a note of irritation. "I left Jared alone with the vultures."

Dabbing away the excess gloss with a tissue, I smile at her in the reflection of the mirror. "I'm sure he'll survive for an hour."

I check on Pirate one last time before dashing after Mattie down the stairs.

It's dark already. The garden is lit with fairy lights that are draped around the trees and lanterns that are burning on the tables. Going on tiptoes on the terrace, I scan the crowd.

"He left," Mattie says in a dry tone.

I feign ignorance. "Who?"

"Angelo."

So, that's his name. It's fitting.

"Angelo who?" I ask, enjoying the sound of his name on my tongue.

"Russo."

"Where's he staying?" I ask, trying to sound

nonchalant. "At the guesthouse or at a hotel?"

Her manner is curt. "He went home."

Disappointment surges through me. He won't see me in my dress. He couldn't even wait until the end of the party. Corsica is on the other side of the world. I may never see him again.

"It's a good thing he left," she says. "He had no business showing up at a family event."

"Wasn't he invited?"

"He and his father invited themselves. Dad only told them to come because it was the polite thing to do."

"How come you know so much anyway?"

"Ryan told me." Mattie steps in front of me, cutting off my view. "He's trouble, Bella, with a big T."

"I wasn't even looking for him."

"Right." She crosses her arms. "Stay away from him and his family. They're bad people."

"How can you say that? You don't even know him."

"Do you remember that guy in primary school, the one who always had scruff here?" She draws a finger around the base of her neck. "He got his school uniforms from the trunk with the second-hand throwaways in the gymnasium. His jersey had holes under the armpits."

I frown. "Isaac?"

"Yes. Angelo is like him. Well, not in the way he was dressed tonight, but his family comes from the same place as Isaac's family."

"I liked Isaac. He was clever and better with math than anyone in school. And he was good with animals. He was really kind to the stray cats who lived in the drainpipes behind the toilets."

She sighs. "Just trust me when I tell you that the Russo family is the worst kind of bad."

I want to say they can't be that bad if Dad considers

them good enough to do business with, but my dad walks up with a proud smile.

He kisses my cheek. "You look beautiful, darling."

My mom follows short on his heels, stumbling her way over the grass. "You almost ruined everything, Sabella. I'm only glad no one decided to leave."

Taking my arm, my father says, "Shall we make the toast?"

When Mom doesn't look, he winks at me.

I'm not so enthusiastic now that *he* has left. To be honest, I'm a little hurt. Fine, a lot. The evening has lost its sparkle. I only endure the party for the sake of my parents. Like a good hostess, I do the rounds and talk to the guests, offer them refreshments, and listen politely to Uncle Fred's story about the bank robbery.

When it's time to open my gifts, I blow out a quiet sigh of relief. That means the cake will soon be cut and served with coffee, which announces the end of the party.

The Russo family gifted me an intricate gold bracelet shaped like interlinked daisies with a diamond in each flower's center. It's exquisite. They must be loaded. If Dad felt obliged to invite them to my party, they must be very important to his business. He never invites his colleagues or associates home. He doesn't believe in mixing business and pleasure.

Everyone admires the bracelet, except my mom. She seems upset about the fact that I like it so much, but it's only because she doesn't want anyone's gift to outshine hers. My parents' gift is a grand piano wrapped in white velvet and tied with a gigantic pink ribbon. I've never played the piano, and I don't have the talent to or ever will. When I point that out to Mom, she says the piano will make a good impression in my living room, one day, and that I have lots of friends who can entertain me by playing.

By *lots of friends*, she means Colin, my childhood friend and neighbor. None of my other friends are musically talented. Colin and I were born a week apart, and we were in the same class for the whole of primary school. We were only separated in high school because my parents sent me to a girls-only private school while Colin got shipped to the boys' school. My mom is still secretly hoping we'll marry one day. Fat chance. Colin is like a brother to me.

After the lychee sponge cake topped with a rose-flavored ganache has been served, I stand in the entrance and dutifully shake each person's hand as I thank them for coming. By the time I finally close the door, I can hardly stand on my feet. Despite my tiredness, a strange listlessness comes over me.

Kicking off the heels that pinch my toes, I wander aimlessly through the empty house. The catering team has already removed the hired cocktail tables and tidied up. "It's what I pay for," my mom always says with a grateful sigh when she wakes up the next morning with a slight hangover in a clean house.

My feet carry me automatically to Dad's study. Saying goodnight has been a habit since I was little. He always works for an hour or two when everyone's gone to bed, never making any exceptions, not even on weekends or after parties.

My mom's heated voice comes through the wood before I even reach the door.

"I'm not going to say I told you so, but I did warn you not to do business with those people. You can't let this happen."

"I won't," my dad grumbles. "Now, give it a rest."

"Give it a rest," she exclaims. "Nothing good is going to come from this."

"You stick to your business, and I'll manage mine."

"You mean run your household and raise your kids but don't have an opinion when it comes to how your business impacts our lives."

"Don't be so dramatic, for heaven's sake. I'll take care of it. Don't I always?"

"Dramatic?" Her voice quivers. "Sometimes, Benjamin Edwards, you can be a patronizing son of a bitch."

A moment later, the door flies open in my face. I bounce back as my mom charges through the doorframe, her face streaked with black mascara. She glares at me before flouncing down the hallway on her bare feet with her heels swinging in one hand.

I don't take her animosity personally. She simply doesn't like showing weakness. No one is allowed to witness her in any state of dress or composure that isn't perfect. I've never seen her in pj's or without her make-up. She's always immaculately groomed when she comes downstairs in the morning.

Hesitantly, I put my head around the doorframe. My dad sits behind his desk, scribbling in his little black book. I knock to make him aware of my presence. As always, he closes the book and puts it in his top left drawer.

"Am I interrupting?" I ask.

He smiles, but the usual easy tilt of his mouth is strained. "Never."

I throw a thumb in the direction of Mom's flight. "I couldn't help but overhear some of that."

"All of it?" he asks with alarm.

I frown. "Only the last part. Is everything okay?"

He sighs. "Come here. Don't look so worried. You know your mother overreacts when she's tired."

That's not an understatement.

I enter the room and inhale the familiar fragrance of wood polish and leather. When I was little, I used to fall asleep on the sofa while my dad was working. I'd always wake up with a blanket covering me, feeling safe and protected. I'd lie awake and listen to the sound of his pencil scratching over the paper. My dad is old-fashioned when it comes to computers. He's still scribbling in his notebook instead of using the programs Ryan installed on his laptop.

Flopping down on the sofa, I tuck my legs under me. "I don't like it when you fight."

He comes over and takes a seat next to me. "It's a silly disagreement. Tomorrow, it'll be forgotten."

"I hope it's not because of me."

"Why would you think that?"

"I ruined the party for Mom, didn't I?"

Pinching my cheek, he says, "You were perfect. Did you have fun?"

I hate lying to my dad, so I simply shrug.

He winces. "I'm sorry about the piano. Your mother wouldn't be dissuaded."

"It's okay." I grin and rest my head on his shoulder. "I can use it as a table when I get my own apartment one day."

A soft laugh shakes his body. "Don't let your mother hear that." Taking a small box from his pocket, he puts it in my lap. "I have something for you."

I sit up quickly and look at his handsome face, gratitude warming my heart. "You shouldn't have."

He waves away my protest. "Open it."

A smile splits my face as I flip back the lid to reveal a delicate gold chain with a sea turtle pendant. "Oh, Dad." I throw my arms around his neck and hug him. "Thank you. It's gorgeous."

"I thought you'd like it," he says with a conspiratorial wink when I let him go.

I caress the lines of the pendant. "I love it."

"Good." He pats my hand. "That's all that matters."

"Did you hear about the kitten?"

"Your mother told me."

Hiding my expression by pretending to study the pendant, I probe carefully, "I thought you didn't invite business associates to family gatherings."

"I don't. They happened to be in town for a meeting. Extending an invite couldn't be avoided."

"You say it as if you don't like them."

"Sabella."

The rare use of my full name makes me look at him.

"You have to stay away from that boy. He's no good for you. Do you understand?"

"Why?" I ask, my voice hoarse.

"He has a reputation. Trust me when I tell you he's not the kind of man you want in your life."

My dad has always been strict about letting me go out with boys, especially boys older than me.

"I don't want you to mix with him or any of his family. Do you understand?" he asks again. "I absolutely forbid it."

He's never spoken to me so sternly.

Swallowing, I nod.

"Good," he says. "Now, go get some sleep."

I kiss his cheek and wish him goodnight, leaving him to his work.

An odd sensation nestles in the pit of my stomach as I walk through the dark, deserted house to my room. I can't explain what happened, tonight. I only know that my solid, trustworthy mind is no longer in control.

Somewhere between sunset and now, my heart became the master of my decisions.

CHAPTER
FIVE

Angelo

An hour before dawn, I pull on a tracksuit and search my hotel room for items suitable for a kidnapping. I settle on the laundry bag and one of my socks. The thick black bag won't let light through, and the sock won't leave marks. Then I scribble a note on the hotel stationary to inform my father that I'm going for a jog on the beach. After slipping the note under his door, I snatch a pair of golf gloves from the kiosk in reception on my way out.

In the car, I pull the address I'd taken from the HR records at Edwards's office up on the GPS. Selecting the shortest route, I head out to an affluent neighborhood on the outskirts of George and park in front of a modern house that overlooks the valley.

The morning is misty, the sun battling to break through the clouds on the horizon. Cows graze on the green hills behind the sea. I switch on the car heater to defog the windscreen. While I wait, I fire off an email from my phone, instructing our best man to get on the next available flight to South Africa. I give him detailed instructions and demand a daily report.

I'm finishing an email to clear the payment for his expenses when the door of the house across the street opens, and Edwards's junior accountant steps out. Elijah Johnson is a short, thin man with manicured nails and perfectly styled brown hair. He wears skinny pants and a Karl Lagerfeld jacket with a matching waistcoat. Transferring a leather satchel from one hand to the other, he checks his wristwatch and hurries to a BMW parked in the driveway.

He gets behind the wheel and inspects his reflection in the rearview mirror before pulling out of the yard. I wait until he's turned the corner, and then I don the gloves, start the engine, and follow at a reasonable distance. When he hits the secondary road that runs through the empty field before joining the national road that goes to town, I cut him off.

His shiny black car skids over the tar as he plucks the wheel to avoid hitting me. The tires squeal as he slams on the brakes. I get out and walk to his side of the car. The gearbox complains as he obviously fails to throw the car into reverse in his flurry of nervous clumsiness.

I knock on his window.

He glances up, squinting like a child peeping through his fingers at a horror movie. When he recognizes me, his shoulders slump.

He winds down the window. "I almost crashed my car. Are you out of your fucking mind?"

"Get out. You're taking a ride with me."

He turns paler than Snow White. Watching me with a panicked expression, he jabs his finger on the button to raise the window. I've seen it coming. I'm already reaching inside and pressing the button on his armrest to unlock the doors. He screams like a banshee as I open his door and pull him out by his arm.

"What do you want?" he shrieks, plastering his arms against his sides and holding his hands in the air as if I'm pointing a gun at him.

"Behave, and you'll get to the office without a crease in your suit."

"It's not a suit," he says, sounding offended.

I drag him to the rental and slam him facedown over the hood, keeping an eye on the road to make sure it remains clear.

"Oh, God," he cries in a thin voice. "Are you going to rape me?"

I chuckle. "You're not my kind."

"Oh God, oh God, oh God," he chants as I grab his wrists behind his back in one hand and take the sock from my pocket with the other. "You're going to kill me. You're going to kill me."

"Shut up." I tie his wrists and pull him to his feet. "As I said, cooperate, and you'll be sipping your organic filter coffee at your desk before eight."

"This isn't how it works," he squeals as I open the backdoor and push him inside. "I know how people like you operate."

His eyes grow round when I take the bag from the door compartment.

Despite twisting from side to side and bucking like a pig with rabies, it doesn't take much effort to pull the bag over his head and shove him down on the seat.

"Stay low," I say. "If you show your face, I'll cut off your nose."

He whimpers at the threat.

I shut the door and lock the car in case he gets it into his head to run with a hood over his head and his hand bound behind his back. I'm not in the mood for chasing him through cow dung and muddy fields.

It's early. The road is deserted, but the morning traffic will start soon. I get into his car, push the ignition button, and drive it to the side road a few meters up ahead where I park it on the wide shoulder. I leave the key inside and go back to the rental. With the high crime rate in the area, a luxury car won't be left here for long. He can attribute his late arrival at the office to his car having been stolen. At least he won't have to lie about that.

He alternates between whimpering and shouting obscenities as I take the road along the coast to an abandoned, unfinished house on a clifftop near Victoria Bay. It's one of many grand houses on the coast that had never been completed due to funds running dry.

A short gravel road leads to the building site. The spot is perfect. The construction is far enough from the road to be out of earshot. A high wall marking the perimeter hides the entrance. In the front, the cliff plunges into the sea.

I park behind the wall where the car is out of sight and drag him kicking and screaming into the ground level of the raw concrete building. The top floor has no walls, only pillars and a flat roof, which makes being spotted from there too probable.

Our steps echo on the dusty floor. He finally falls quiet, most likely realizing his pleading and screaming are useless. I steer him around rusted metal spikes sticking from half-finished pillars to the center of the floor where a heap of concrete bricks are stacked. The blue sky is visible through the gaping window frame on the cliffside of the building. I push him down on the bricks, facing the window, and pull the bag from his head.

He drags in air and, blinking a few times, casts a bewildered glance around him. "Where am I? Why am I here?"

I prop a foot on the bricks. "You're here to tell me some things."

He leans away and asks in a high voice, "What things?"

"Things I want to know. I'm going to ask you some questions. You're going to answer them. Easy."

He watches me with wariness etched on his face as I pick up a brick and weigh it in my palm. With his hair standing in all directions and his fancy jacket hanging askew on his frame, he's a pathetic sight.

"Your boss bribes a few high-ranking government officials," I say. "Let's start with their names."

Shifting to the end of his makeshift seat, as far away from me as possible, he says, "I don't know anything about that."

"Come on, Johnson. I'm not an idiot, and I don't have time for games."

Moving around him, I set the brick aside.

"What are you doing?" he shrieks, craning his neck to follow my movements.

I untie his hands and place them palm-down next to him. "For every lie you tell, I'm going to flatten one of your fingers."

He yanks his hands aways and buries them under his armpits.

"Put down your hands, Johnson. If you don't spread your fingers, I can always crush your balls."

"I don't know," he cries. "I mean, I know about the bribes," he stammers. "But I don't know who the money goes to."

"Mm." I pick up the brick and round him again. "I'm not sure I believe you."

"I swear it." He crosses his legs in a feeble effort to protect his junk. "No one does. Only Mr. Edwards."

"Someone pays them." I throw the brick in the air right above his head and catch it before it hits his skull. "Therefore, someone must know."

"Not me," he screeches, ducking to the side. "Mr. Edwards takes care of the payments himself."

"However, you have access to the accounts."

"He pays the money into offshore accounts that are set up in several company names." He pulls his shoulders up to his ears. "It's impossible to trace it back to an individual. The payment system is designed to be untraceable."

This, I do believe. I know how it works. "What about Mrs. Thomson?"

He shakes his head. "I told you. No one knows."

Should I believe him? The reason I didn't pick up Thomson, the CFO, is because she's a much tougher cookie than Johnson. It would've taken a lot more effort to get answers from her, and I don't have much time.

Is he telling the truth about Thomson being in the dark too? Johnson only cares about himself. I've already come to my own conclusions about him by watching him in action at the office. He's sly, ambitious, and self-absorbed. The only things that matter to him are money, status, and a promotion. He's eager for Thomson to retire so that he can move into her corner office. He won't sacrifice himself to save that taciturn woman's hide.

Johnson follows my movements with his gaze, his pupils jittery in their sockets as I bounce the brick on my palm.

"Edwards keeps a record of the sums he pays somewhere," I say. "The recipients must acknowledge receipt of those payments. Edwards is way too thorough not to keep a proof of delivery. You should be able to get your hands on that information. How difficult can it be to do a little snooping at the office?"

"If the information was captured electronically, it would've been possible." He swallows. "Difficult but possible. The problem is that Mr. Edwards writes everything down in a book."

"A book? That sounds old-fashioned, even for Edwards."

"He has this … this little black book." He makes a gesture with his hand, and then, seemingly thinking the better of it, quickly hides his fingers again. "Thomson once mentioned that Mr. Edwards keeps note of how much he pays to whom in that book."

"That's risky."

"Not as risky as keeping the data on a laptop. Encryption programs aren't safe. It only takes a good hacker to crack the code. The information is much too sensitive to let it lie around in cyber space. The people taking bribes from him sign their names in that very same book to acknowledge the receipt of the money. The book doesn't only contain the information that can condemn every woman and man whose names are recorded on its pages, but it also contains the proof that can bury those officials behind bars for a very long time. It'll cause a national scandal, if not a complete collapse of the ruling party."

I grin. "In that case, your job is even easier."

He blinks. "You want me to steal his book? It's impossible. He keeps it locked in his desk at home. He never invites us to his house. He doesn't believe in mixing with his employees outside of work. Even if someone tried to break in, it would be useless. I've seen the precautions he took because I paid the security companies who installed his burglar bars and alarms. From the details on the invoice, there are even burglar bars inside his ceiling to prevent robbers from coming through the roof. The place is like Fort Knox. Mr. Edwards has one of the most sophisticated alarm systems in his world. It's foolproof. He's a stickler for security, which is why he lives in this quiet, godforsaken place and runs an office in George instead of in Cape Town. It's a lot safer here."

After that long speech, he sucks in a breath.

"Fine," I say.

He regards me with mistrust. "Fine?"

I drop the brick. "I believe you."

His features contort with alarm. "What now? What are you going to make me do?"

"Nothing."

"Nothing?" he cries out.

"You're of no use to me."

He's not competent enough to play the thief. I'll have to make another plan to get my hands on that book.

Cowering, he whimpers, "You're going to kill me. I know it."

I laugh, moving around him to tie his hands again. "Not if you keep this *meeting* to yourself." I pick up the sock. "However, if you say a word—"

Before I have time to finish my sentence, he jumps to his feet and charges to the window like a man with the devil on his tail.

"Wait," I cry out, diving after him but grabbing nothing but air.

It's too late. Before I can grab his jacket, he's sailing through the window like an athlete jumping hurdles. The windowsill digs into my hips as I slam my body against the bricks.

Dumbfounded, I watch him flail through the air, trying to navigate a drop he clearly didn't anticipate. A dull thud sounds as his body hits the rocks at the bottom of the cliff. He lies there motionless, his arms at his sides and his left leg bent in an awkward position while a red circle bleeds out from beneath his head. I don't need to climb down to know he's dead.

Stupid, crazy fucking bastard.

A wave crashes over him and tugs his body toward the sea when the water pulls back. The next wave drags him a little farther. In a minute, his body will be taken by the current.

I spare the idiot a last glance before getting to work, using a leafy branch I break from a nearby tree to wipe out my tracks. I drive to the tar road and do the same with the marks the tires left in the dust. Bringing the branch with me, I make my way back to George. On the way, I chuck the branch through the window down a ravine.

Fuck.

I still can't believe Johnson was such an idiot, trying to escape through a window without knowing what lies beyond. His fear of me must've outweighed his fear of taking such an uncalculated risk, which is proof of how much terror I inspired in him.

He's not the first man I saw dying. Witnessing torture and death is part of my inheritance. My father never sheltered me from who we are. I've seen men beaten, carved to pieces, and shot since I turned ten. Johnson is the first man who died by my hand though. He's the first man I killed in the name of my future bride, and my gut tells me he won't be the last.

CHAPTER
SIX

Sabella

My mom knocks on my door early, telling me I have a visitor. Anticipation sparks in my belly as I jump out of bed. I dress hurriedly, pulling on a pair of shorts and a T-shirt. When my mom sticks her head around the doorframe to ask if I'm ready, she gives me a disapproving look and instructs me to wear something more presentable like the red dress she takes from my closet.

"Who's here?" I ask, shimmying into the fitted dress that's overly formal for a Friday morning, too excited to argue about my mom's choice of outfit for me. If she's making me dress up, my visitor must be someone important to my parents, someone with business ties to Dad.

Someone like Angelo.

She hands me my red sandals. "Fix your hair and come

down quickly." On her way out, she adds from over her shoulder, "Don't forget to brush your teeth."

My stomach flutters as I take care of my grooming and brush my hair. I apply mascara and lip gloss and give myself a once-over in the mirror before charging to the door.

Wait.

I turn on my heel and hurry to my dresser where I take the bracelet Angelo's family gave me from the drawer and secure it around my wrist.

There. Perfect.

Not two seconds later, I'm rushing down the stairs. I bet Angelo returned to offer an excuse for leaving the party early. He won't go back to Corsica without saying goodbye. Something happened last night. I can't put my finger on what transpired between us, but I'll bet all the money in my bank account he's aware of it too.

I take the turn to the lounge so fast my sandals slip on the tiles, and then I slow my steps. My spirits sink. Colin sits on the sofa, framed by the view of the sea and the brilliant sky at his back. The sunlight crowns his blond head with a silver lining. He's dressed in a striped shirt, beige chinos, and loafers without socks. His blue eyes crinkle in the corners when he sees me.

"Oh, it's you," I say, unable to keep the disappointment from my voice.

He frowns. Usually, I'm ecstatic to see my best friend, especially when he's just returned from a holiday abroad. He must be pondering the sudden change.

My mom, who must've entered short on my heels, clears her throat behind me.

"I'm very happy to see you," I continue quickly, which is the truth. I *am* always keen to hang out with Colin. He's just not who I was hoping to see today.

He gets to his feet, takes a bouquet of multicolored flowers wrapped in cellophane from the coffee table, and holds it out to me. "Happy birthday, Bella. I'm sorry I couldn't be here for the party. Our flight landed at six this morning."

"That's okay. You don't have to be here for every birthday party." I take the flowers. "Thank you. They're beautiful."

He leans in and kisses my cheek. "You're welcome."

"You shouldn't have rushed over straight away." I hook my hair behind my ear, feeling overdressed and uncomfortable. "You must be tired."

This setup is so awkward. We normally swim or play volleyball on the beach, not meet each other in the formal lounge reserved for important guests with my mom sitting in like a chaperone.

"Are you kidding? Of course I had to come." He winks. "If I didn't need a shower first, I would've woken you up even earlier. Did you get my video message? It's not the same as saying happy birthday in person, but it's the next best thing."

"Yes, thank you. I'm sorry I haven't replied yet. The party finished late."

My mom pokes me in the ribs, which is my cue to turn the conversation to him.

Resisting an urge to glare at her, I ask, "How was New York?"

Of course, he'll tell me all the juicy details later when we're alone, but since my mom isn't showing any signs of leaving, I'm just making polite conversation.

"Freezing. My mom got her New Year on Times Square, but she couldn't last outside for more than ten minutes before we had to head back to the hotel."

"How are they—your parents?" Mom asks. "And your sister? Clara must've had fun."

"Dad enjoyed it less than Mom, seeing that she mostly did shopping and towed him along. Clara caught a cold on the second day. Needless to say, she was miserable."

"Poor dear," Mom says. "I'm sorry to hear that."

He shrugs. "It happens." Reverting his attention to me, he continues, "More importantly, how was the big event?"

As my mom can't see my face, I roll my eyes while saying with enthusiasm, "Great."

A grin stretches his cherub cheeks. Colin is handsome in a blond-and-tanned surfer kind of way, but he hasn't outgrown the baby fat on his face.

"There's cake left over," my mom says. "Would you like a slice? It's from a renowned French baker."

He replies with a brilliant smile. "That sounds great, thank you, Mrs. Edwards."

My mom lifts the receiver of the intercom phone on the wall and dials the kitchen, ordering Doris to serve tea and cake.

"While you're at it, please bring a vase with water," Mom adds before hanging up. Facing me, she rubs her hands together. "Colin has a surprise for you."

I look at him. "You do?"

"Sit," he says, taking the flowers from my hands and leaving them on the table. "It's your birthday gift."

Flopping down on the sofa, I give him an anxious smile. I hate surprises. "I thought the flowers were for my birthday."

"This is your real gift," he says, walking to the grand piano.

Oh, no. I cringe inwardly when he takes a seat on the bench and shakes his fingers to warm them up. Sometimes, he can be such a nerd. He's an all-rounder, good at academics, music, and sport. He's always considerate and friendly. His manners are impeccable. He never loses his cool, and he never says something bad about anybody, not even to side with me when I'm having a tiff with one of the kids in our neighborhood. I'm not sure why his flawless character irritates me so much today. I just wish he'd sometimes be a little less perfect.

He runs his fingers over the notes from C to B or whatever they're called, testing them.

"It hasn't been tuned," my mom says, taking a seat next to me and crossing her legs. "The technician can't come out until next week."

"It's a mighty fine piano, Mrs. Edwards."

She beams. "Thank you."

Diving into a saloon-style version of Happy Birthday, he sings, "Happy birthday to you. Happy birthday, dear Bella."

I make a gagging gesture.

He laughs and changes direction, letting his fingers fly over the keys as he launches into a complicated modern piece of music.

While I admire his skill, the music isn't my style. Call me unsophisticated, but I find it awful. I clench my hands in my lap while he loses himself in the music.

It feels like it's gone on forever before the beat slows and he pauses dramatically before hitting the final key. The high note still reverberates in the space when Doris enters with a tray.

Colin shoots me an expectant smile.

My mom claps. "Bravo. That was outstanding, Colin."

I join in the applause, but my effort lacks enthusiasm.

"What is it called?" Mom asks.

"I composed it for Bella," he says. "I haven't titled it yet. Maybe I'll call it Sweet Sixteen."

Doris leaves the tray on the coffee table and straightens. "Bella has another guest."

I jerk my head in her direction, expecting her to tell me my visitor is waiting in the entrance to be invited in, and then I do a double-take. Angelo stands in the doorframe with a huge box in his hands. My stomach lurches as if I'm on a rollercoaster. Blood surges through my body, and heat burns on my cheeks.

Wearing black jeans, a leather jacket, and a dark expression, he looks sinister and angry. The rings on his fingers and the chunky bracelets on his wrists add a bad-boy slash alternative-artsy vibe. I find the male accessories hot, but my mom's upside-down smile as her gaze homes in on his hands says it's too much jewelry for her liking.

He sweeps his gaze over the room, taking in the flowers, my dress, and the fine china reserved for special occasions. When he fixes his attention on Colin, the look in his glacial eyes turns diabolical.

Colin blanches. Who wouldn't under such a stare? That glare promises torture and murder and all the unspeakable horrors of nightmares.

Shifting on the bench, Colin glances between Angelo and me.

"Angelo," Mom says, turning as stiff as cardboard. "We didn't expect you."

He nails her with a piercing look. As if finding the sight boring, he quickly moves on, his next target me. I'm frozen in place, exposed and vulnerable, my secrets spilling out in the color of my cheeks and the breathless gasp that's squeezed from my chest.

Tilting his head, he inspects my features. What he sees amuses him. He quirks an eyebrow. A knowing smile curves his lips.

He knows.

He knows the effect he has on me.

I'm such a damn open book.

"I brought the rest of Sabella's gift," he says in a suave voice, his accent barely detectible.

My mom says through tight lips, "As you can see, Sabella has a guest."

Angelo's tone is dry. "I noticed."

"I'll fetch another cup and slice of cake," Doris says, enjoying the spectacle with a little too much glee. She's never been a big fan of my mom.

My mom's cutting look is lost on her as she leaves the room.

Always following the protocol of good manners, my mom stands and straightens her skirt. "Angelo, this is Colin, Sabella's very special friend. Colin, this is Angelo, a business associate of my husband."

At *business associate*, Angelo gives my mom a mocking smile. He crosses the floor and puts the box on the table.

Colin stands and rounds the piano. He offers Angelo a hand. "It's a pleasure to meet you."

Angelo's long lashes dip as he glances at Colin's palm before gripping it in a handshake that makes Colin wince. "Is it?"

Colin frowns.

Dismissing Colin with an air of disinterest, Angelo addresses me. "I brought some things Pirate may need."

Colin looks between my mom and me. "Pirate?"

"Um, Angelo gave me a cat."

Colin raises a brow. He knows about my mom's aversion to pets and her so-called allergy.

"I thought he may need a bed, toys, and a litter tray." Angelo motions at the box. "There are all kinds of soft and dry food as well as different types of litter. That way, you can test everything to see what he prefers."

"Wow. Thank you." I smile at him. "That's so thoughtful. I was going to beg my sister to drive me to the pet shop to buy all of that."

"Colin wrote a ballade for Sabella's birthday," Mom says. "Would you like to hear it?"

"I heard it." Angelo's smile is flat. "I think all your neighbors did. I hope they have earplugs."

A choking sound slips through Mom's lips.

Colin simultaneously frowns and smiles as if to say, *What the fuck is your problem?*

"I have to be on my way. Our flight leaves in a few hours." Angelo offers me his arm. "Will you walk me out, *cara?*"

Even though it was a question, he phrased it like an order.

I stand on shaky legs, place my hand on his forearm, and mumble, "Excuse me," in Colin's direction as Angelo walks me out.

"What about your tea?" Doris asks when we pass her in the foyer. She's carrying a tray laid with a cup and a plated slice of cake.

"Another time," he says, inclining his head and leading me outside.

On the front patio, he steers me to the swing bench in the corner and lowers his arm. I don't have a choice but to remove my hand. Watching me with cunning attention, he leans a shoulder on the wall and takes a joint from his pocket.

"Is that a habit?" I ask.

"It helps to relax me when business is tense." He scrutinizes me. "You don't like it."

"I hate the smell of tobacco smoke. It has a way of clinging to a person's hair and clothes and leaving a horrible stale smell in a room." I wrinkle my nose. "Not to mention cigarette breath."

He breaks the joint in half and shoves the pieces back into his pocket.

Something warm spreads through my chest, knowing he did that just because I hate the smell of smoke.

Silence stretches as he continues to study me with a penetrating stare.

"What?" I say when I can't stand it any longer.

He grips the chain around my neck, fingering the sea turtle pendant. "Did he give this to you?"

"Who, Colin? No. It was a gift from my dad."

He drops the chain. "Is he your boyfriend?"

"No," I exclaim, not wanting him to get the wrong idea. "Colin is my neighbor and my best friend. We grew up together. He's like a brother to me." I push a finger on his chest. "Which is why you can't treat him like that."

"Like what?" he drawls.

"As if he's your enemy. I saw how you shook his hand."

"You want me to go easy on him?" he asks with a chuckle.

"I want you to be polite. You can't be rude to my friends."

He drags his gaze over me. "Is that how you dress up for all your friends?"

I cross my arms. "The dress was my mom's idea, not that what I choose to wear is any of your business."

He rubs a thumb over his bottom lip as he considers my answer. After a beat, his lips curve into an indulgent smile. "It seems like your mother has a different idea about your brotherly friend."

"Okay, I'll admit that was awkward."

He scrutinizes me. "Does your mother always play matchmaker?"

Mom can be infuriating at times, but I'm not going to let him judge her. "She means well."

"I'm sure Colin will agree."

"I can assure you that Colin was just as uncomfortable as me."

"You've never had the tiniest attraction to him, not even when you played house when you were young?"

I pull my back straight. "We didn't play house. Why is this starting to sound like an interrogation? I don't care much for being questioned like this."

"You've never kissed him?" he asks, his tone incredulous.

The fact that he doubts my honesty makes me angry. "Like what I wear, that's also none of your business."

He raises a thick, dark eyebrow. "Isn't it?"

The meaning behind that statement sends a shiver of anticipation through me, but I won't let him bully me. "Is this conversation going somewhere, or are you just being rude?"

He steps so close that the heat of his skin is like a warm mist around me. "Yes, this is going somewhere, but you already know that." He adds with a wicked glint in his eyes, "Despite what your mother and father may say."

My heart starts galloping in my chest. His masculinity is overwhelming. I'm no match for the power he exudes or for the experience that comes with his age, but I can't bring myself to care.

"Now, tell me, *cara*," he says in a soft voice, leaning closer. "Is it sweet sixteen and never been kissed, or has that card been claimed?"

Annoyingly, the heat burning on my cheeks gives me away again. I hate that he knows how inexperienced I am.

Satisfaction bleeds with something darker into his black eyes. "Good. Keep it like that. Your first kiss is mine."

Awareness of him, his smell, and how tall and strong he is washes over me. Goosebumps run down my arms.

He leans closer still and continues in a possessive tone. "*All* your firsts are mine."

With those words, he invades my spaces, my dreams, and my hopes, and builds an indestructible nest for himself in my future.

My pulse pounds in my temples. Angelo Russo wants my first kiss. And more. So much more.

He fixes his gaze on the bracelet on my wrist. The approval that sparks in his eyes warms me. I have an inexplicable urge to please him. My parents have always showered me with love and acceptance. I'm not starved for approval, but I crave *his*. No one's appreciation matters as much as his. Until yesterday, my dad was my hero. My everything. Somewhere between then and now, Angelo has challenged that first place my dad held in my heart.

Urgency infuses his words. "Tell me you understand. Make a promise. To me. Now."

"A promise?" His sudden intensity scares me. It pushes my newly empowered heart into the background and allows my logical reasoning to take center stage again. "You're going back to Corsica in a few hours."

"I'll always come back for you. Remember that. No matter what anyone says."

He's so serious now, so overbearing, that I can't help but take a step back to breathe, to focus. To put distance between us.

This isn't how relationships develop. This isn't a guy asking me out on a date. He's skipping everything in between, jumping straight to what sounds an awful lot like a serious commitment.

"I don't understand what you're asking from me," I say, my throat tight as I stare up at his beautiful face.

His gaze drills into mine. "I'm asking you to be patient. To wait."

"We only met yesterday."

"When we met doesn't matter." He holds out his hand. "Give me your phone."

"I don't have it on me. It's in my room."

"Give me your number."

My mom pops her head around the front door. "Sabella, your guest is waiting, and your father is on the phone. He wants a word with you."

"I'm coming," I call. "I'm just saying goodbye."

Mom purses her lips but goes back inside.

"Give me your number, Sabella," Angelo says.

Not, *will you please give me your number*? No. He's demanding it like it's his right to have it.

A calculated look comes over his face. "I can get it easily enough, but it'll be sweeter if you give it to me."

The part of me that doesn't like to be told what to do wants to resist, but another part of me, the part that needs to please him, wants to do as he demands. Do *I* want to? There's not even a question about it. I wanted him to own more than just my number before he'd even spoken to me. From the moment I saw him, I wanted things I can't put in words.

"Sabella," my mom calls from inside the house, her tone carrying a warning.

If I'm not back in the house in the next second, my mom will come out and drag me inside. Having been embarrassed once in front my instant crush is more than enough.

I quickly rattle off my number.

The approval I want so desperately shows in the curve of his sensual lips. "Good girl."

That warm feeling of earlier spreads through my whole

body. I focus on his lips. His bottom lip is fuller than his upper lip, giving his mouth both a sexy look and a determined set.

"I'll text you my number," he says. "If you ever need anything, you only have to call."

The enormity of the statement takes me aback. He doesn't owe me anything, yet he behaves as if he's already much more to me, even more than a boyfriend.

Shoving his hands into his pockets, he strolls to the car parked next to the fountain. This time, when he drives away, he doesn't look back, but it's as if a part of him stayed behind. Inside me.

CHAPTER
SEVEN

Angelo

When I get back to the hotel, Edwards is waiting in the reception. He gets up from the chaise by the window, his face ruddier than usual. Holding my gaze with a moody expression, he adjusts his jacket and meets me halfway across the floor.

"Have a coffee with me," he says, tilting his head toward the bar.

I smile as I follow him, knowing what's coming.

We take a seat at the counter where it's quiet.

"Two espressos," he says to the barman. Then, turning to me, "I want you to stay away from my daughter. I don't want you going near my house again."

The barman puts a coffee in front of each of us.

Pulling mine closer, I take note of the thin layer of sheen on his forehead, how he'd rather sweat in the heat than take off his jacket. "News travels fast."

"My wife called me at the office when you turned up at our place." He rips the packet of sugar open and pours it into his coffee, messing grains over the counter. "I left an important meeting to have this discussion with you."

"I'm flattered. However, seeing me off in person wasn't necessary."

His jaw tightens, but his tone remains patient. "I thought we should talk before you go."

"Without my father."

"Yes." He stirs his coffee and taps the spoon on the rim of the cup. "It's better that we do this alone."

The *this* he's referring to is going to be interesting. "I'm listening."

"You're a young man with your whole life ahead of you. Being tied in a marriage to a girl you don't know can't be something you want."

"Don't assume to know what I want."

He stiffens. "I can assure you it's not what Sabella wants."

I raise a brow. "Are you sure about that?"

The spoon clatters on the saucer as he drops it. "Arranged marriages may still be practiced where you come from, but it doesn't work like that here."

"Where I come from, family and duty come first. We honor our promises."

His face turns red. "I did not make any promises. Your father is mistaken."

"My father is many things, but he's not a liar. I was there, remember? I might have been young at the time, but I did pay attention to your conversation, especially since your discussion involved me."

He balls his hand into a fist on the counter. "If you're not willing to back down from this ridiculous idea, you won't leave me with a choice but to find another service provider."

My smile is cold. "Meaning you'll cut us out?"

He lifts his chin and says in an unwavering voice, "Yes."

Up to now, we've always received our orders via third parties. No emails. Nothing on paper. No trails that can lead back to him. He's clever, but I'm cleverer.

"If you're bringing it up, Mr. Edwards, you must already have someone in mind."

He raises his chin another inch. "I do."

I study him as I sip my espresso. Judging from the sweat stains under the armpits of his jacket, he's not as certain of himself as he likes to appear. Still, this is Africa. Nothing is impossible here. The continent has no lack of powerful criminals. We don't have a legally binding contract that will prevent him from getting his services elsewhere. Our kind of deals are sealed with a handshake and retained with bloodshed.

I put my cup on the counter. "I see."

He scrunches his eyes into slits. "Does that mean you're going to do something about it?"

"I guess I am."

He pats me on the shoulder and gets to his feet. "I'm glad we could come to an understanding. I'll leave it in your hands to deal with your father. You'll know best how to convince him." His lips curve into a semblance of a smile, but the gesture is flat and formal. "I'm glad we'll continue to do business."

Leaving his espresso untouched, he walks to the door.

I stare after him with pity, because I *am* going to do something about it.

And he's not going to like it.

I take a two-hundred-rand bill from my wallet and slide it over the counter.

If Edwards misinterpreted my meaning, it's his bad.

CHAPTER
EIGHT

Sabella

I hug a pillow to my chest where I lie on my bed as I replay the morning in my head, or more accurately, the part involving Angelo. Pirate is curled up against my side, his warm little body soothing.

I pick up my phone and check the screen like I did not five minutes earlier. There's still nothing, no word from Angelo. Maybe he's in the plane. Does he even remember my number? What if he forgot it? No. Somehow, an inadequate memory seems beneath him. He comes across as one of those people who's both insightful and good at memorizing facts. Intelligent. Like someone who breezes through life, navigating the pitfalls effortlessly and efficiently, he's clever on all levels.

Maybe he'll send me a text message when he lands in Corsica. Can you even fly there directly? Do you have to go via France? My knowledge of geography is good, but

I've never traveled abroad, so I don't know how it works. I make a mental note to look it up.

A fresh pang of guilt hits my conscience. My stomach twists. I lied to my dad. It's a line I've never crossed, and it makes me loathe myself. I hate the feeling, but what choice did I have?

When Dad called, I've never heard him so angry. He never loses his cool, especially not with me. I told him Angelo had delivered the rest of my gift and that was all. He asked if Angelo had initiated any contact, and I said no without blinking. If I'd told the truth, Dad would've confiscated my phone, and I couldn't let that happen. I'll die if I don't hear from him.

Urgh. Why must Dad be so difficult? It's obvious he doesn't trust Angelo with me. He made that clear when he said Angelo is never to set foot in our house again. When I asked Dad why he disliked him so much, he gave me the same answer as last night, that he's a bad person and no good for me.

A knock falls on the door, pulling me from my thoughts. Mattie enters without waiting for my reply.

She comes over and sits on the edge of the bed. "Mom said you're grounded."

"I can't believe she ran straight to the phone and called Dad." I push the pillow over my face and utter a scream before throwing it against the wall. "I'm so mad at her."

Pirate jerks awake at the sudden movement, his big yellow eyes alert and wild as he looks around.

"Sorry, Pirate," I mumble, stroking his fur.

He settles with a purr and curls up in a ball again.

"Don't blame Mom," Mattie says. "She did what she thought was right. Dad obviously agrees."

Mattie's words stir a sense of betrayal in me. "Hey, whose side are you on?"

"Everyone told you to stay away from that boy. It's for the best." She gets to her feet. "Do you want to look at wedding brochures with us? Jared and I are getting some ideas for the venue."

I'd rather swallow needles. "Why don't you just elope and have an island wedding?"

"I want a big wedding with all the frills. If it's the most I'm getting out of the deal, I may as well go the whole nine yards."

Mindful not to disturb Pirate again, I sit up carefully. "How can you be so accepting of everything? How can you sacrifice getting a degree and having a career for Jared?"

She shrugs and turns for the door. "I love him." Calling from over her shoulder, she adds, "We're in the informal lounge if you change your mind."

"Thanks," I mumble, but she's already closed the door.

In exactly ten minutes, Mom is going to barge in here and tell me to be a good sister by showing an interest in Mattie's wedding. It's not that I'm uninterested. I just don't want to pore over glossy magazines and browse cake decorations for hours. What can be more boring?

I quickly strip out of the red dress and pull on my bikini, a pair of shorts, and a boyfriend shirt that I knot in the front. After making sure Pirate has food and water, I close the door behind me and run barefoot downstairs.

Mom is talking to Doris in the kitchen, giving her dinner instructions.

"I'm going to Colin's," I say as I scoot past the door, not giving Mom a chance to object. Not that I expect her to, seeing how hard she's trying to push Colin and me into each other's arms.

"Be home by five," Mom calls after me. "Your father won't be later than six."

That's new. Usually, on Fridays, he has drinks after work with his clients. It's a company tradition. As he never gets home until after midnight, we have our Friday night dinners without him. I hope he's not making an exception in coming home early to lecture me again. Keeping a straight face while lying to Dad is neither easy nor pleasant.

After letting myself out through the pedestrian gate, I walk the two hundred meters to Colin's house and ring the intercom at the gate. Our gardens touch on the eastern side, but their mansion doesn't have a sea-facing view.

When the gate clicks open, I jog down the paved driveway to the front. The house is modern with angular lines and lots of glass. I like the design and the sparse, contemporary furniture much better than our imposing, palatial structure with its stiff and formal sofas.

Colin opens the front door, wearing a pair of Bermuda swimming shorts and holding a maxi bag of potato crisps in one hand. His ridiculously perfect abs and hairless chest didn't retain an ounce of the baby fat that gives his cheeks their chubby appearance. Besides his blond-hair-and-blue-eyed look, his well-proportioned pecs, biceps, and washboard stomach are some of the biggest reasons why the girls in my school are chasing so hard after him. Other reasons include his family's money, his good grades, his promising future, and his faultless manners. Oh, and did I mention that he's the town's rugby star?

"Hey," he says, stuffing a handful of crisps in his mouth. "What's up?"

"Mattie and Jared are choosing wedding colors and themes."

"Ouch." He sucks air through his teeth. "Sounds like a nightmare." He holds the bag out to me and says with a full mouth, "Want a chip?"

I make a face. "No, thanks. Your hand's been in there, and I don't know where your hand has been."

He cocks a shoulder. "Your loss." Turning back into the house, he says, "My parents went grocery shopping. There's not much to munch in the house."

I follow him inside. "I'm not hungry."

Not today. Usually, I always have an appetite. I'm just too out of sorts to be in the mood for snacks.

We walk through the television room toward the deck at the back and stop next to the pool where Clara is swimming a length underwater.

She surfaces at the shallow end and wipes drops from her eyes. "Hey, Bella."

I give a little wave. "Hi."

She kicks away from the side, dives under the water, and resumes her swimming.

Colin goes to the bar and opens the fridge. "There's only Pepsi and tonic water."

"I'm not thirsty."

He pulls his head from the fridge and gives me a mock-horrified look. "What? Sabella Edwards not hungry or thirsty? It's going to snow, and I've had enough of that in New York."

My tone is sarcastic. "Ha-ha."

He grabs a can of Pepsi. "Sure you don't want one?"

"I do," Clara says, pushing herself out of the water.

He throws the can to his sister and takes another for himself. After cracking it open, he plonks down on a deckchair.

Clara takes a few gulps before setting the soft drink on a table and snatching a towel from the pile on the shelf next to the bar.

Colin and Clara are three years apart, but if you didn't know they were brother and sister, you'd never guess. Their resemblance ends with their golden hair and clear blue eyes. Her face is narrower and her small body pixie-like in build.

She wags her eyebrows. "I'm going for a shower to give you two time to, you know, catch up." At *catch up*, she makes a heart shape with her hands.

Colin flips her off. She giggles as she waltzes past me and into the house.

"You won't grow taller by standing there," Colin says. "Grab a seat."

Too agitated for lounging, I shove my hands in my back pockets and kick at the pebbles on the border of the deck.

He sits up and swings a leg over each side of the chair, clasping the can in both hands. "Clara is going to a sleepover at five. I have to watch her until then, but I'm free after. Do you want to go catch a movie?"

"Nope." I sigh. "I'm grounded from going to town."

"Grounded? Wow. What happened?"

I exhale through my nose. "Angelo."

"What did you do?"

"Nothing." I throw my hands in the air. "I got grounded for talking to him." Alone. Outside.

He takes a sip of his drink, watching me from over the rim of the can. "Just for talking to him?"

"Yes."

He rests his elbows on his thighs. "That's harsh."

"Tell me about it." I go over to the ping-pong table and pick up the ball and a bat. "My dad said I should've refused the stuff he bought for Pirate. He's angry that I walked him out. He wanted to know what we talked about alone outside as if I'm a child who can't be trusted. I'm supposed to tell Angelo he's not welcome if he ever shows up again."

"Why?"

I bounce the ball with the bat. "Dad said he comes from a bad family and that he's only doing business with them because he doesn't have a choice."

"Don't you believe your dad?"

"You know my dad is overprotective. I looked Angelo up on Google. There wasn't a lot of personal information, only that his family owns tons of businesses in Corsica. They donate shitloads of money to charity. His mom is an angel investor in several startups and the patron of a program that reintegrates runaway teenagers into society."

"Anything can look good on paper. You have to admit, the dude *is* weird."

I look at him quickly, missing a hit. The ball hops off the table and rolls under a rosebush. "Why do you say that?"

"He looked like he wanted to rip my head off and eat my brains for breakfast."

Busying myself with going after the ball, I avoid his gaze. "You're exaggerating."

"What's the deal with the two of you?"

Heat pushes up my neck. I take a moment to gather myself before straightening. "There's no deal."

"Come on, Bella. I don't know you from yesterday. The guy walks into a room and you turn redder than a stop sign."

I throw the ball and catch it mid-air. "I was surprised, that's all. He didn't have to buy all those things for Pirate."

"I've never seen you blush in the sixteen years I've known you."

I can't argue that fact.

"Are you in love with him?" he asks in a quiet voice.

The heat travels from my neck to my face. Ignoring the question, I dribble the ball with the bat on the table.

"You are." He adds in a disbelieving tone, "After only meeting him last night."

I can't deny it. He won't buy the lie. If anyone knows me inside out, it's Colin.

Dropping the bat, I turn to face him. "Maybe I am. So what?"

"So what?" He utters a laugh. "You don't even know him."

I frown. "You say it like you disapprove."

"How can you fall in love without knowing the first thing about him?"

I stiffen. "I know plenty of things."

"Yeah? Like what?"

"He's kind."

He snort-laughs. "Is he?"

"Yes," I say, my tone defensive. "He made my mom let me keep the cat."

"How did he manage that anyway? Wait. How did he know you wanted a cat?"

"He didn't. I found the cat in a trashcan and took it home. When my mom saw it, she wanted to take it to the SPCA, but Angelo happened to be there, and he told her he gave me the cat for my birthday."

"And she agreed? Just like that?"

"Yes." I brush my hands over my shorts. "Their business must be really important to my dad."

He glances toward the horizon and back at me. "He lied and then manipulated your mom into letting you have a cat. You base your feelings on *that*?"

"Why not?" I say, irritation bubbling up inside me. "He didn't lie with bad intentions. It was only to help me."

Chuckling, he tips back the can and takes a long drink. After wiping his mouth with the back of his hand, he says with a wry expression, "Because of him you finally have a cat, and I wrote you a stupid fucking ballade."

"It's not stupid." When he raises a brow, meeting my gaze with a challenge in his, I add quickly, "Okay, you have to be honest, the situation was weird. That's not our dynamic."

"No?" He searches my face. "It could be."

I walk to his chair and poke him in the chest. "You're my friend, my best buddy."

He squints up at me. "Exactly. We know each other's faults and weaknesses. I know you hate avo and that you mash bananas on your peanut butter toast. We're perfectly suited. Everyone says we make the handsomest couple in town. We're both high achievers and good sportsmen. They all think we're going to end up together. Why shouldn't we?"

"There's no spark," I say, raising my palms and lifting my shoulders.

"Sparks are overrated. I think friendship is much more important."

Propping my hands on my hips, I scrutinize him through narrowed eyes. "This is all because of this morning. My mom put you up to that. The ballade was her idea. Admit it."

He scoffs. When I don't budge, he cuts his gaze toward the pool. "She may have mentioned that they'd gotten you a piano for your birthday and that, since you don't play, a little performance would be a nice gift."

"I knew it," I say with a measure of triumph and relief. "I'm so embarrassed about her meddling. I'm really sorry she's like that."

"Gah." He waves a hand. "It's nothing." His Adam's apple bobs as he swallows. "You don't have to apologize."

I straddle the chair, facing him. "Are we seriously

having this conversation? I don't want things to get awkward between us."

He tips back the can and drinks, pretending to look at the ocean.

"Because you're my only real friend." I make a puppy face. "My best buddy." Dipping my head, I catch his gaze and say in my pouty voice, "My buddy bear. My cuddly pooh."

A grin tugs at the corner of his lips even though he tries hard to keep a serious face. He gives me a gentle shove. "Okay, okay. I get it."

Laughing, I lean back with my weight supported on my arms and tickle his side with my toes. "Come on. Smile. You know you want to."

He pushes my foot away, but his features soften as his resolve crumbles. He's never been good at pretending to be angry. "So you want sparks, huh?"

I let out a dreamy sigh. "Yep."

"If your parents don't want you to see this guy, what are you going to do? Anyway, your mom mentioned that he lives abroad. Corsica, right?"

"Right." I bite my lip, considering how honest to be, but Colin *is* my bestie, and I trust him. He won't tattletale on me to my parents. "I gave him my number."

"Have you heard from him?"

My chest tightens as I admit, "Not yet."

Caution slips into his voice. "Say you do hear from him. Then what?"

"Then we're going to text and talk on the phone. Isn't that why you give someone your number?"

"How is this going to work if you don't see him again?"

"I will," I say, emphasizing the words with conviction more for my own sake than for Colin's. "He said he'd come back."

"Will you meet him in secret?" He studies me with something that looks too much like pity. "How will that work in the long term? Can you hide seeing him from your parents forever?"

The obstacles in my path are dampers on my short-lived excitement. The unknown difficulties lying ahead constrict my chest. But I won't be a minor forever. As an adult, I'll be able to make my own decisions. Even then, I'm not looking forward to disappointing my dad.

Putting on a carefree smile, I say, "I'll cross that bridge when I get there."

Concern passes through his eyes. "Just be careful, Bella. Don't do something that'll get you hurt. I don't want that for you, because you're my best friend too."

"Thanks." My smile wavers. "Anyway, it's not serious. It's not like I'm making plans to marry him. Like you said, we only met yesterday."

"Okay," he says, not sounding convinced.

My phone pings. Taking it from my pocket, I check the message.

It's from Angelo.

My heart starts pounding, sending a rush of blood through my veins.

Angelo: *Are you thinking of me?*

I type out a quick reply. *Are you thinking of me?*

His answer comes a second later. *Funny. And clever. Yes.*

Simple and honest. He doesn't mince his words. I like that.

Aware of Colin's gaze on me, I get up. "Sorry. It's him. Give me a minute."

I turn my back on Colin and type, *Yes too.*

Angelo: *Good. I'm having a phone delivered for you tomorrow.*

My cheeks turn hot, knowing he anticipated the fact

that my parents may confiscate my phone or check my messages.

Angelo: *The delivery will be made at ten. Can you wait outside?*

So that my parents don't find out.

Me: *Yes, but tell the courier company to meet me at the bottom of the street.*

Angelo: *Done.*

Me: *Where are you?*

Angelo: *On our way to Cape Town.*

I think a moment, trying to come up with an appropriate reply. It's too soon to tell him I'll miss him. I don't want to come on to him too strongly.

Me: *Bon voyage?*

I wait a few beats, but when he doesn't reply, I write, *At what time is your flight?*

His answer comes immediately. *Midnight. I'll let you know when we land in Marseille.*

My finger hovers over the kissing emoji, but as he hasn't used any emojis, I decide against it. I stare at the screen for another three seconds, and when the dots indicating that he's typing remain absent, I pocket my phone.

"What did he say?" Colin asks.

I set my gaze on the ocean, trying to imagine Corsica on the other side. "That he's thinking of me."

"Damn, Bella."

I turn around.

Colin stabs his fingers through his hair, messing it up. "Nothing good can come of this."

That sounds an awful lot like what Mattie said, but I pay the pessimistic prophecy no heed. My stomach does that funny thing again, and suddenly, the world is a wonderful place.

CHAPTER
NINE

W hen we land in Marseille at eleven in the morning, I send a text message to Sabella, asking if she received her new phone. I went to some lengths to arrange a secure line with unlimited data for a good reason. A few reasons, actually.

The calls won't be traceable, meaning her father won't find out what I'm up to, and the location tracker I activated will give me her whereabouts. I'll have eyes on her not only via the man I dispatched to keep her safe and to report on her activities, but also via her phone.

I want to have a means of communication with her every minute of every hour. I want to be able to get hold of her twenty-four-seven. I'll teach her to keep that phone on her day and night like one uses treats to teach an animal to do tricks. I'll send her messages when she arrives at school and when she leaves. I already know she's anxious to hear from me.

I'll pull her in and spin a web around her, charming my way into her heart until she won't be able to go a day without hearing from me. I know how to turn people into addicts. I'm a good manipulator. I'll throw a few breadcrumbs, luring her closer little by little until she eats out of my hand like a bird. She won't even realize it's happening. She'll wake up checking her phone, and it'll be the last thing she does before going to bed.

I won't text her when she's in school. I don't want to disrupt her concentration or have a negative influence on her grades. Outside of school, however, I'll control her life, and no one will be any the wiser. The thought is sweet. The day Edwards finds out, I want to be there. I want to look him in the eyes and see his disillusionment when he realizes I stole his precious princess right from under his nose.

As I anticipated, her reply comes immediately, thanking me for the phone and asking how the flight was. I like that about her, that she's honest and direct without indulging in games. Only women who are uncertain of themselves play hard to get. Sabella is straightforward and uncomplicated. She doesn't see a need to hide her feelings, which counts in my favor. It'll be easier for me to get to know her and to learn what makes her tick.

In my line of work, being an open book is a weakness, but I prefer that trait in women. Sabella is sweet and innocent. Some would say naïve. I see the characteristic for what it is. She's unspoiled, not yet poisoned by the toxic side of life. She's fresh and gorgeous, a beautiful young woman on the precipice of adulthood. I could've done a lot worse for a wife.

At the harbor, I snap a photo of me on our luxury

yacht that we use to sail to Corsica. The sky is a cerulean blue and the sea a translucent turquoise. The scenery makes a pretty picture. It's never too early to get her acquainted with what her future home looks like. I send the photo with a message to take care of herself.

The weather conditions are good. It takes us roughly seven hours of cruising at twenty-five knots to reach Bastia. At the familiar sight of Terra Nova, a centuries-old citadel with ramparts that was built by our Genoese ancestors, the tightness in my chest eases. I breathe easier, inhaling the familiar smell of salt and sea with the crisp air.

I'm happiest on the water, a quality I inherited from our seafaring forefathers. On land, Bastia is where I'm most at home. My father comes from a long line of Italian ancestors. My grandfather came to Corsica when Italy occupied the island in 1942. My mother is from local origin. For that reason, my sister and I didn't speak Italian until we went to school. My father was hardly involved in our lives when we were young. He was too busy building his business and making his riches.

My uncles and cousins wait for us when we cruise into the marina. It's a cold winter's day with a clear, sunny sky. They have cars waiting, but my father says he wants to walk for exercise. Uncle Nico sends the drivers ahead. While we stroll to a bar in town, he fills us in on what's been going down in the business.

The owner clears the bar when we enter, sending the clientele outside. No one argues as they carry their espressos to the tables on the pavement. They know who we are.

Uncle Enzo closes the door. My father's younger brothers are identical twins. They look so much alike, it's difficult to distinguish them, but if you know them as well as I do, you can easily differentiate them by their mannerisms. Uncle Nico is the more boisterous one. Plus, he's rounder around the waist than Uncle Enzo. My mother says their extra weight is the result of eating so unhealthily since both their wives passed away at a young age. Uncle Nico's wife died in childbirth. Uncle Enzo's slowly faded away after her menopause medication triggered a stroke at the age of fifty.

My father sits down at a table and wipes a handkerchief over his brow. Despite the cold, he's sweating. I order a glass of water and coffee. The owner serves them personally, leaving both at my father's elbow. A waitress brings a tray with pastries and coffee for everyone else while we remove our coats and get comfortable.

"How is she?" my cousin, Tommaso, asks, nudging me in the ribs.

His gleeful expectation rubs me the wrong way. I play dumb. "Who?"

"Your bride. Who else?"

"Do you think I'm going to discuss my betrothed with you?"

"I just want to know if she has nice—"

I give him a slap upside the head.

"Hey." He leans to the side. "What was that for?"

"If you insult my wife, I'll break your nose."

"Future wife," he says with a disgruntled look.

"Same thing," I say.

"Tomma," Uncle Nico grumbles.

Tomma rubs his head. "I didn't mean anything, Papa. I just wanted to know, seeing that it's my turn next." He adds in a sulky tone, "And I'm not even eighteen."

I hit him again. "Show some respect for *your* future wife."

"Hey," he cries out. "I was just saying."

Uncle Nico says in his gravelly voice, "Don't give the

impression that you're not keen on meeting her. Angelo is right. It shows disrespect and a bad character."

Gianni pats Tomma on the back and grins. "Tomma only just lost his virginity. He's not keen on being reminded he'll be shackled soon."

When Tomma turns red, the men chuckle. No disrespect intended. In our circles, seventeen is considered late for being initiated into manhood. Normally, that's taken care of on a son's fifteenth birthday. Tomma had issues, it seems. The hookers his father paid didn't do it for him.

No man sitting around this table knows I'm as virginal as they come. I have no intention of throwing something sacred away for the sake of experience. The whore I got for my birthday was only too happy to be sent away without having to bed a boy. I paid her extra to keep her mouth shut. As far as my father and uncles know, she did the job. I want my bride to wait. So, I'll wait.

"On a serious note," Uncle Enzo says. "How did your meeting go? How soon can we expect an integration?"

"The sooner the better." Uncle Nico's expression is somber. "The casinos are losing money. Our contact in Marseille and Nice wants to increase his cut to fifteen percent. Refusing will be declaring war, and it'll be a bloody one."

"That's what the French government is hoping for," Uncle Enzo says. "As long as we keep our noses clean, they can't bring evidence against us. The slightest show of violence, however, will give them the excuse for a cleanup they're waiting for."

My father clears his throat. He slurps his coffee, trying to hide a cough but not quite succeeding. It takes a moment before he speaks. "Edwards denied he made the deal."

Tomma and Gianni's mouths go slack. Uncle Enzo looks at my father, dumbfounded.

Uncle Nico clenches his jaw. "That's an insult to you and your family. You can't let it slide."

My father glances at me. "I'm not."

"I'm dealing with it," I say, dragging a gaze around the table.

"How?" Uncle Nico asks.

I take my time to finish my coffee before answering. "I need a year."

Uncle Enzo sits up. "Why a year?"

"For my plan to work, I need compliance from both Edwards and his daughter. Convincing Edwards to honor his promise won't be difficult—I can bend him to our will tomorrow—but she has to believe our relationship is her idea. At least for now."

My uncles consider that.

"You can always threaten her with her family's lives," Tomma offers.

I pin him with a stare at which he quickly shuts his mouth.

Gianni whistles through his teeth. "Looks like you've got your work cut out for you, Angelo."

Always quick to catch on, Uncle Enzo says, "You'll have to find something to hold over her father's head while making her fall for you."

"She won't be so quick to fall at your feet when she finds out that you're blackmailing her father," Uncle Nico points out.

My smile is flat. "By that time, it won't matter." She's mine, and I'll do whatever it takes to claim her.

"One year," my father says, as the oldest, his word final. "Then we do it our way."

Our way means kidnapping Sabella and forcing a ring

on her finger while holding a gun against her father's head. We'll put a pen in his right hand while, one by one, cutting off the fingers on his left until he signs the contract. But that won't happen until she turns eighteen, and if my plan works, it won't have to happen at all.

"Good," I say. "Then it's decided."

And with those words, I seal Sabella Daphne Edwards's fate.

CHAPTER
TEN

Did Angelo know I'd think of him every time I cuddle Pirate when he told my mom to let me keep the cat? Whenever I set my eyes on Pirate, I'm reminded of Angelo. These days, he occupies most of my thoughts as well as my daydreams.

We communicate daily. He's interested in my life, peppering me with questions about everything from my favorite food to my favorite books. He wants to know what I like for breakfast and why I love the ocean so much.

The attention is flattering. It's got my head spinning, but not enough to be blind to the fact that he's not sharing as much information with me. When I point that out, he says his life isn't that interesting. All I know about him is that his family is filthy rich, that he's involved in his father's business, which he'll take over one day, and that he lives in Corsica.

During one of our many chats, I ask him what his job title is.

Angelo: *Jack of all trades.*

Me: *You're not a master of none.*

Angelo: *You flatter me.*

Me: *I mean it. You're one of those people who are good at everything.*

Angelo: *Some won't call me good.*

Me: *I do.*

Angelo: *Does that mean you like me?*

Me: *Would I be chatting to you if I didn't?*

Angelo: *One day, bella, you'll change your mind about that.*

Me: *Never. I'll always like you.*

He goes quiet then, making me worry that I've scared him away by implying too much, but then he asks me what else I like, a clever way of changing the subject.

Me: *The ocean. As always. You know that already.*

Angelo: *Why?*

Me: *I don't know. Because I feel at home in the water. I think I want to become a marine biologist.*

He says nothing at that.

I think about it often, about what I want to do with my life and why Angelo isn't as interested in my career choice as in everything else that concerns me. I'm ninety percent certain I made him uneasy by saying I like him. Some guys aren't comfortable talking about mushy subjects like that. From then on, I refrain from giving away too much of what's in my heart.

During the course of the year, I become more certain that I want to become a marine biologist. I've researched several career options with my parents, but I've always had my heart set on working with sea life. The admission criteria for a BSc degree are strict, and places at the University of Cape Town are limited. I can't mess up my grades. I have to score high in science, biology, and mathematics.

When I'm not swimming for our school team, I'm studying with Colin. He wants to become a civil engineer like his dad, which is an equally competitive course. We get our learner driver's licenses on the same day, and work hard toward our academic goals. Instead of distracting me, Angelo is amazingly supportive, cutting our conversations short when I need to study and checking in to make sure I get enough sleep.

I told no one but Colin about the phone Angelo had delivered. As I can't share my lovesickness with my family, I only have Colin, whose ear I chew off about how great Angelo is, how handsome, how mature, and how utterly considerate. Colin bears my ravings without a word, listening like a good friend. Since that first day, he's never warned me about speaking to Angelo in secret again. He's accepted with quiet tolerance the fact that I'm in love with a man who lives thousands of kilometers away on an island.

I carry the knowledge like a precious seed inside me, and as time passes, it blooms like a flower in a secret garden, nourished by attention and affection. Before I know it, the year is gone, and the preparations for my seventeenth birthday celebration leave me with a bittersweet longing, reminding me of when Angelo and I met.

Seventeen is not a milestone year. Luckily, this year, there won't be a string quartet and people crammed onto our lawn. My father makes a dinner reservation at a new restaurant on the beachfront in Wilderness.

During the dinner, I sneak to the bathroom and check my phone, the one Angelo gave me, but there's no message from him. He hasn't wished me a happy birthday. Has he forgotten? Doesn't he remember the day we met? The absence of any news and no word from him puts a damper on the evening and steals my appetite.

I splash water on my face, put on a bright smile, and go back to the table. Mattie and Jared are there. They finally secured a wedding venue for October, and it's all my sister can talk about. Ryan and his wife, Celeste, couldn't make it. Celeste is pregnant with their first baby and due to deliver any day.

"So," Mattie says when I'm seated. "What did you get for your birthday?"

"An underwater camera from Mom and Dad." I smile at them. "Colin gave me a new scuba mask."

"What a pity he couldn't make it, tonight," my mom says.

"Oh, no," I say quickly. "It's better that we kept it in the family."

Mattie mixes her pink gin and tonic with a bamboo straw. "If Colin isn't family, then I don't know what he is." She elbows Jared. "Isn't that so?"

Jared straightens his glasses. "Oh." He glances at Mattie and clears his throat. "Yes. I have a friend I'd like you—"

"I don't want to meet him," I say.

"Come on, Bella." Mattie stabs the ice with the straw. "Just meet the guy for drinks."

My dad checks his watch for the second time in five minutes. "What's taking them so long? Are they catching the prawns?"

Mom picks up her wine and asks with thin lips, "Do you have somewhere else to be?"

"Just tired," my dad says, winking at me. "It's been a long day."

I watch him closely, taking in the bags under his eyes

and the extra weight he picked up around his waist. "Is everything okay at work?"

"Of course," he says. "There's nothing to worry about."

"Are you sure?"

He leans over the table and pats my hand. "It's the spillover of the end-of-the-year stress. You know how it goes." As he looks over my shoulder, his expression lifts. "Ah. Here are our starters."

Mom and Mattie launch into a conversation about the wedding arrangements while Dad wolfs down his food and Jared seems to tune out. I fish my phone from my bag on my lap and check the screen under the cover of the table.

Still nothing.

"Sabella," my mom says.

I jump, guilt painting my cheeks with heat.

She frowns. "No phones at the table."

"Sorry." I put the phone away. "I'm expecting a message from Colin."

Lying became easier as the months passed. I'm doing it now without as much as wincing. Guilt still plagues me, but not nearly as much as in the beginning. I guess you grow immune to it after a while.

The pleats on her brow smooth out. Somewhat pacified, she says, "You can check your messages at home."

For the rest of the evening, I push the food around on my plate while I think up a hundred reasons why Angelo forgot my birthday. It's the anniversary of our first meeting after all. Doesn't that hold any importance for him?

Dad excuses himself when we have dessert to make a call outside.

"What's so urgent that it can't wait until the morning?" my mom asks when he gets back. "Does your CFO still work at this hour?"

Ignoring her, Dad waves over a waiter and orders a coffee.

Things have been hectic at the office since his junior accountant was murdered. Dad is still battling to find a good candidate to replace him. The ones he employs don't stay long. I overheard Ryan tell Celeste that the staff turnover has never been as high.

The online article said the police suspected that the victim was hijacked on his way to work. The assailants must've thrown him over a cliff. His body washed up two weeks later near Buffels Bay. I shiver at the thought. The traffic police later spotted his car on a highway near Cape Town.

They arrested the driver, who claimed he bought the car from a private seller. The seller had been convicted of several car thefts throughout the Western Province. He'd been arrested on charges of theft and murder but was released due to a lack of evidence. These crimes happen so frequently that no one blinks when it's on the news any longer. It's the first time it happened to anyone in our close circle though.

While Dad settles the bill, I drive home with Mattie and Jared. Jared kisses Mattie goodbye and leaves just as Mom and Dad arrive. Dad goes to his study to work for another hour, and Mom and Mattie go to bed. I have a shower, dress in my favorite T-shirt and boy shorts, and go downstairs to say goodnight to Dad.

"Happy birthday, darling," he says with a smile, shutting his notebook in the drawer before switching off his desk lamp. "I'm going to call it a night too."

Dad locks the doors and sets the alarm as I go in search of Pirate, who now has access to the garden as well as the entire house. As it turned out, my mom outgrew her allergy.

Pirate comes out of the lounge when I call him, knowing there's a treat waiting for him. I tuck him under my arm and carry him upstairs.

When I get back to my room, my phone pings. I leave Pirate's snack in his bowl and rush over to retrieve the phone from my bag.

It's the wrong phone. It's Colin. My shoulders slump.

Colin: *How was dinner?*

I sigh. *Thank me later for sparing you from sitting through that.*

He sends a laughing emoji. *I would've liked to go.*

Trust me. You wouldn't have enjoyed it.

Night, Bella.

Smiling, I type, *Night, Colin.*

I dump the phone on the nightstand and check the other one.

Nothing.

After switching off the light, I crawl into bed with Pirate, as always, taking comfort from his warm body pressed against mine. I'm about to doze off when my phone pings again.

Rubbing my eyes, I reach for the phone to tell Colin to go to sleep, and then my heart jumps in my chest.

It's not Colin.

I grab the other one from where I've hidden it under my bed.

The screen lights up with a text message from Angelo.

Open the gate, bella. I'm outside.

CHAPTER ELEVEN

Sabella

Angelo Russo is here, outside, in front of my gate.

I want to believe it, but I'm scared to. If it's a joke, I won't be able to handle the disappointment.

My heart hammers in my chest as I throw back the covers and get out of bed. I open my door and stick my head around the doorframe. The hallway is dark. No light falls from under Mattie's door. At the end of the hallway, my father's snoring is already coming through the door of my parents' bedroom.

Not daring to switch on a light, I walk barefoot through the house. The moonlight that falls through the big windows illuminates my way. I stop in the kitchen to check the screen on the intercom. Angelo Russo stares right into the camera, his face a clear black-and-white picture that steals my breath and makes my palms sweat.

He's here.

A mixture of excitement, surprise, and anxiety slams into me. It takes a moment to find my bearings and to somewhat calm my breathing. I don't even want to think about my dad's reaction if he finds out.

But he's here.

Angelo Russo flew across the whole of Africa because he didn't forget my birthday.

It takes a split-second to make a decision. Quickly crossing the floor, I open the steel door of the control room where our security equipment is located. The room is basked in the blueish light from the monitors on the desk. It's cold inside. I shiver and glance over my shoulder—a nervous, guilty reaction—as I flip the switch to deactivate the cameras.

What I'm doing is wrong. I'm disobeying my father, but my joy at seeing Angelo outweighs my fear of getting caught. No one ever watches the camera recordings anyway. It's a precaution in case of a burglary.

When the screens go dark, I leave and quietly close the door behind me. At the front door, I switch off the alarm in the house as well as the perimeter alarms in the garden. I turn the three locks on the door as noiselessly as I can. With each squeak, I hold my breath.

Finally, the front door is open. A button on the wall unlocks the security gate. Grabbing my key from the bowl on the entrance table, I cut across the lawn to the pedestrian gate.

Angelo is visible through the bars. He stands on the pavement under the yellow light of the streetlamp with a hand shoved in his pocket and his jacket slung over his shoulder. He looks like an apparition in the mist rolling in from the sea. In dark slacks and a fitted white shirt with the top three buttons undone, he's both the same and different, familiar and a stranger.

Exhilarating and frightening.

His demeanor is vigilant and alert. He's observing the surroundings even as his attention is trained on me. Like a seasoned soldier, he seems to be aware of every sight and sound, of every leaf that stirs in the breeze.

For a moment, I can't do anything but look at him. I take in everything, the thicker curls of his hair, the harsher, more angular lines of his face, and the stubble on his jaw. His forearms are exposed where his shirtsleeves are rolled up. The hair dusting his skin is dark. His biceps are bigger, and his chest is broader.

The difference between us hits me all at once. He's a man, even more so now than last year. He's twenty-one, and I'm seventeen. Compared to him, I'm a child. He has experience I'm lacking. Yet he's interested in me. A year didn't wipe out the spark of two fleeting meetings. Time only strengthened our attraction.

The curve of his lips is sensual. His voice is rich and deep, his accent still slight but also deliciously different. "Hello, Sabella."

This isn't a dream.

He's here.

"You're here."

He tilts his head. "You didn't think I'd miss your birthday, did you?" When I don't move, his smile turns amused. "Are you going to let me in, or are we going to do this through the bars of your gate?"

This.

So many possibilities are contained in that one little word, so many meanings and interpretations.

Are we going to do this?

My stomach flutters. Jumping into action, I slip the key in the slot and unlock the gate. He steps into the garden, holding my gaze as he pushes the gate closed.

We stand toe to toe, me staring up and him looking down.

I make the first move, taking his hand and closing my fingers around his. The minute we touch, I become aware of my body in a different way, a powerful and scary way. I become aware of him. This isn't me imagining how it feels to hold his hand. This is real.

His skin is warm. The contrast makes me aware of the dewy grass that's cold under my bare feet. I look at our hands that are clasped together. His big palm barely fits in mine. The tone is darker than my tan.

I tear my gaze from our hands to look at his face. My heart is beating so hard it aches. It hurts to breathe. For a beat, I'm scared, but I don't know of what. Of getting caught? No. It's a fear born from self-preservation, a little voice warning me that this man has the power to destroy me. I feel too much. It's the third time I see him, and he's already the center of my life.

He seems to sense my hesitation. "Don't be afraid, Sabella. I'll always take care of you."

Always.

Always means forever.

He's not the kind of person to throw words like that around carelessly. The statement is huge but so is his presence. Everything about him is bigger than life. The world is too small a place for him. I sensed it that first time, but now it's so visceral I can taste it on my tongue.

Then he smiles, and the warmth of it penetrates me, melting all those internal warnings and scary feelings. A sense of safety wraps around me. How can I ever be afraid while I'm holding his hand?

Returning his smile, I pull him to the house. As I lead him through the door and up the stairs, our grasp changes. When we get to my room, I'm no longer guiding him by the hand. He's taken over, his strong fingers wrapped around mine in a firm and secure hold. We stop outside my door, facing each other.

We don't need words to communicate. I get it. I know he's waiting for my permission. He understands me. He knows I want him to do *this*, whatever that means, not in a grainy night through the bars of the gate, but here in my room where I've touched myself thinking of him.

His smile never wanes. The gesture offers me gentle reassurance as he pushes down the handle and opens the door. He pauses, waiting for me to enter, giving me a choice. Only, with him, there's never been a choice.

When I step into my room, he closes the door. I turn. He looks at me, not vigilant and alert like outside, but cutting a slow path with his gaze over me, taking his fill. He starts at my toes and ends on my face, and then, finally, on my lips.

He takes a step forward. I take one back. I don't want to run. The room just feels too small with him in it. His energy is overwhelming, his masculinity drowning me.

In the light of the moon, something dark flashes in his eyes. He likes this—my flight and his chase. I may not be experienced, but I know it instinctively. Like on that first day, I'm out of my depth.

He advances. I retreat. I'm not sure why. Maybe because he likes the game. Maybe because I like it too. My back hits the wall. He closes in on me, leaning a hand next to my face. Deliberately, he gives me an escape route, slipping his free hand in his pocket and leaving one side of our bodies open.

His eyes are so dark they glow like a demon's in his face. Even more captivating than those gleaming pools is what I see in them. Something deep and darker flows underneath, something simultaneously disturbing and hypnotizing.

"Did you keep it for me?" he asks, fixing his gaze on my mouth.

I'm incapable of speaking. My chest heaves as I stare up at him, painful breaths trapped between my ribs where my heart is pounding.

He pulls his hand from his pocket and brushes a strand of hair from my forehead. The touch is careful, tender. "Did you save your first kiss for me?"

He knows the answer, but he wants me to say it.

"Yes," I whisper.

Instead of softening his features, satisfaction turns them hard. The possession in his expression is so fierce it almost makes him look cruel.

When he lowers his head, I inhale sharply. His smell envelopes me, a combination of citrus, cedar, and a man's clean skin.

We've never been suggestive or physical in our messages. No sex talk or naked pics. He made the rules and set the boundaries. At some stage, I was worried our exchange was too platonic, that he wasn't interested in me like that, but all those doubts fly through the window as he lets me see the intention in his eyes. He keeps them open as he slowly aims for my mouth, searching my gaze and reading my reaction.

My eyes flutter closed. I'm not brave enough to keep mine open. The anticipation drags on, the waiting like torture as his warm breath fans over my mouth with a hint of mint. I want to breathe him in, to taste him.

Seconds pass, the world spinning, and then he does it. He closes the distance. His lips are warm and soft, their pressure gentle on mine. The kiss is dry and pleasant. Too fleeting. I'm not prepared for my body's reaction, for the arousal that tightens my nipples and the heat that gathers between my thighs. I squeeze my legs together. My breath catches as the warmth vanishes from my lips. I lift my chin, chasing after the intoxicating heat, but it's gone.

Confused, I open my eyes.

Angelo stares at me with a shuttered expression. He cups my jaw in his big hand and lifts my face to his. "I can't go further with you, *bella*. You're only seventeen."

I bite my lip, both disappointed and frustrated.

Brushing our cheeks together, he brings his lips to my ear. "Happy birthday, *cara*."

My skin tingles where the roughness of his stubble grates over it. My mouth is dry. "Thank you."

"One day, you'll thank me for more than kissing you."

The nuance of his words makes me burn. I recall what he told me, the promise he made on the morning after my party.

All your firsts are mine.

Taking my hand, he pulls me off the wall. "How's Pirate?"

The change of topic gives me time to gather myself. It's a clever and deliberate effort on his part.

"See for yourself," I say, motioning to where Pirate sleeps half-covered under my duvet.

He goes over and strokes Pirate's fur. "He's grown a lot. He looks bigger than in the photos."

Pirate meows, stretches, and curls into a ball again.

"It's been a year," I say. "He's an adult now."

He sits down at the foot of the bed and pats the space next to him. "Come here."

I don't hesitate. Now that the initial sensations and the shock of seeing him are over, I'm more at ease. The moment is stolen. I have to make the most of it.

I flop down next to him. "How long are you staying?"

"I'm flying back tomorrow night."

"Oh," I say, unable to keep the disappointment from my voice. "It's very far to come for just one day."

"No," he muses, studying me. "For you, even a minute is worth coming across half the world."

The compliment warms me inside. "Did you fly to Cape Town again?"

"To George this time."

"Where are you staying?"

"At the golf estate."

I look at him sideways, considering how to phrase this. "I can skip summer school tomorrow."

"No." His voice is harsh. "You will do no such thing."

I wince, feeling embarrassed for suggesting it.

He continues in a softer tone. "I have to see your father about business tomorrow. I won't have much free time."

"He knows you're here?" I exclaim. "In town, I mean?"

"No." He grins. "It's better that I surprise him. I'm not his favorite person."

I frown. "Why is that? I don't understand why he feels so strongly about us not seeing each other if he's working with you."

His face remains serious even as he says in a playful way, "He doesn't want me to take his princess away."

I slap his arm. "He's not like that."

He raises a brow. "Isn't he?"

"No." I laugh, taking care to keep my voice down. "He's strict, especially when it comes to letting me go out, but he's not one of those fathers who keeps a shotgun in case someone shows an interest in his daughter."

In a flash, his eyes darken. "He should."

"He didn't with Mattie when Jared started dating her."

"With you, it's different."

"Different how?"

He lifts his hand to my face but drops it before touching me. "You're mine."

The words are spoken with so much conviction, they leave me speechless. Will I ever get used to his intensity?

Wiggling a gold signet ring from his finger, he says, "Give me your hand."

"What are you doing?"

"Give me your hand, Sabella."

The way in which he says my name prompts me to action. His uncompromising tone demands obedience. A part of me likes it. I like that he's strong, that he's not scared to take control. He grips my right hand and pushes the ring over my thumb. It's too big to fit on any of my other fingers.

"It's yours," he says, rubbing a fingertip over the embossed crest.

"Angelo," I exclaim. "This looks like a family ring."

"It's our emblem." He motions at the intertwined wolves. "Every firstborn son in our family gets one when he turns eighteen."

I gasp. "You can't give this away. It obviously has special meaning."

He wraps his hand around mine, squeezing the ring between us. "It'll keep you safe. Everyone in my country knows what it means."

I'm here, not in his country, and I don't need to be kept safe, but I assume it's some kind of superstitious symbol like a lucky charm that keeps harm away.

The notion is sweet, but it's a family heirloom. "I can't keep it. It's too valuable."

"Keep it for me." Lifting my hand to his lips, he kisses the ring. "Promise me you'll wear it until the day I replace it with another."

My throat goes dry. I must be misinterpreting his words, but he doesn't give me time to ponder their meaning. He takes off his jacket and kicks off his shoes, and then he stretches out on my bed, pulling me down with him. We're pressed together on one side of the queen-sized mattress because Pirate takes up my side.

"Can I stay for a while?" he asks, rubbing a lock of my hair between his fingers.

"Of course." I lay my head on his chest where I can hear his heart beat. "Even if you wanted to, I wouldn't let you go, not if I only get to see you for a few hours."

Wrapping one arm loosely around me, he hugs me closer. "I'll never miss a single one of your birthdays."

I want to ask if that means I'll only see him once a year, but I don't want to spoil the moment. Surely, if he's meeting my father about business, there's a chance he'll travel to George more often.

I don't know for how long we're lying there in an amiable silence in the dark, simply enjoying each other's presence while Angelo runs his fingers over my arm, but at some stage, I must've dozed off, because when I wake up, he's gone.

Angelo

I go downstairs on socked feet with my jacket slung over my shoulder. I don't have to search. I remember the way to the study from my first visit to the house.

After pushing the door open, I take a second to inspect the space like I always do when I'm in enemy territory. I inhale the air, the smell of wood polish and leather, and slide my gaze over the formal arrangement of books on the shelves. They're not well-loved and often-visited books, but books with golden letters on the spines of matching green leather covers meant to decorate rather than entertain or educate.

I'm not in a hurry. I take my time to cross the floor. At the desk, I drape my jacket over the back of the swivel chair and take my phone from my pocket. I use the screen light to look over the contents on the desktop, which include a laptop and stacks of papers.

A framed photo of the Edwards family is posed on the corner. They're in a vineyard, smiling and looking happy. Edwards has more hair, and his frame is leaner. He appears proud. His wife stands with a straight back, her smile polished. A young Matilde mimics her mother, standing tall and staring with a closed-lip smile at the camera. Ryan looks up at his father. He must've been about twelve. That would've made Sabella two. Her dark hair is tied into pigtails, the ends curly. She made a cute kid. If we have a daughter, I hope she'll take after Sabella. I notice how Matilde poses next to her mother while Sabella is on her father's side, her small hand wrapped around one of his fingers. Ryan is in the middle, separating Edwards and his wife. They're not touching or posing with their arms around each other like loving couples do in photos. How close are they really?

As there's nothing else of interest, I go through the drawers. It doesn't take me long to find what I'm looking for. Edwards puts a lot of faith in his security system to leave his precious notebook lying around in an unlocked drawer. It's a mistake, a flaw in the system, and I'm good at sniffing out flaws and using weaknesses to my advantage.

I turn the cover of the small, black book. The handwriting is cursive and neat. The first inscription is dated eighteen years ago. Each page contains a list of names, dates, and amounts. Next to each amount, there's a signature. Proof of receipt. I flip a few pages, skipping to the date when Edwards made the deal with my father. Sabella was only ten. I scan the names, recognizing some of them. A few big ones jump out, people who were high up in government and had since retired.

The names change as the years move on. It's like a map of the county's political history, of who's been in power and who replaced who, but I also notice a few international players—foreign ministers and big names in the mafia. Two of those names are specifically familiar to me. One is connected to the French and the other to the Corsican mafia. A quarter of the book is still empty. It will take at least another decade to fill those pages.

I don't take photos of the incriminating evidence. I can't be bothered to go through the pains of proving they're not forged. Nothing beats the real thing.

The screen of my phone lights up with one or the other notification. I don't read it. It's not important. I shut the book and slide it with my phone into the pocket on my jacket. Through the window, the horizon is tinted with deep purple. Sunrise is about an hour away.

I don my jacket and walk through the sleeping house back to Sabella's room. When I open her door, she's sitting up on her bed, rubbing her eyes. Her dark hair is wild around her face, and her manner is alarmed. She's pushed the blanket I covered her with aside, revealing long legs with a golden tan.

She blinks. It takes her a second. Her chest deflates, and the tenseness eases from her shoulders. "I thought you'd left."

I close the door. "I wouldn't go without saying goodbye."

Almost absent-mindedly, she pats Pirate. "Where were you?"

The lie falls easily from my lips. "Bathroom."

Her eyes grow large. "What if someone saw you?"

The moon has shifted. The darkness in the room is deeper, thicker. It's impossible to distinguish the black of her pupils from the rich brown color of her irises. It makes her look like a fragile doll with pretty glass eyes, utterly vulnerable and completely breakable.

"I was careful," I say, resisting the urge to cup her face

and sample the smallness in my palm. I've already broken too many promises I made myself.

She follows my movements with her gaze when I sit down and pull on my shoes.

Hugging her knees to her chest, she asks, "Can't you stay a little longer?"

I hear the longing in her voice, the desperation. I planted it there when I ensured she'd crave my presence. A year is a long time, but it's only a drop in the ocean in the bigger scheme of forever.

"It's almost four." I keep my voice gentle, softening the unpleasant business of saying goodbye. "It'll be light soon."

She nods, biting her lip.

It's tempting to promise that I'll visit more often. It's even more tempting to take her with me. What her father says doesn't matter anymore.

Instead, I stand.

She's seventeen.

I shouldn't forget that.

I'm too weak when I'm with her.

Until she's eighteen, it's safer to keep my distance.

Having done too much already, I kiss the top of her head. It's the only indulgence I allow myself before taking her hand and pulling her to her feet.

I look around. My gaze falls on a sweater draped over the back of a chair. I take it and lift her arms before pulling it over her head.

"Put on some socks and shoes," I tell her. The mornings are fresh here, cooler than the evenings, and the grass is always wet with dew. "You'll catch a cold."

She takes a pair of socks from her dresser and obediently slips them on. I give Pirate a pat on his head while she fastens her sneakers. When she's ready, I lead her downstairs.

"Put the alarm back on," I instruct when she's seen me out.

She hugs herself, nodding, looking small behind the bars of the gate.

"I'll wait until you're inside," I say.

She offers me a last smile before doing as I told her, returning inside and shutting the door. I appreciate the fact that she didn't make a big deal out of saying goodbye.

When the red lights of the cameras on the walls blink on, I make my way to the rental I parked in the cul-de-sac. The notebook sits snugly in my pocket, the ticket to my rightful place, and in it, the evidence that will change everyone's future.

CHAPTER
THIRTEEN

Sabella

The news of last night is so exciting, I can't wait to tell Colin about it. It's his mom's turn to drive us to summer school, so I can't say anything in the car. We arrive at my school, where the mixed classes for the eleventh-grade boys and girls are presented each summer, with only a minute to spare, which means my big news will have to wait until we get home after five.

The whole day, I'm in the clouds. I can't stop touching the heavy gold ring on my thumb. I barely manage to concentrate on the math exercises. When the tutor asks me a question, I look up from my book in a daze, lost in my daydreaming. Colin, who sits one row in front of me, looks over his shoulder with a frown. I never get a question wrong, let alone having to ask the tutor to repeat the question.

"What's up with you today?" Colin asks when we

finally gather our books at five.

"I'll tell you later," I say with a grin, swinging my backpack over my shoulder.

"You need that A for math if you're to make it to the final selection for uni." He takes the heavy bag from my back. "You can't afford to screw this up."

I skip ahead of him to the exit. "I won't."

When we come down the steps, Mrs. Taylor, Colin's mom, honks the horn to pull our attention to where she's parked in the shade of an oak tree. She gets out and leans against the car, waiting for us with a smile.

Emmaline Taylor is petite with blond hair and blue eyes. On days like these, when her hair is tied into a ponytail and she's wearing her gym leggings and T-shirt, the resemblance between her and Clara is uncanny.

Colin dumps our bags in the trunk and shifts behind the wheel. Mrs. Taylor takes the passenger seat in the front. Since we've gotten our learner driver's licenses, Mrs. Taylor lets us take turns to drive when it's her week to carpool.

"Hi, Mrs. Taylor," I say, getting into the back.

"Hey, Bella." She twists in her seat. "How was class?"

"Okay."

Colin shoots me a look in the rearview mirror, but he doesn't say anything. He starts the engine and focuses on driving.

Mrs. Taylor asks how my birthday dinner was and if we have news about Ryan and Celeste's baby. Ryan and Celeste live in Cape Town where Ryan runs Dad's city office, so we don't see them very often. They only come to Great Brak River for family events like birthdays and Christmas.

As we drive up our street, I spot my mom's Audi parked in front of the house. It's strange, almost as if she left it there in too much of hurry to open the gates. She always parks inside the garage because she doesn't want her windows to get sticky and dirty from the sea air.

I thank Mrs. Taylor when they drop me off and tell Colin I'll see him later. We're planning on doing geometry exercises together. We'll be working in his library where no one ever disturbs us, and I'll be able tell him about last night.

The canteen at summer school is horrible. I didn't eat much of the lukewarm fish pie, and I'm starving. I let myself in through the gate and slow down when I notice the cars in the driveway. Dad's Rolls Royce and Ryan's BMW are there. My dad never comes home this early. And what is Ryan doing here? He's not keen on traveling far from home since Celeste developed complications with the pregnancy.

I push the front door open and close it quietly behind me. My dad's heated voice booms from his study. Ryan says something, his tone placating. I drop my bag and pad down the hallway. Sniffling comes from the lounge. I stop in the doorframe. My mom is perched on the sofa, crying into a tissue. Mattie sits next to her, rubbing her shoulder.

Shit.

What happened?

Coldness invades my body.

Mattie looks up. Her expression is grave when she meets my gaze. She gets to her feet and crosses the floor, her steps quiet on the marble tiles like in the way people walk at funerals as if they're afraid of making noise.

Putting an arm around my shoulder, she leads me to the kitchen. Doris stands at the counter, rolling out dough. For once, she doesn't shoo us away and tell us not to get under her feet. She dusts her hands on her apron and disappears into the scullery.

"What's going on?" I ask, my heart beating in my throat. "Has someone died?" Aunt Judith or Uncle Fred?

Mattie leans on the counter and crosses her arms. "There's been an incident."

My voice comes out hoarse. "What incident?"

She's calm, taking after Ryan in that sense, but I don't miss the tension in her face. "Someone stole Dad's notebook."

I battle to make sense of it. "What?"

"Someone broke into the house and stole Dad's book, the little black one he kept in his desk drawer."

"But…" Shaking my head, I open and close my mouth, finally only managing, "Why?"

"The book is important."

"I don't understand. Why is Ryan here? And why is Mom crying about it?"

She lowers her voice. "Dad's been involved in some bribing."

"Bribing?" My breath catches. "What do you mean?"

She waves a hand. "He paid some people under the table."

I go colder still. "I don't believe it. Dad would never do that."

"It's how business is done here. Everyone does it. The thing is not to get caught."

"What does that mean?" I lean my hand on the table to steady myself. "What does that mean for Dad?"

"Dad and Ryan are dealing with it."

"What's going to happen to us?" I ask, panic constricting my chest.

"Nothing," she says, her voice stern. "What's important right now is to figure out how it happened because it can never happen again." She glances at the scullery and continues in a quieter tone. "Someone cut the alarm and the cameras last night."

Her words hit me like bullets. Blood pumps through my body and rushes to my head.

She straightens. "Naturally, we can't involve the police."

I hear her through the gushing in my ears, her words distant and distorted. I look at her, see her lips move, but I don't register what she's saying any longer.

Someone cut the alarm and the cameras.

And I know.

I know who took the book.

I don't know what's worse, the betrayal that burns like acid in my stomach and pushes up with bile in my throat or the shame that cripples me. The shame, I think. Of being stupid and naïve. Of being an accomplice. Of being selfish and hurting my family.

I draw back my hand, noticing how much it's shaking, noticing the flour stuck to my palm.

"…just have to give them a moment. Dad isn't himself."

Mattie. I stare at her. She's still talking.

I nod, the movement mechanical.

She grips my shoulder on her way to the door, a rare show of affection. No, not affection. Support.

My thoughts are scrambled, my body shaking with the devastating blow of deception. Blazing red-hot in the wake of that deceit is nauseating fear. It's my first taste of the ugly sentiments, and I don't care for them.

What have I done?

I glance over my shoulder at the straight set of Mattie's back, how strong she is when she needs to be.

"I'm going to Colin's," I say, making a rash decision.

Mattie turns to me. "You can't tell anyone about this."

"I know."

She sighs. "Maybe it's not a bad idea to hang out at Colin's for a while, at least until the worst of it has blown over. I suppose Dad will want to speak to us before dinner. Make sure you're home by then."

Her heels click down the hallway, her steps that strange funeral march again, cautious and subdued.

Before Doris has a chance to return and question me, I escape to the entrance and snatch my mom's car key from the table where it lies next to her handbag. I'm too upset to think about taking her car registration papers or my license. I walk out of the door and push through the gate. The Audi is an automatic. It's not difficult to drive. I get in and start the engine, not bothering to check the mirrors or to adjust the seat.

At the bottom of the street, I floor the gas. My eyes burn, but they remain dry. Good. Angelo doesn't deserve my tears. The line in the middle of the road blurs and doubles. I rub my eyes with the heel of my palm, trying to clear my vision. I'm driving like a maniac, way too fast, and it's only sheer luck that I don't get pulled over by a traffic cop before I reach the golf estate.

I park in front of the main entrance of the hotel and stalk inside, ignoring the valet who stares after me. At the counter, I catch a glimpse of my reflection in the mirror. My mascara is smeared in dark circles around my eyes and my expression looks wild. The people in the reception area steal glances at me. They're dressed in fancy golf clothes or formal office attire. My favorite T-shirt with the whale on the back dating from an aquarium visit two years ago stands out like a sore thumb. So does my faded and authentically ripped jeans, but I don't care.

As I don't have a bag with me, I shove the car key in my back pocket. Drumming my fingers on the counter, I wait. There's no one else but me, but the concierge is in no hurry to help me.

Anger makes me brazen. I lean an elbow on the counter and put myself in the concierge's space. "Mr. Russo's room number, please."

The man's voice is neutral. "We're not allowed to give out room numbers, ma'am."

"He's expecting me," I say, smiling sweetly, speaking too loudly.

The concierge glances around. They don't like people to make scenes in upmarket places like these, especially not underdressed and underaged girls who ask for grown men's room numbers.

I lift my hand, showing him the gold ring on my thumb. "Why don't you call him and check for yourself?"

Something passes over his face as he takes in the ring, some recognition that gives life to his otherwise cardboard-like countenance.

He doesn't have to check the guest list. "The penthouse suite."

Of course. There's only one penthouse suite.

I slam a hand on the counter, palm-up. "Give me a card."

His mouth tightens. "I'll need your name, please."

"Sabella Edwards."

He quirks an eyebrow but says nothing. His long, spidery fingers clack over the keyboard as he types. A moment later, he pushes a keycard in a paper envelope toward me.

"Thank you," I say.

He doesn't bother with a reply.

I grab the card and cut across the foyer. When I look back over my shoulder, he's got the phone pressed against his ear, no doubt alerting Angelo that I'm on my way.

There are only two floors, but my legs are too wobbly to navigate the stairs. I stab the button of the elevator to call it down, repeatedly hitting the button until the doors slide open. The man and woman who were also waiting for the elevator step aside, not getting in with me.

I jam the heel of my palm on the top-floor button. The doors close, shutting me in. I turn in a circle like an animal in a cage, willing the numbers to light up more quickly. The soft, generic music that plays through the speakers in the ceiling does nothing to calm me. It only agitates me more.

When the elevator stops, I squeeze through the doors before they're fully open. There's no hallway, just a foyer with a burgundy carpet and silver wallpaper embossed with fleur-de-lis's.

The only door on this level opens before I reach it. Angelo stands in the frame, wearing a black shirt, dark pants, and an inscrutable expression.

All the fury I felt since Mattie's words had ripped into my heart bubbles to the surface. I'm blind with rage as I storm across the floor, plant my palms on his chest, and shove him with all my might.

My effort doesn't move him an inch. He steps back into the room of his own accord, letting me in.

Raising my arm, I slap him hard across the face. My handprint lies red on his cheek when I pull away. I lift my hand again, but this time, he catches my wrist.

I yank free. "How could you?"

He moves around me and closes the door.

I turn, circling with him, unwilling to give him my back. "How could you do something like that?"

He only looks at me with gleaming eyes.

"You used me," I say, stepping away from him, my palm burning and my hands shaking.

He doesn't deny the accusation.

"You planned this for a whole year." My voice quivers. Tears prick at the back of my eyes when I realize how deep his deceit runs. "That's why you gave me a phone."

"Not only," he says with a stoic face.

Fuck. That hurts. I gnash my teeth, forcing back the tears. I will not show him how effectively he's broken me into pieces. The only thing he deserves to witness is my loathing.

I shove him again. "How could you?"

He just stands there, taking my abuse.

"Damn you, Angelo Russo. Tell me." The volume of my voice rises to a hysterical level. "Why? Why did you do it? What are you going to do with the information you stole?"

Still, he says nothing, shows nothing. No emotion. No regret.

Done. I'm done with *this*. The *this* he didn't want to do through the bars of a gate last night had nothing to do with me. It was all about stealing information from my dad.

I utter a wry laugh. He couldn't steal that through the bars of our gate. No. He needed me to switch off the alarm and let him in. And I did it. I invited him in, welcoming him like a wolf in a lamb's pen.

He walks to a wet bar in the corner and pours a glass of water. I take in the surroundings for the first time, the spacious lounge that opens onto a balcony with potted trees, the canopy bed in the adjoining room, and the home gym in front of the big windows.

He puts the glass on the coffee table in front of me. "You need a drink."

I feel like throwing that water in his face, but I've already assaulted him physically, and it's not how my parents raised me. I don't like this person, the one I become when I'm with him.

"Juice, perhaps?" he asks.

"You're an asshole."

His mouth lifts in one corner. "Maybe I should add some sugar for that mouth of yours."

I've tried. I'm not going to get answers from him. There's no closure for me here, no reasons or excuses.

I hold out my hand. "Give me the book."

"It won't make a difference. The information has already been copied and stored in the cloud."

"I'm going to tell my dad. You know that, don't you?"

"It doesn't matter. He already knows."

"That was your business with him?" I exclaim. "You son of a bitch. What do you want? Money? Are you blackmailing him? Is that it?"

His tone is level. "If your father was a man of his word, this wouldn't have been necessary."

"I don't know what you're talking about, but it doesn't change the fact that you manipulated me or that you're using stolen information to blackmail my dad."

"I did what had to be done for us to be together," he says matter-of-factly.

"Us?" My chuckle is ugly. "Do you seriously think I'll ever be with you after what you've done?"

"One day, you'll understand."

"Never," I spit out. "We'll never be together."

His look turns calculated. "Then you better think again, *cara*. You're mine. We belong together. Nothing will change that. I'll kill for you if that's what it takes."

Oh my God. He's not just bad. He's the definition of evil. The love he kindled inside me and so carefully cultivated is like poison. If I don't cut it out of my heart, it'll kill me.

My dad was right. I've been Angelo's fool, and I'm no longer playing the idiot for him.

Stripping the ring from my thumb, I throw it on the table. It clatters over the glass before rolling off the edge and hitting the carpet with a thud. "I don't ever want to see you again. Stay away from me and my family."

I turn on my heel and head for the door, but I don't make it two steps before Angelo wraps a big hand around my throat and pulls me back. The action breaks my momentum. I stumble, my back hitting the wall of his chest.

He squeezes, pressing his fingers on sensitive spots. "You're not so quick to like me now that you've seen my true nature." It almost sounds like an accusation. Lowering his head, he brushes a whisper over my ear. "That ring stays on your hand until I replace it with another. Have you forgotten so quickly?"

I step away and spin around. "Keep your ring. I don't want it."

"You'll wear that mark on your finger or branded into your skin. Your choice."

My lips part. He must be joking.

He's not. He bends, picks up the ring in no hurry, and takes a Zippo lighter from his pocket. It's the same one he used to light a joint when we first met. I watch, horrified, as he flicks the lighter and holds the ring under the flame.

He's bluffing.

I look between his impassive face and the blackening surface of the ring, unable to believe he'll go through with it.

"I prefer that you wear it on your finger," he says. "But as I said, it's your choice."

When he kills the flame and reaches for me, I shrink back. His fingers curl around my bicep, dragging me closer.

I fight his hold, clawing at his forearm, but my efforts have no effect. He brushes my hair over my shoulder, taking care not to touch my skin with the ring, and kisses a spot on my neck.

A shudder runs through me.

He's going to do it—right there where he pressed his lips on my skin.

"Wait," I cry out, straining in his grasp.

He blows over the spot that's wet from his kiss, making my skin contract. "It'll hurt, but I'll put you out first."

Wait. What? Put me out? What does that even mean?

"No." I claw at him again. "I'll wear the ring."

He stills. "What was that?"

I push him off me. "I'll wear the ring."

"Definitely the better choice."

He goes to the table and drops the ring in the glass. It makes a hissing sound when it hits the water. He stirs the water a few times with his finger before taking the ring out and rubbing the black off on a napkin. Gripping my hand, he pushes it back onto my thumb.

He closes his fingers around my nape again, pulling me closer and bringing his lips to my ear. "If you ever take it off, I'll know."

I don't ask how. I don't want to own that knowledge. My legs buckle a little. I just want to go home.

Not daring to look at him for fear of seeing the smug victory in his eyes, I walk to the door.

He steps in front of me, cutting me off. "How did you get here?" I push past, but he grabs my arm. "Who brought you?"

"I drove."

"By yourself?"

"Yes."

Not letting go of my wrist, he grabs his jacket from a

hook on the back of the door.

"What are you doing?" I ask.

"Driving you home."

"Are you out of your mind?"

"You have a learner license. Driving alone is illegal and dangerous."

I gape at him. "You're worried about illegal driving after you broke into our house?"

"I didn't break in." He lets me go to pull on his jacket. "You let me in. And it's your safety I'm concerned about."

"I may have let you in but only because you tricked and deceived me."

Taking my arm again, he opens the door. "You'll get over it."

"Fuck you."

"We're going to have a serious talk about that mouth."

"Let me go."

"Stop struggling, Sabella." He tightens his hold. "I told you I'm going to see you home safely."

"Don't pretend to care about my safety."

"I don't have to pretend."

He drags me across the foyer and into the elevator. We get out when the doors open on the ground level. People stare as he steers me through the lobby, but he pays them no heed. A man with a shaved head dressed in a dark suit waits outside.

Angelo takes a key from his pocket and throws it at the man. "Follow us." He motions at my mom's Audi. "Is this her car?"

The man nods.

Angelo dips his hand into my back pocket and pulls out the key.

"Hey." I try to grab it from him, but he holds it out of reach. "Give that to me."

The man gets into a Mercedes parked in the lot while Angelo bundles me into the passenger side of my mom's car.

"Who's that man?" My tone is sarcastic. "Your bodyguard?"

"Yours," he says, starting the engine.

"What?"

"His name is Roch." He pronounces it like *rock*. "He'll be keeping an eye on you."

I cross my arms, facing forward. "To make sure I don't run to the police?"

He only chuckles, knowing very well if my father is involved in paying bribes, going to the police isn't an option.

Some of the fight has left me, bringing on sudden exhaustion. Without the armor of anger, I'm frightened. How will my dad react? Will he hate me? Will my naivety and disregard for his wishes ruin our relationship?

We drive in silence, Roch following in the Mercedes.

At our house, Angelo stops in front of the gates and cuts the engine. "See you soon, *cara*."

"I don't think so."

He only smiles, gets out, and closes his door.

When I don't move, he comes around to my window. "Go inside."

He doesn't get to tell me what to do, but it's almost dinner time, and I don't want my parents to go look for me at Colin's house. I don't want them to see me outside our house with Angelo.

He opens my door and offers me a hand. Ignoring his proffered palm, I take the key from the console between the seats and get out. His eyes burn holes at the back of my head as I let myself through the gate, but I don't look back. Not this time. Never again.

CHAPTER
FOURTEEN

Angelo

On my way to the airport, I stop at a lookout point, get out, and watch the sea. It's a clear but windy morning. Angry waves break on the shore. Seagulls dive low over the water, their cries piercing the crushing noise of the surf.

The scenery is growing on me. I can get used to this, but I prefer the rugged coastline of Cape Town. It's closer to home, except for the Atlantic current that makes the water cold, even in summer. It's much more pleasant to swim here in the warmer Indian Ocean.

As I have a few moments to spare before my flight, I let my thoughts wander. It's not a luxury I often have. I've been taking on more responsibilities at home and in the business as my father has been weakening. It meant cutting my studies short, but I don't mind. Life is the best school. I learned more from being involved in the business than what any book can teach me.

The family is my priority. My uncles and my mother's family, although we've never met them, are dependent on our business. The money we make feeds many mouths, including the families of the four hundred and something employees we have on contract. I can't let them down. Soon, Sabella will be one of those people depending on me. I'll be a husband, my duty not only to protect and care for my wife but also to ensure the bloodline continues. To produce an heir.

I take my phone from my pocket and video call my father. A moment later, my sister's face comes onto the screen. In the sunlight falling over the dining room table, her hair has a red glow. Except for that difference and being more feminine in bone structure and build, we're an exact replica of each other.

"Hey, Ang," she says, shoving a spoonful of cereal into her mouth. "Wow. Nice view. Where are you?"

"Close to the airport. Why aren't you having a proper dinner?"

Adeline rolls her eyes. "This is a proper dinner."

"You know there are hardly any nutrients in that junk you're eating. You're just stuffing your face with sugar and fiber."

She points the spoon at me. "Just because you were born three seconds before me doesn't make you older and wiser."

"Obviously wiser where nutrition is concerned. What kind of a wife will you make for your husband?" I say that last part only half-playfully.

She scoffs. "I'll marry a man who knows how to cook."

"You'll marry a man who'll be a good provider."

The phone dips, the camera pointing at her legs as she

swings them over the chair before her face comes on again. "Unlike you, I'm in no rush to get married." Her hair bounces on her shoulders as she walks. "I'll finish my degree and see the world first."

My twin is neither romantic nor maternal. "How's school?"

She enters a room—the kitchen, judging by the big windows overlooking the garden—and makes a face. "You asked me that before you left." She taps a finger on her lips. "Let me see. Yesterday?"

"Cut out the sarcasm. You had an economics test. You didn't think I'd forget?"

She's all bubbly and sparkly, her grin showing off her white teeth. "How sweet of you to remember."

I can't resist a smile. "Sarcasm, Adeline."

"Of course it went well. What did you expect?"

"Nothing less." I turn serious. "How's Papa?"

She sobers. "As well as he can be. Maman is feeding him soup. He was waiting for your call. He asked me to answer his phone while he was napping."

"Can you put him on? I have news. Good news. It'll cheer him up."

"Sure. Let me put my bowl in the dishwasher, and I'll take the phone to him." She moves down the hallway and up the stairs. "Want me to pick you up at the airport tomorrow?"

"Absolutely not." My tone is stern. "You're not driving the boat to Marseille."

She bats her eyelashes. "You do."

"It's different."

"You're such a macho guy, you know that? Sexism went out of fashion like five decades ago."

"The answer is no. In any event, you have school."

"Fine." She blows out a dramatic sigh. "Just don't

overdo your practice run as head of the family." The moment the words are out, she bites her lip. "I didn't mean it like that."

I wince. "I know."

"Here's Papa." She blows me a kiss. "Bon voyage."

There's shuffling, the camera zooming in on blankets before my father's face fills the screen. His eyes are red and sunken with bags underneath. The ashen color of his skin shocks me like it does every time I look at him. My mother is next to him, pressing a cloth on his forehead.

"I'm good," he croaks, pushing her hand away.

"Hello, Angelo." My mother leans closer to my father, her smile warm albeit a little strained. Her dark hair is knotted in a bun, wisps falling around her oval-shaped face. At thirty-eight, she hardly has a wrinkle. Her skin is smooth, and her features are youthful, yet a permanent tiredness makes her seem older. "Are you well?"

"Hello, Maman. I've never been better."

She picks up a tray. "I'll make ratatouille tomorrow."

"That sounds good."

We say goodbye, and then she leaves my father and me to talk business.

"How did it go?" he asks in a raspy voice.

"Exactly as planned."

He nods, closes his eyes for a moment, and drags in a long, rattling breath.

My gut clenches. As if in an empathic response, it becomes difficult to breathe.

Time is running out. The specialist's words repeat in my head. Without an operation, my father has a few months. A year at most. If only he wasn't so pig-headed about having the surgery.

So precious little left. So much I still want to give.

I won't let him go to his grave with the worry of unfinished business.

For that reason alone, I take comfort in telling him, "It's done." I grip the phone hard, feeling the absence of my signet ring. "Edwards signed."

CHAPTER
FIFTEEN

Sabella

The house is strangely quiet. The clang when I drop my mom's car key on the table in the entrance sounds unnaturally loud. A smell of apple pie wafts from the kitchen, but the delicious aroma of home baking doesn't warm me inside and welcome me like it usually does.

Something changed. I don't feel at home in the house any longer. Angelo destroyed my haven with his despicable betrayal. I'm like a stranger in the place I grew up in. The walls close in on me, but I don't feel safe outside either. Angelo's words repeat in my head, that someone will always be watching me. That he'll always come back for me. But I don't want to think about him. I can't. Not now. I have to push those disturbing thoughts aside and do what has to be done.

Taking my phone from my bag that still lies on the

floor next to the door, I send a text message to Colin to tell him I won't be over tonight, making up a feeble excuse of being tired.

Mattie exits from the kitchen as I shove my phone in my pocket.

"There you are." She scrutinizes me, studying me more closely than usual, and says in a manner much friendlier than her norm, "We're having dinner in ten minutes. Go wash up quickly."

Picking at a cuticle, I glance down the hallway. "Where are they?"

"In the study."

I nod and swallow.

"Are you all right?" she asks, phrasing it as if I shouldn't be.

I'm not, but I nod again.

"Okay." She brushes down her skirt. "I'm helping Doris with the final touches to the dinner. Come give us a hand to set the table when you're done."

When she goes back to the kitchen, I walk with leaden steps to the study. I stop in the doorframe. My mom sits on the sofa, her eyes unfocussed as she sips amber liquor from a tumbler. Ryan leans against the windowsill with one hand in his pocket and a glass of the same liquor in his other. My dad sits behind his desk, staring into space, his drink standing untouched in front of him.

All three of them turn their gazes to me. As always, Ryan's face is impassive and his expression neutral. My mom's jaw is set into a hard line, her brown eyes glittering with something akin to helpless anger. My dad appears tired and dejected, and it sends a jolt of panic through me, because Dad is invincible. I've never seen him looking so beaten.

My mom clears her throat. She's the first to speak,

always taking charge of the difficult conversations like the birds and the bees and lessons in morals. "Did Mattie bring you up to speed?"

"Yes." I avert my gaze, unable to look them in the eyes. "It was me."

Silence falls over the room.

When I raise my head, my mom is sitting up straighter, staring at me with colorless cheeks.

"I'm sorry," I say, my tongue tripping over the words. "I didn't know. I didn't know—"

The glass makes a sharp clink as my mom puts it down on the table. "What did you say?"

I glance between them, from the shock on Mom's face and the sorrow on Dad's to the nothingness on Ryan's. "I deactivated the cameras and the alarm. It was me."

Mom stands, her arms stiff at her sides. "Why would you do something like that?"

I fix my gaze on a spot on the carpet. "To let Angelo inside the house."

Another stretch of silence follows, tying my stomach in knots. I wish someone would say something. The quiet judgment is worse than the verbal lashing I deserve. When I dare to lift my head again, my parents are observing me with disappointment. Incomprehension. Even Ryan's habitual emotionless face shows pity.

"Why?" Mom exclaims, the word no more than a whisper.

"He wanted to wish me a happy birthday." I wring my hands. "I didn't know he planned on taking the book."

Mom balls her hands into fists. "You brought him into our house? Into your room?"

"Nothing happened," I say quickly. "I swear. He sent me a message to say he was outside. He came all the way to say happy birthday in person." I pause. "So, I let him in."

My dad's voice is hard. "What happened, Sabella?"

"Nothing. We just talked. I fell asleep. When I woke up, he was gone. I thought he'd left, but he came back, saying he'd been to the bathroom. Then he said goodbye, and I let him out." I shrug, feeling miserable and stupid and small. "That's all."

My mom pulls back her shoulders and walks to the door without sparing me a glance.

"Mom," I say, my tone pleading.

When she all but shoves past me, I don't have a choice but to step out of the way.

I bite my lip, turning to my dad. "I'm sorry." My voice breaks as the tears I'm trying to hold back slip free and roll over my cheeks. "I'm really, really sorry, Dad." Sobs wrack my shoulders. "I didn't know. I didn't know he was only using me to steal your book."

Blowing out a heavy sigh, my dad gets to his feet and rounds his desk. I'm a slobbering mess when he puts his arms around me and hugs me close. I nearly collapse with relief in his embrace, taking the comfort he offers.

"Shh." He rubs my back. "It's not your fault."

"At least now we know how he got his hands on it." Ryan utters a wry chuckle as he sips his drink. "He didn't hire someone to break in, which means the alarm system is still foolproof." His smile is cynical. "I suppose that's something."

I pull back with a hiccup. "Aren't you mad at me?"

Dad's face hardens. "Angelo Russo is a vile creature. He used you as a pawn in this nasty scheme of his. How can I be angry with you when he's the one to blame?"

"Thank you." I wrap my arms around him. "You have no idea how scared I was to tell you."

"You did the right thing."

I step away, searching his eyes. "What's going to happen?"

My dad and Ryan exchange a look.

I turn to Ryan. "Why did he take the book? What is he going to do with it?"

In my peripheral vision, Dad clenches his jaw.

Ryan pushes off the windowsill. His tone is calm, as if none of what happened affects him. "He wanted shares in the business." He twirls the glass. "Instead of only taking a cut of the profit, he also wanted power."

"Is it true?" I ask my Dad. "About the bribes?"

Dad's smile is drawn. "A necessary evil."

I take his hand, brushing my thumb over the onyx wedding ring on his finger, tracing the square stone like I used to do when I was little and Dad held my hand. "Isn't there another way?"

Dad checks his watch. "Your mother is waiting for us. We better have dinner."

"I'm sorry." I squeeze his hand. "I'm sorry I didn't listen to you." Fresh tears build behind my eyes. "It'll never happen again."

"I know, darling." Dad pauses. "You only saw him this once? If there were other times, you have to come clean about them now."

"Only last night."

Dad considers me for another beat, and then he nods. "Go clean up your face. The food is getting cold."

My shoulders sag as I walk to the bathroom and wash my face. My father lost shares in his business, and it's my fault. Because of me, he had to give a part of his hard-earned company to the Russo family. If Angelo used the bribing to blackmail my father into signing over a part of his business, then Angelo is condoning the bribing too.

It's a bitter pill to swallow. A part of me wishes I never learned the truth. I don't like to think this house and everything else was bought with dishonest means. Dad has never involved us in his business. I've never understood much about it because he's gone to such great pains to keep his private and professional lives apart.

I've always put him on a pedestal. He's always been my hero, and today made a dent in the image I upheld for so long, proving that even my strong, successful, and invincible dad is only human. That he has faults. I suppose he feels the same about me, realizing that his little girl isn't so perfect or obedient after all.

After drying my face, I go downstairs. Ryan stays for dinner. Mattie keeps on stealing glimpses at me during the meal. I'm sure Ryan told her what happened. Mom stares at her plate, saying nothing. Dad is equally quiet. I'm relieved when the ordeal finally comes to an end.

Mom wants Ryan to sleep over, seeing how late it is, but he prefers to get back to Celeste. After saying goodbye to my brother, I can finally escape to my room.

I lie awake for most of the night, finding comfort in petting Pirate. When dawn breaks, I send Colin a message to say I'm not going class. He asks if I'm sick, so I think up another lie and tell him I'm having my period. The cramps and headaches are often so bad that Mom lets me stay at home instead of going to school. It's a feasible excuse.

Dad has already left for the office by the time I go downstairs. Mom isn't surprised when I tell her I'm not going to class. She meets the news with an uncharacteristically indifferent attitude.

I'm not hungry, but I force myself to eat peanut butter and banana toast. Then I pull on my bathing suit, grab my beach bag, and slip past Mattie who's having her breakfast on the veranda while talking to Jared on the phone. She's no doubt updating him on yesterday's events, telling him what I've done. The way everyone is tiptoeing around me only makes my guilt worse. I feel dumb and humiliated. Awful. I just have to get out of the house.

I use the footpath to climb down the dune and jog to the beach. It's peak holiday season, but the nearest umbrellas are planted on the other side of the lagoon. Thanks to being private, our beach is always quiet.

Grateful for not having to face people, I leave my bag in the cave and take out Angelo's phone. There are two new messages, one from last night and one from this morning. I delete them without reading either. I should've told Dad about the phone, but I couldn't bring myself to hurt him more than I already have.

I drop the phone in the bag with the underwater camera that I clip to a utility belt around my waist and step out into the sun. The heavy ring on my thumb catches the light. I grit my teeth as I look at it, wishing I could throw it into the sea, but Angelo said he'd know if I'm not wearing it. His threat is still too fresh in my mind. The seriousness of his actions told me he wasn't joking. He wouldn't think twice about branding me like an animal. How could I have been so wrong about him? I must be a bad judge of character. Like Dad warned me, Angelo isn't the man I thought he was.

Is Roch here now, watching me? I look around as a shiver crawls down my spine. The dunes and the beach are deserted. I should've told Dad and Ryan about that too, but I don't want to spook them unnecessarily. I've done enough damage. Surely, now that Angelo got what he wanted, he'll leave me alone. I'll wait a few weeks and do a test by going to town without wearing the ring. If nothing happens, I'll throw it in the trash. For now, there's no one here to witness my actions.

With that thought somewhat soothing me, I take the ring off and chuck it inside the cave. It's a pity there's no one around to steal it. From time to time, people cross the river at low tide and walk along the beach toward Glentana. Whenever that happens, Mom calls the police and lodges complaints of trespassing. Sometimes, youngsters from the island drive their jet skis and motorboats up and down the surf of our beach just to piss her off.

Today, the sea is flat and quiet. I walk in, embracing the coolness, and dive under the waves until I reach the swell. From there, I swim with strong breaststrokes deeper into the sea.

Despite the stillness of the water, the currents running under the surface are strong. They're especially treacherous where the river runs into the sea. Almost every year, an unsuspecting holidaymaker drowns here. Since the lagoon became popular with day visitors as well as people camping in the nearby caravan park, the municipality put lifeguards in place. That doesn't prevent the tragic accidents from happening every summer.

I swim until my arms ache and my legs cramp. It's too far. I know it. But I want to punish myself. I want to purge myself of Angelo Russo. I never want to hear his name or see his face again, not in my thoughts or in my dreams.

When I'm too tired and too cold, I drift on my back for a while. From this distance, our house is a small white beacon on a green hill, framed by a sandy dune. The colorful umbrellas and towels on the left are pinpoints on the pearly sand. I fit the new scuba mask Colin gave me, suck in a lungful of air, and sink under the water, but I find no joy in the quietness today.

A school of sardines torpedoes past on my left, their movements staccato and synchronized. They change direction, heading like one body toward the beach. When they behave like this, it's because they have a predator on their tail. Maybe it's a tuna or swordfish. I turn in a circle under the water, and then I see it. Not even five meters away, a great white shark of at least ten meters glides through the water. I've never seen such a big one, and never in the sea. My only acquaintance with great whites was at the aquarium.

My pulse spikes. The beat of my heart thrums in my temples. I forget that I need air. I forget everything but the sight in front of me. Unzipping the bag on my belt, I take out the camera and activate the video. The majestic hunter passes a few meters in front of me. The visibility is good, the light that pierces the dark blue water making the gray body and white underbelly shimmer. As my hands are occupied, I have to pedal with my feet to turn, following the predator as it circles me.

The blood pumping through my body gushes in my ears. The shark swims away, turns, and heads with full speed straight at me. I try to remember what I read. Don't swim away. Don't behave like prey. The best defense is a fist on the gills, not on the nose.

I take in the eyes, glassy like marbles, and the half-open jaw studded with spiky teeth that oddly resembles a smile. It's so close I can make out the sandpapery surface of its skin. I brace myself for the impact. I don't know how much it weighs, but I have no doubt a collision will do damage, if not knock me unconscious.

At the last minute, it changes direction, zipping to the right. It's probably sniffed me and figured out I'm not a snack it's familiar with. Great whites aren't aggressive by nature like Zambezi sharks. Most accidents happen because they mistake surfers for seals.

The shark turns around and circles me again. I'm

calmer now. I think it knows I'm not food. The adrenaline coursing through my body is more from a rush of excitement than fear. The predator passes me slowly, and then it shoots away, disappearing into the same direction as the sardines.

Desperate for air, I kick up and break the surface. For long seconds, I do nothing but drag oxygen into my lungs. When my breathing settles, I switch off the video, making sure to save it. I'm high from the experience, my body and brain fueled by the incredible beauty and grace I witnessed. I just hang there in the water, savoring it for a while.

I don't feel cold any longer, but when I start to shiver, it's my cue to turn back. Before I swim for the shore, I do what I came here for. I take Angelo's phone from the bag and let it drop to the bottom of the ocean.

CHAPTER
SIXTEEN

Angelo

Our house is a stone structure that stands on a cliff. The wall of rock dives straight into the sea. To the left, a small bay with a strip of sand provides enough protection to tie a boat. Beyond the bay, terraced gardens lead up the hilly side to the house. On the east side, an Olympic-sized pool overlooks the sea. The garden is planted with rosemary, thyme, lavender, and olive trees. A vineyard stretches down the hill at the back. It's a small vineyard that produces a few bottles of mediocre quality wine a year, but it was never meant to be an industrious enterprise. It's my father's hobby. It was always his dream to own a vineyard.

I throw the rope of the yacht to one of our men who waits on the jetty. He greets me with a nod. Once the yacht is secured, he goes on board to close everything and pull the covers over the fittings. I look at the gray sky, taking in the thick bank of clouds as I climb the stone steps that cut through the garden to the front of the house. There will be snow on the mountains, tonight.

My mother waits on the veranda. Wisps of dark hair showing the first streaks of white blow around her face. She's wearing a beige rollneck sweater and white slacks, the clothes hanging loosely on her frail frame. She's lost too much weight. My father's illness has taken a toll on all of us.

Spreading her arms, she pulls me into a hug. "Angelo."

Her hair smells of fried butter and zucchini. She's been cooking.

"I kept you some lunch." She pulls away to look at me, her brown eyes piercing. "How was your trip?"

"Good. How's Papa?"

"Better." Her smile gives nothing away. "He's over the worst of the cold. He's waiting for you instead of lying down. I told him you wouldn't be here before three." She turns for the house. "Come on. I'll dish up a plate for you."

I linger a moment to appreciate the view. The sea runs from turquoise into a darker ring of blue. The colors are lighter here, not blackish blue like the deep, stormy waters of the Cape.

"Angelo," my mother calls from the house.

I go inside and close the door. The house is warm. The high ceilings and big windows allow for plenty of natural light, but today, the soft, golden ceiling and floor lights expel the grayness of the day.

Thanks to the yellow color of the sandstone walls, the three-story building isn't gloomy like most of the other strongholds guarding the coastline. Not like the hovel in which I was born before my father made enough money to buy and renovate this place. With teak floors and whitewashed ceilings, the house looks spacious and bright.

Heidi, our housekeeper, takes my coat. The man who took care of the yacht enters with my bag and satchel. He hands me the satchel and takes my bag upstairs.

A clanking of pots and cutlery comes from the kitchen. Classical music plays in the background. My mother likes to cook while listening to Mozart or Bach. The radio in the kitchen is always on, tuned to a classic station. A fragrance of garlic, oregano, and bell peppers hangs in the air.

It's home.

These are the things I value—my mother humming in the kitchen, Mozart playing on the radio, the smell of fried aubergine and garlic, and the sourdough rising in my late grandmother's big porcelain bowl under a kitchen towel on the table. It's the only thing my mother brought with her when she married my father—that bowl with the blue flowers painted around the rim.

A bout of coughing pulls me from my peaceful state. I walk to the library. My father sits on a chaise in front of the fireplace with a blanket over his knees. He's twirling a glass of red wine in front of the flames, studying the color in the light. A box of cigarillos lies open on the coffee table.

I go over, squeeze his shoulder, and pull up a chair.

He takes a sip of the wine and sloshes it in his mouth before swallowing. "The grapes had too little sun, last year. Too much wind, perhaps."

I sit.

After putting the glass aside, he takes a notebook from the table and jots something down. "Did everything go as you'd hoped?"

"Better."

Taking the contract Edwards signed from my satchel, I hand it to him. I had our lawyer draw it up. My father hasn't seen it yet. He was too unwell to accompany me to the appointment. He takes his time to read it, going over every line.

My mother enters with a tray. She puts a plate loaded with deep-fried aubergine and a generous helping of ratatouille as well as a wine glass on the coffee table in front of me.

"Thank you," I say.

I stopped telling her to let the housekeeper do the work a long time ago. My mother needs to do this. She likes to spoil us.

Her smile is warm as she leaves the room.

My father looks up from the papers in his hand. "This is a lot more than we bargained on." He drops the documents in his lap. "What did you do to make him sign? Hold a gun against his head?"

"Something like that."

I remove the black book from my satchel and hand it to my father.

He turns it over and flips the cover. His expression gives nothing away as he scans over the contents. He flicks through a few pages and then lifts his gaze to me. "How did you get it?"

"Walked into his house and took it."

He doesn't ask how. It's not important. "If you have the book, you don't need the girl." He picks up the papers in his lap and waves them at me. "Not with this."

I tense at the mere sound of that. Taking the bottle from the side table between us, I pour myself a glass of wine. "The deal is on."

"Why?"

I taste the wine. My father is right. It's too tannic. "She was promised to me."

"That's your reason?"

"Do I need another reason? You told Edwards to his

face the wedding will happen no matter what. It's your honor I'm protecting, your word."

"Is that the only reason, or is it because you liked what you saw a little too much?"

"No one takes away what belongs to me. Whether I liked or hated what I saw didn't matter before. Why would it make a difference now?"

"Because, by your own design, you have a chance to make a choice. You can pick and choose from all the single women. You can marry for looks or love or money or whatever you please. Few men of our standing have that kind of freedom. Your cousins don't. Your uncles and I didn't."

"You love Maman."

He coughs, gargles, and clears his throat before continuing. "It took time, and I can tell you it wasn't smooth sailing. It helps that your mother is a good woman with an iron will who knows her duty and who loves her family. I'm not an easy bastard to live with."

I chuckle at that. The illness has made him soft, but he's not as bad as he makes himself out to be. Everyone knows he dotes on my mother.

"I made up my mind," I say. "When she turns eighteen, her father will give me his blessing, and she will say yes."

"Why are you so set on seeing this through?"

"They have a good name. It'll be valuable for the business."

He can't contest the fact.

Saying nothing, he hands me the book and the contract and picks up his glass again.

I put the book and the documents in the satchel and eat my lunch. When I'm done, my father is snoring, the empty glass tilting in his hand. Removing the glass carefully, I set it on the table. After pulling the blanket up to his waist, I grab the satchel and exit quietly.

My mother waits on the other side of the door, standing small and almost guiltily in the hallway like someone who doesn't have the right to roam freely in her own house.

I frown. I don't like that she's sneaking around like a mouse, too scared to make a peep. After all this time, she should be used to the luxury and the grandness of everything. My father rules the business, but the house is her domain. She should be queen here, not creeping down the hallways and tiptoeing through the rooms. The kitchen is the only place where she lets her guard down and where she truly seems carefree. Is it a coincidence that it also happens to be the only room in which my father never sets foot?

"What are you doing out here?" I ask.

"Waiting for you."

"Is something the matter?"

She juts her chin at me. "Tell me about the girl."

I'm not keen on discussing Sabella. It's private. "She's nice."

"Kind?"

"Yes."

She waits.

"Unpretentious. Honest."

"She sounds nice."

"That's what I said."

My mother holds my gaze. "Does she want this? You?"

"Does it matter?"

"She liked you."

I take in the permanent circles under her eyes and the fragile bone structure of her face, how the hollows beneath her cheekbones leave shadows on her clean-scrubbed, olive complexion. How happy is she truly?

"I never said she liked me." I motion with my head toward the library. "Have you been listening to our conversations?"

She shrugs. "The walls have ears."

My mother never oversteps her boundaries, but I sometimes forget how perceptive she is. She's so quiet, I sometimes forget she's here. "What are you getting at?"

"That you shouldn't have spoiled that."

"Spoiled what?" I ask, the muscles around my eyes tightening.

"Spoiled good feelings. There are little enough of those in life as it is."

It's not her business, but I know she means well. Still, I can't help my curt answer. "There wasn't another way."

She clutches her hands together in front of her. "Than stealing information from her father?"

"Yes." My tone is clipped, my impatience winning out. "Without something to hold over Edwards's head, he'd never let the marriage happen. Even if she was willing, he would've turned her against me."

"If you waited until she was older—"

"Feelings are fickle," I say, repeating my father's words. "One day, she'll understand why I had to do it."

"She doesn't know?"

"Not why I did it. Her father hasn't told her about his promise or about us. She's young. In another year's time, she'll be more mature and better equipped to handle the truth."

"You should tell her. Keeping her in the dark won't make it easier for her later."

The handle of the satchel pushes into my palm as I

tighten my fingers around it. "I'll deal with it as I see fit. The discussion is over. Don't bring it up again."

Something like hurt passes through her eyes, but before I can get an accurate read on her, she averts her gaze.

"Ang!" Adeline cries out, barreling down the hallway.

I just have enough time to drop the satchel before catching my sister as she throws her arms around my neck.

She smacks a kiss on my cheek. "You're back." Laughing, she lets me go and wipes something from my face, presumably her lipstick. "You should've told me. I would've come home straight after my last class instead of going to the library."

My mother gives an awkward smile before slinking away, allowing us space as if she's not welcome in our circle. Like an outsider. Guilt constricts my chest as I follow her retreat with my gaze over Adeline's shoulder.

"Hey," Adeline says, punching me in the stomach. "I'm talking to you."

"Quiet." I glance at the library. "Papa is sleeping."

She blows out a breath. "It's been hard." Then her expression brightens. "But the doctor reckons he'll be fine in a couple of days. It's only a cold." She picks up the satchel and hooks her arm around mine. "Have you eaten? If I know Maman, she's been cooking all day. Let's grab a hot chocolate and you can tell me all about the love of your life."

I scoff. "She's hardly that."

She swings the satchel around and punches me with it. "Be nice."

"Love takes time to grow. It doesn't happen overnight."

"Pff. You're such a cynical man." Pulling me toward the kitchen, she continues. "What did you give her for her birthday? I hope you made an effort with the gift. Women pay attention to small details like that. The bracelet was nice, but Papa chose it. It's not the same, you know?"

Adeline's enthusiasm and love of life are always contagious. Smiling despite myself, I say, "I did give her a cat."

"You said she rescued it."

"I got everything the cat needed."

Drawing me into the kitchen, she shakes her head. "Nope. That doesn't count."

"A phone?"

She dumps the satchel on a chair. "Getting better, but that's still last year. What about this year?"

I take a seat at the table and fold my hands on the top.

A kiss.

No. That was for me.

"So?" Adeline asks with her head buried in the fridge. "I hope you didn't have something impersonal delivered." She straightens with a carton of milk. "Like flowers or chocolates." She makes a face. "That's for men who don't want to take the time to think about it and put effort into picking out something themselves."

"I gave her my ring."

Silence wraps around us as my sister freezes on her way to the stove, gaping at me with round eyes.

Why did I tell her that? It wasn't my plan. It wasn't *not* my plan either. If anyone notices that my ring is missing, I have no issue about telling them what I've done with it. Maybe I just wanted to shut her up.

It takes her a moment to come to her senses. She glances at the naked ring finger of my right hand and back at my face. A slow smile curves her lips. Pointing the milk at me, she says, "Now that's a birthday gift with meaning."

"I'll replace it with her own ring of course."

"Of course." Her expression is radiant. "And like a considerate fiancé, you'll let her choose it."

I don't reply.

I doubt Sabella will want a ring, especially not from me. Not that it matters. There won't be a choice. Not in the ring she wears, and not in the husband she marries.

Sabella

A man stands on the shore. I recognize the dark suit and his shaved head even before I reach the first breaker. The coldness that travels through my body isn't from the water alone. Roch is a solid, all too real reminder that Angelo wasn't bluffing, at least not about having me watched.

Anger fuels my body, giving me the energy I lacked a few minutes ago to surf the big waves. My exhaustion is so complete that I give up when I surface behind the last wall of foam, letting the tide push me out onto the beach.

Roch comes running.

I'm lying flat on my stomach in the shallow water, too tired to push onto my knees, when a pair of black shoes and dark trousers enter my line of vision. A firm hand grips my arm and drags me out of the water onto the sand.

I register Roch's drenched pants and shoes through my choking. A fresh surge of fury pumps through my veins.

I jerk free. "Don't touch me."

Surprisingly, he lets go.

Rolling onto my back, I cough until tears roll down my cheeks. I pinch my eyelids shut against the glare of the sun and just lie there for twenty seconds or more, sucking in air like a suffocating person.

When I open my eyes again, a round face is staring down at me, blocking out the sun.

"I have permission to touch you when necessary," Roch grumbles.

"You don't have *my* permission."

"You almost fucking drowned," he all but growls.

I scoff. "I'm a good swimmer. I know what I'm doing."

"Yeah?" He narrows his eyes. "It didn't look like that when you washed up like a piece of driftwood. If this is a habit of yours, I'll have to get a fucking boat, and there's no place to tie a boat on this no-good beach."

Sitting up, I lean my weight on my arms and squint at him. I don't tell him boats can be tied on the lagoon. Not that many people go out to sea from there. The river is too unpredictable. The sandbank that forms the riverbed is forever changing. Sometimes, the passage is deep and the flow so strong even a seasoned swimmer like me risks her life crossing it. At other times, it's so shallow, you can walk to the other side. A jet ski will be more practical, but I don't tell him that either.

Even though I'm dizzy and lightheaded, I make to get up. I've never pushed myself this hard or far. He grasps my arm and helps me to my feet.

I pull away again. "I said don't touch me."

The line of his jaw hardens. A trickle of sweat runs

down his temple. He must be dying of heat wearing that black suit in the hot sun.

Good.

Dusting wet sand off my butt as best as I can, I ask, "What are you doing here anyway? Checking up on me? What am I going to do? Swim to the nearest police station?"

His nostrils flare as he dips his hand in his pocket and pulls out a phone. "I brought you this." He adds with an evil smile, "As yours died."

I grit my teeth. He knows what I did. He knows I threw Angelo's phone into the sea.

I don't take the new phone. I turn on my heel and head for the cave.

He cuts me off.

For a few beats, we're in a stare-off, neither of us moving.

Fine.

I plonk down in the sand and pretend to be sunbathing.

From the corner of my eye, I see him stomping away, his dress shoes sinking into the sand.

Not ten seconds later, he's back with my clothes bundled in one hand and my towel in the other.

He dumps everything on my chest. "Get dressed."

"Is that part of your job, telling me what to do?"

"It's keeping you from harm, including letting yourself burn and get skin cancer."

"I don't burn that easily."

"Doesn't matter. You need to wear sunblock."

Making a face, I say, "Did Angelo give you a rule book with a list of things I'm not supposed to do?"

The moment I say his name, a deep, searing ache settles in my chest. I may not want to see him again, but it's going to take more than saying so to get him out of my system. He's wormed his way in deep. I fell hard and completely. Exorcising him isn't going to happen overnight.

I swallow the lump in my throat.

"Get dressed," Roch mumbles again, crossing his arms and turning his back on me.

I glance at the top of the dune. The windows of our house look out over the sea, but you can't see the beach directly below unless you're standing on the lawn. My mom and Mattie hardly ever come down here. They don't want to spoil their perfect complexions or get wrinkles from the harsh southern hemisphere sun. Both of them hate the sand. Dad is too busy at work to enjoy the beach. The only other person who comes here is Colin, and he's at summer school. No one is going to spot Roch and ask me about him. Just as well, because I won't know how to explain. My parents don't know that I confronted Angelo or what transpired during that conversation.

I consider arguing, but I was planning on heading home anyway. I hate to admit that Roch is right. Being spiteful will only leave me with a painful sunburn. It's almost noon. The sun is at its highest.

"Is this going to be regular thing?" I ask, unclipping my utility belt and letting it drop on my towel. I hop on one leg to pull on my shorts.

"Is what going to be a regular thing?"

"You interfering in my life." I push my arms into the sleeves of my shirt. "Am I going to have to look over my shoulder every time I leave the house?" Although I infuse my tone with a good dose of sarcasm, the thought makes me shiver.

"The idea isn't to make you feel uncomfortable."

"No?" I force a laugh. "Stalking isn't supposed to make me feel uncomfortable?"

Turning, he regards me through the slits of his eyes. "Don't do anything stupid, and you'll forget I'm here."

I snort. "Right."

He mumbles something in French, I think, something that sounds like a string of profanities, and shoves Angelo's ring at me. "You shouldn't let this lie around."

Snatching it from his palm, I push it over my thumb. "You preferred that I swim with it? Maybe I will. You can tell your boss you insisted when you explain to him why it dropped off in the sea." I add under my breath, "Where it belongs."

"Don't be a wiseass."

"Don't overstay your welcome."

A thin smile stretches his lips as he tilts his head, shaking it while studying me.

My beach bag hangs over his shoulder. I grab the strap and yank it free. He watches with a broody expression while I shove my towel and utility belt into the bag.

"Your phone," he says, taking it from his pocket and holding it out at me. When I don't move, he drops it in my bag. "Keep it on you and charged at all times."

I cross my arms. "Or?"

His smile stretches into a grin. "Or be prepared to see a whole lot of me."

Not sparing him another glance, I charge toward the lagoon. The river isn't coming down strongly today. The water has eaten away the sandy banks on the sides, leaving a deep sandcastle canyon, but at the bottom, the washout is shallow.

Digging my heels into the edge of the bank, I slide down as the sand gives way under me. Somewhere behind me, Roch curses. I make my way through the water and climb up the embankment on the other side. Looking back, I take perverse pleasure from how Roch sinks knee-deep into the middle of the river with his shoes in one hand and his socks in the other. The riverbed is like quicksand in places. If you don't know where to walk, you can be sucked in up to your waist. You have to look for the darker patches of harder sand.

I quickly make my way past the children splashing in the shallow water of the lagoon and the men fishing farther along the shore. The sand burns my soles when I cut across the beach to the bridge.

Among the holidaymakers in their swimming trunks and bikinis, a man with a suit will attract attention. I dare a glance over my shoulder again and spot Roch walking over the scorching hot sand with his jacket slung over his shoulder, appearing to have no worries in the world. He looks like one of those holiday commercials with the French guy strolling in a tux, trouser legs rolled up, on a beach in Saint-Tropez.

Breaking into a run, I cross the island via both bridges and turn right onto the road that goes up the hill. I'm sweating and sticky from the sea and the sand when I finally arrive home. I burst through the gate, but I don't feel safe on the other side of it. Even slamming and locking it doesn't make me feel better.

"Everything okay?" Doris asks, coming out onto the porch.

"Yes," I say, trying to sound normal as I reach her. "The tar is hot. I forgot to take flipflops."

She clicks her tongue. "You shouldn't be so careless."

I push past her into the house and sprint up the stairs. After showering, I grab a snack and close myself in my room. When I've eaten, I download the video on my laptop and watch it several times, unable to get over the exhilarating experience.

I'm itching to share it with my family, but Mom will

freak out and Dad will ground me from swimming. They don't understand sharks like I do. They just think danger instead of beauty when anyone mentions the word. Besides, if they know how far I went out into the sea today, I'll probably be grounded for life.

Pirate is stretched out on my unmade bed. I lie down next to him, drifting into a fitful nap, and when I wake up, the room is basked in a gloomy light.

The hour hand on the clock on my dresser stands on six. The room is stuffy and hot. I forgot to close the blinds and switch on the AC.

I get up and open the balcony doors to let the breeze in. Pirate jumps from the bed and rubs against my leg. Something squeezes in my chest when I crouch down to pet him. I can't look at him and not think of Angelo, and I can't think of Angelo and not hurt.

A knock on my door startles me from my thoughts.

My mom opens the door and sticks her head around the doorframe. "You're awake." Her smile is stilted. "Colin is here. Can he come in?"

"Oh." I straighten. "Sure."

Colin enters with his backpack slung over his shoulder, carrying a six-pack of ginger ale and a bag of gummy bears. "What's up, Bella? I took notes for you in class. I brought the exercises we did so you can catch up." He offers me the snacks. "These are for your period. Ginger and sugar always help."

My mom clears her throat. "I'll leave you to work. Would you like something to drink, Colin?"

"I'm good, thanks, Mrs. Edwards."

She closes the door and leaves.

"How are you feeling?" he asks. "Do you want me to prepare you a hot water bottle? It always works for Clara."

"No." I flop down on the bed. "But thanks."

"You look like death warmed up. Are you sure you're not coming down with something?"

Pulling my knees up to my chin, I shake my head.

"Hey." He drops his bag on the floor and sits down next to me. "What's going on? Did something happen? It's not Celeste or the baby, is it? I saw Ryan leaving your house late last night."

"No," I say again. "Celeste and the baby are fine. I mean, Celeste is due any day now, but that's not why Ryan came."

"Why did he come?" He studies me. "He's so seldom here, I was worried something may be wrong."

"Something is wrong." I cover my face with my hands. "Oh, Colin."

"Bella." He puts a hand on my shoulder. "Talk to me. You can tell me."

Yes, I can. I trust him, so I tell him the story, omitting the part about the bribes. I only say that Angelo took sensitive information concerning my dad's business.

He stares at me when I'm done, his mouth agape. "He stole information? To do what with?"

I cringe when I say, "Industrial espionage." That's what stealing incriminating evidence to blackmail someone into signing over shares is, isn't it? Well, in a way.

Colin takes a can from the six-pack, cracks it open, and offers it to me. When I shake my head, he kicks off his shoes, shifts to the wall, and sits crossed-legged with his back resting against the headboard.

"I can't believe that slimy son of a bitch did this to you." He takes a long drink. "He must've been planning it right from the start." He clenches his jaw. "That asshole used you."

Rolling my hair into a bun, I secure it with a pencil. "Don't rub it in. I feel bad enough about the whole thing.

It's silly, but I feel like my privacy has been invaded. After all, I *did* let him in."

"It's not silly." He gives me a stern look. "He lied. He tricked you. If you knew what he was planning, you never would've let him in. That *is* an invasion of your privacy." He adds with scorn, "In the worst possible way."

"No, that's not the worst." I bite my lip, contemplating if I should say more, but the sinister promise is too scary to face alone. "The worst is that he said he'd come back for me." I add in a barely audible voice, "Always."

"Fuck, Bella." He sits up straight, anger flashing in his eyes. "You have to get a restraining order against that bastard."

That's not an option, not as long as I can't go to the police, and with what Dad's done, I can never go to the police.

"I'm serious," he says. "I'm going to talk to my dad. He knows people in the force—"

"No." I lay a hand on his knee. "He was just bluffing, trying to scare me. He got what he wanted. He has no reason to come back."

"I still think—"

"No," I say more forcefully, thinking fast. "My dad doesn't want the news to leak out to the media. It won't be good for his company's shares on the stock market. You can't tell anyone. Understand?"

The look that passes over his features is conflicted. "I still think you should get protection, but I'll never do something you don't want."

I blow out a shaky breath. "I knew I could count on you."

If he feels this strongly about going to the police for a restraining order, I'm not telling him about Roch. It'll only make matters worse. Angelo is gone. He won. There's nothing we can do about it. But Roch is here. Colin won't let such a blatant trespassing slide. He'll see it as his duty to tell my dad. If my dad finds out a man is shadowing me, he'd rather get himself arrested and thrown in jail in the midst of a bribe scandal and destroy our family in the process before letting me keep my mouth shut. I'm sure Angelo is only covering his ass, making sure I don't step out of line. In a few days, when he realizes no one is talking to the police, he'll call Roch back.

"Yeah." Colin ruffles my hair, messing up my bun. He doesn't seem convinced. "Anything for you."

"Shall we work on those exercises?" I ask, forcing brightness into my tone. "That's why you came in the first place."

"Why not?"

He puts the ginger ale on the nightstand and picks up his bag, but his actions lack enthusiasm.

For the next hour, we go over the notes he took and do a couple of exercises. My mom calls me down just after seven and invites Colin to stay for dinner. Colin and I work another two hours after clearing the table and helping to tidy the kitchen before he says goodnight.

"You sure you'll be fine?" he asks, hovering in the doorframe when I see him out.

"Yes." As he doesn't budge, I add, "I'll tell you if I'm not."

He nods once, climbs down the steps, and stops at the bottom. "Are you coming to class tomorrow?"

"Yes."

Colin was right. I can't afford to mess up my future, and I sure as hell won't let Angelo be the cause of missing out on my dreams.

Trying to lighten the mood, I say, "Only if I'm driving."

I meant to tease, but his response is serious. "Sure."

I watch him walk away, feeling like a fake and a liar because I pretended it's not serious. Because I pretended it doesn't matter. Because I lied when I said that Angelo coming back for me is the worst.

The worst is far from that. The worst isn't even mourning the loss of my first love.

The worst is that my heart can't bear the thought of Angelo never returning.

CHAPTER
EIGHTEEN

Angelo

My mother comes downstairs as I exit the dining room after breakfast. She's wearing a camel-colored Dior coat, a Hermes scarf, and a Louis Vuitton handbag over her arm. Since we made our money, my father has turned her into a walking luxury brand. It's an overkill. He's trying to make up for those days none of us can forget but will never mention.

"Morning," I say, the nagging guilt and questions from yesterday still burrowing like splinters under my skin.

She pulls on a pair of gloves and stops at the bottom of the staircase with a soft smile on her face. Her words are equally soft, as if she's scared to speak up, scared she'll be heard. "Good morning."

I stop in front of her. "Where are you going?" It's early. My father is still sleeping.

"To the store. We're out of rice. I'll get some oranges

while I'm there. I know how much you like those ones from Morocco. They're sweeter than the local varieties. Has Adeline left?"

"Five minutes ago."

She frowns. "I was going to say goodbye. I lost track of time while getting ready. Do you need anything while I'm out?"

"I'll drive you," I say on impulse.

She looks taken aback. "That's very kind of you, but I know how busy you are."

She says it as if I never have time for her, because I don't. I don't give her the attention she deserves. I'm taking her too much for granted. We all are.

"I don't have anything planned for the morning." I take my key from my pocket. "The sun is out. A drive will be nice."

She blinks.

She doesn't believe me. She knows better than anyone the paper stack on the desk in the study is higher than the Tower of Pisa. There's much to be dealt with, too much, and the pile is only getting bigger while there's never enough time.

"All right," she says, her smile uncertain, but she goes ahead and picks up the basket next to the door.

As I escort her outside, she shoots me a sidelong glance. She's questioning my motives for driving her. I can't blame her, seeing how seldom I go anywhere with her. I rarely make time for anything or anyone outside of business.

The man who takes care of the cars is new. He's polishing my father's Mercedes in the driveway.

I throw him the key. "Get my car. Is the tank full?"

"Yes, sir," he says, catching the key and running to take the basket.

When he brings the car around, I seat my mother and take the road over the mountain to the village in the valley.

My mother looks at me as I park in a lot on the outskirts of the town. "We're not going to Bastia?"

"There's a good market here. It's quieter. Less pollution."

She says nothing as I get out of the car. I go around and get her door. She pushes oversized sunglasses over her face while I get the basket from the back.

The market is set up on the square under the canopy of Corsican pine trees. The morning is fresh. Our breaths make white puffs in the air. I pull my coat tighter and flick up the collar. The cobblestone street is wet, already scrubbed clean by the bar and café owners who've put their chairs out on the pavement. Despite the cold, a few elderly people sip espresso at the tables. They look up as we pass, avert their eyes, and turn their faces away.

"We should go straight to the supermarket," my mother says. "We can get everything there. It'll save time."

I watch her closely, trying to read her. She's nervous.

"I'm not in a hurry," I say, the muscles around my eyes tightening in an involuntary reflex. "Let's go through the market. I'd like to see it."

My mother walks a step ahead of me with her head held high and the basket swinging from her arm. She looks small and thin against the backdrop of the sturdy villagers, more like a malnourished child than a grown adult.

A bustle of activity greets us on the square. Local farmers are offloading crates of parsnips and leeks from vans, and women are filling baskets with olives, tomatoes, goat's cheese, and bunches of dried thyme that they display on the tables.

We walk through the rows, my mother inspecting the

goods, and at each table, we're met with the same reaction. The men turn their backs, and the women look away.

I witness the behavior with a nasty suspicion growing in the pit of my stomach. Anger pushes up inside me as we're given the same disrespect stall after stall that we pass. My mother doesn't stop anywhere, not at the rice seller from Camargue or at the fruit vendor from Morocco. Instead, she heads for the supermarket on the other side of the square where a teenager with a nose ring sits behind the cash register.

The guy doesn't look up from his phone when we enter. He rings up the oranges and rice that my mother puts on the counter without as much as glancing at us.

Yeah. That's not going to work for me.

Grabbing the basket, I take my mother's arm and drag her to the door.

"Hey," the guy says, finally lifting his head. "What about this stuff? Are you buying it or not?"

I don't bother to answer.

"Angelo," my mother exclaims. "What are you doing?"

I cross the road and push open the door of the general store. The chime of a bell announces our entry.

"I'll be right there," a man calls from a room at the back. "Help yourselves in the meantime."

The place is a far cry from the supermarket with its wilted vegetables and soggy lettuce that are crammed into rows of refrigerators. Here, the fresh produce are presented in crates and neatly arranged on trestle tables. The tomatoes are fat and red and not half-frozen. Local and organic products are displayed on wooden shelves. Dried sausages hang from the beam over the counter. A whole salted ham stands on a slicing block. The space smells of paprika and cloves. It's warm inside, cozy, not freezing like in the generic supermarket.

My mother looks at me like she did in the car.

Ignoring the quiet plea in her eyes, I push the basket into her arms. "The quality looks better here."

Her voice is soft. "Angelo."

"You wanted rice. Get it. And the oranges too. Take some extra. Papa likes his orange juice freshly squeezed."

Her manner is quietly accepting like when my father gives her an order. She's never said no—neither to him, nor to us—but she has that way about her that says, *Don't say I didn't tell you so*. It's the same look she wore when she warned us not to go too high on the swing, but we did it anyway and came home with scraped knees and bleeding shins.

She takes wild rice, my father's favorite, and a few oranges.

A man, who I presume to be the owner, comes out of the backroom just as she carries the basket to the counter. Dusting his hands on the striped apron tied around his waist, he slides his gaze from my mother to me. His expression becomes shuttered. He's in his fifties, old enough to know who we are.

My mother unclips her handbag and takes out her wallet.

Pursing his lips, he pushes the basket back toward my mother.

The fury that's been building since we set foot in the village explodes. In two long steps, I'm in front of him, curling my fingers around his nape. His eyes bulge as I squeeze.

"Ring it up," I grit out.

He shakes his head as much as he can in my hold.

I push, knocking his head three times on the counter. "Ring. It. Up."

He braces himself with his hands on the wood, not fighting my grip, but he shakes his head again.

I'll crack his fucking skull open.

My mother leans her back against the counter. She looks away, yet she doesn't tell me to stop. She knows I won't listen. Whatever she says won't matter. She's not a stranger to the violence running in our veins. My father has been careless at times, letting her witness things she shouldn't have seen.

I bang the shop owner's head on the counter again. "Why won't you take our money?"

He grunts at the impact.

My voice is mocking, my smile thin. "Do you think it's dirty?"

"I didn't mean to disrespect you," he stutters. "I can't charge you. It's on the house."

I don't think so. Holding him down while digging my fingers into his neck, I take a few bills from my pocket and slam them down in front of him. "Look at the money."

He lifts his gaze to me.

I apply enough pressure to make him shuffle his weight. "I said look at the fucking money." A little more, and I can make him pass out. I know exactly where and how hard to press, but I want him lucid.

Slobbering, he squints at the bills.

"Good," I purr. "Does it look dirty?"

"No." He sniffs. "No, sir."

Shifting my hold, I grab a fistful of his hair and rub his nose in the money. "Does it smell bad?"

He mumbles something unintelligible.

I push harder, flattening his nose. "I can't hear you."

"No," he cries out in a nasal voice.

I let him go with a shove, slamming his nose down hard. He bounces to his feet, cradling his nose between his palms. A drop of blood drips from his nostril and splashes on the hundred-euro-bill on top of the stash of money. It paints a big splatter in the middle with a few red dots around.

"Keep the change," I say, taking the basket and handing it to my mother before leading her out by her arm.

We say nothing on the way home.

I only speak when I stop in front of the house. "How long has it been like that?"

She stares straight ahead. "You know how it is in small villages."

Just about forever then.

I turn to face her. "From now on, you take a man with you when you go shopping."

She lets that sink in before reaching for the door handle.

"And you go to the village." I clench my jaw. "You will shop at the market and anywhere else you damn well please."

My mother gets out. So do I, but I hang back, leaning in the open door as I watch her walk to the house with her shoulders squared and her expression hidden behind those glasses that obscure half of her face.

Heidi exits and comes down the steps to take the basket.

At the front door, my mother turns around. "Aren't you coming?"

"I have business to take care of. I'll be home for lunch."

She nods and disappears into the house.

My grip on the roof of the car is hard. I feel like punching something. Someone. I loosen my fingers one by one and get back into the car.

The new man runs up. He takes off his cap and

clutches it in his hands. "Do you want me to park the car, sir?"

"No." I study him through the window, lowering it a crack. "It's Cusso, right?"

"Yes, sir."

"It'll probably need a wash when I get back."

"Yes, sir."

He steps back when I pull off. I don't close the window. I open it all the way, letting the cold air clear my head. Anger has a way of messing with my mind. I don't see things straight when fury obscures my reason.

Even though I haven't been there, I don't need to put the location where I'm headed into the GPS. I know this island like the back of my hand. I know the roads and where they lead, even the ones I've never travelled on.

While I drive, I activate my phone via voice command. Our lawyer left a message to say he'll pick up the contract Edwards signed in the afternoon. He'll ensure that copies are made and validated with a police affidavit before the original is locked in the safe. That's good to know, but it's not the message I'm interested in. There's still nothing from Sabella. Roch sent me a text yesterday to let me know he replaced the phone Sabella threw into the sea.

If she thinks she can get rid of me that easily, she's got me figured out all wrong.

My thoughts alternate between Sabella's visit at the golf estate and what this morning's events mean until, a good two hours later, I take a dirt road that snakes into a crevice between two hills. It's only a little over a hundred kilometers from our house, but the narrow, treacherous mountain roads make driving slow.

A layer of snow covers the ground. The white is a dirty brown at the bottom of the gorge where it's been trampled to slush. A few tents and shacks stand haphazardly around a big fire pit near a frozen stream. It's neither a village, nor a farm. It can't even be called a settlement. A funnel of smoke rises from the dying embers in the pit, dispersing into the air. Even the sky looks grayer here, like a scene belonging in a black-and-white picture.

I don't dare drive all the way to the bottom. The tires will get stuck in the mush. I pull off where the road widens, not that I expect other traffic here, and get out.

A few kids come running at the sight of my car. They're black-haired and snot-nosed with weather-hardened skins.

"You want weed?" the oldest of the lot asks.

Freckles dust his nose. On closer inspection, I notice that his skin isn't as freckled as it's dirty. Their clothes are tattered. Roughly knit jerseys of mixed colors and threads hang on their frames. Their toes stick through the holes in their shoes. One kid's shoes are stuffed with crumpled newspaper to fill up those gaps.

"You want fucking weed or not?" the kid says, taking a flip knife from his pocket and showing me the blade.

My tone is emotionless. I'm still processing the sight, not sure what to make of it. "No."

He swings the knife in my direction. "Then what the fuck are you doing here?"

"Yeah." A younger kid wipes snot from his nose with the back of his hand. "What's your business here?"

"Where are your parents?"

The oldest who's obviously in charge shrugs. "Who knows?"

A tiny one with a musical voice says, "They haven't been home in a long time."

The voice belongs to a girl. Her hair is cropped short, and her tiny frame is wrapped in dirty rags. At first sight, I mistook her for a boy.

"Grandpa is home," she says, pointing with a dirty fingernail at one of the shacks.

I make my way down the slippery path with the oldest boy following closely on my heels and the other kids making a raucous noise.

A stooped old man exits from the shanty the girl indicated. A pipe hangs from the corner of his mouth, and in his hands, he carries a shotgun.

"What'll be your business?" he shouts before I reach him.

"I'm Angelo Russo."

He scrunches up his face. "Who?"

"Teresa's son."

His bushy eyebrows draw together, and then he laughs so hard the pipe falls from his mouth.

I stop in front of him, waiting until he's wiped the tears from his eyes with a grimy hand. He shoves the shotgun into the oldest boy's arms who returns the gun to the shack.

"What do you want?" the old man asks.

"You're Teresa's father?" *My grandfather?*

"Yeah." He hooks a thumb in the suspenders that hold up his pants. "What of it?"

I gave my question a lot of thought. It's the reason I drove here. "Why did she marry my father?"

He scratches his head. "Santino?"

"Yes."

He looks me over, taking in my clothes. "You're just as fancy as that good-for-nothing mother of yours." His upper lip curls. "Whore."

Old or not, I'm a second away from punching him. "Answer my question."

Gurgling, he spits on the ground. "War."

"What?"

"War." He squints at me through one eye. "Your father married her to stop the war between us. We stay here." He makes a circle with his finger. "He stays there."

An old vendetta. It explains why we don't see each other and why my father hasn't mentioned the war. He'll never dishonor my mother by telling us kids about the feud between him and her family. "Don't forget the money."

I know how much we pay my mother's family every month because I've been making those payments for the past two years. The accumulated value is worth a small mountain of gold.

He grins, showing two missing teeth. "You'll be bringing it now in person?"

Looking around, I say, "It's cold out here. Dirty too."

A sneer contorts his features. "Are you coming here and telling me you're better than me?"

"I'm just wondering why you haven't made a nice home for yourself somewhere, a place with heating and running water."

He points a bony finger at me. "Don't you come here and judge us for our way of living. We are what we are. Have always been. Never needed no fancy house with heat and water."

I glance at the children. "What about them?"

"They'll do as they're told if they know what's good for them."

The misery hangs thick in the air. It clings to his clothes and to the stench coming from the hole next to the shack where a swarm of flies are buzzing.

"What are you doing with all that money?" I ask.

"That'll be none of your fucking business."

"He buys gold," the girl says. "He keeps it in the—"

The old man lifts his arm. The girl cowers. Before he

can backhand her, I catch his wrist. It's brittle and skeletal under my fingers. I can snap it with little force.

The kids scatter, some of them laughing, but not the girl. She jumps over the stream and runs in the direction of the forest.

I drop his arm and wipe my hand on my trousers. "From now on, you're not getting money. You're getting a house, food, and clothes. The kids will go to school."

His face turns red. "You won't be changing our ways with your smart mouth and your big car. We do what we want."

"We do what we want," the boys yell, throwing rocks at me.

"You can have an allowance for entertainment or whatever it is you do with the money," I say. "The rest of it will cover your living expenses."

I've decided. I'll drag the old man tied up out of here if I must.

Turning back, I climb the hill. When I get to the top, I let out a curse and charge toward my car. The two in-between kids have broken open the door and are stripping my car of anything they can lay their hands on, which include the mats, a packet of wipes for the leather, and the service book in the glove compartment. The wheel caps are already gone.

They jump on broken pieces of pressed wood and use them as sleighs to slide down the hill with their loot.

I take in the state of my car, the scratch marks on the door where they forced the lock and the mud on the seats.

Fucking savages.

I start the engine and turn the car around, glancing at the sorry camp in the rearview mirror.

No wonder my father never brought us to visit. I understand why he kept us away from here. I always knew why my father was hated and feared. He comes from a bad bloodline of scavengers who poached the riches of others. However, I never knew how much my mother was despised, not only because she's married to my father but also because she comes from here.

We're the scum of the island, and the people here don't forget. Not all the money in the world can change that. Some legendary creatures like Midas turn whatever they touch into gold. Anything we lay our hands on is soiled.

CHAPTER
NINETEEN

The summer holidays have always been my favorite time, but I'm glad when the final school year starts in January. Being occupied helps to take my mind off everything that happened around my birthday.

The rhythm is harsh and the subject material tough. Colin and I work hard, studying together every day. I push myself more than ever, because when I'm busy, I don't have to think. I don't have time to mourn the loss of something that never had a chance to start.

I haven't seen Roch since the day he dragged me out of the sea. That doesn't prevent me from being jittery when I leave the house. I'm constantly scanning the faces of the people in the street or in the mall. Both Colin and Mattie remark how nervous I seem when I'm out, but I'm attributing my behavior to the stress of the matric year.

Celeste and Ryan's baby boy is born at the end of

January. We drive to Cape Town to visit them at the private clinic where Ryan has arranged to sleep until Celeste and the baby are strong enough to be discharged.

Mom, Dad, Mattie, and I stay at Ryan and Celeste's house, a big property with white-washed walls and a gable in the typical Cape Dutch style in Bloubergstrand. Jared booked into a guesthouse. Mom doesn't want him to sleep in the same house as Mattie before they're married.

The name-giving party for the baby is on the day that Ryan and his family arrive home. Mattie and I set tables on the lawn and decorate them with blue tablecloths and white overlays. Mom is overseeing the flowers and the catering. Dad is constantly on his phone, standing apart from the rest of us.

I grab a bottle of sparking water from the ice tub and carry it over to where he leans against a tree.

"I have to go," he says as I approach. "I'll call you back later."

"Here," I say. "You must be thirsty. It's hot today."

Smiling, he takes the water, but he doesn't open it. A frown pleats his brow as he looks out over the sea.

"Who were you talking to?" I ask. "I didn't mean to cut your conversation short."

"Just work. Don't worry about it."

I take his hand. "You look stressed."

"It's the upcoming financial year-end. It's always a stressful period."

"You work too hard. I'm worried about you."

He squeezes my fingers. "It'll calm down once the audit is over."

Tenderness overwhelms me when I study his face. The bags under his eyes have become permanent features. "We haven't been to the aquarium in ages." I remember how relaxed he was when he took me three years ago, how he laughed when he lifted me onto his shoulders for a better view of the shark tank. "We can go to the waterfront tomorrow. We're here anyway."

"Maybe another time." He lets my hand go. "I'm planning on heading back to George early."

"Sure," I say, not wanting to show him how much his rejection hurts.

I hoped my mistake wouldn't cause a rift between us, but my dad has been more distant since the incident with Angelo. We're not as close as we used to be, and I hate how little time he spends at home these days. I hate how it's my fault.

He must've seen the dejection on my face, because he grips my shoulder and says, "You know what? There's a documentary about the lifespan of an octopus on the Discovery channel, tonight. Feel like watching it? We can make popcorn." He grimaces. "If we can find such a thing in this house. There only seems to be seaweed and tofu."

I smile, but his attempt at humor doesn't touch my heart. "Okay."

He's only suggesting watching the program because he feels bad about shooting down my idea of visiting the aquarium. It's not a spontaneous invitation because he wants to spend time with me, not that I deserve his time. I can't expect him to feel the same about me when I betrayed him.

"Sabella," my mom calls, making her way over to us. "Celeste's parents just arrived. Why don't you help them to bring some of the…"—she makes a face—"…origami flower decorations from their car?" She acknowledges my dad with a strained smile. "I was wondering what happened to you. Mattie and Jared want to tell the caterers where to set up the wine spritzers." She adds before walking off, "If it's not too much trouble, you can give them some input."

Celeste's mom is a yogi, and her dad is a non-denominational minister, but he prefers to be called a spiritual worker. Her dad carries out the naming ceremony, which involves burning incense while asking the universe to bless the youngest addition to the family. When it's time for the big revelation, Celeste and Ryan share their baby's name. They decided to call him Bradfield Edwards.

Bradfield is Celeste's maiden name. Mom hates the name instantly. Dad, as usual, is impartial.

"You'd think they'd call him Benjamin Junior," Mom says through tight lips when Celeste and her parents are out of earshot.

"You didn't call Ryan Benjamin Junior," I point out.

My mom shoves her empty teacup in my hand and says with a saccharine smile, "Be a darling and put that on the table."

I don't care what the baby's name is. With his blond curls, he's the cutest thing ever. He looks just like Ryan. I cuddle him against my chest until Celeste pulls him away, saying he's too young to be handled that much.

After the excitement of the birth is over, I fall into a kind of a depression. I never read the texts or listen to the voice messages that Angelo sends like clockwork every day. I always delete them immediately, but I don't dare to get rid of the phone. Getting those messages every morning and every night, even if I don't open them, makes it impossible to forget about him. It makes me spiral into a place of desperation and heartache from which I find it difficult to return.

During that darker period in February, I stop deleting his messages. I tell myself I won't read them, that I just don't care enough anymore, but, like a lot of other things I tell myself about Angelo, it's a lie.

One evening in my bed, when I'm at my lowest, I click on his message.

Angelo: *Sleep well, cara. I'll see you in my dreams.*

An arrow shoots straight into my heart. Tears build behind my eyes. He has no right to say things like that. He has no right to make me keep this phone and force me to think about him day and night. I'll never heal like this, and I have a sneaking suspicion that's his intention. He deceived me, but he won't grant me the mercy of setting me free.

Angelo: *You're awake.*

The double checkmarks on his phone would've told him I read his message. I wipe angrily at the tears on my face.

Angelo: *I miss talking to you.*

Why am I even crying? I hate him.

Angelo: *I miss you.*

Angelo: *Do you need something, bella? You only have to ask.*

I blink more tears away.

Angelo: *How's school? Tell me about—*

Dropping the phone on the bed, I bury my face in my hands. I can't do this. I can't pine for a man who doesn't deserve me, a man who's a deceitful blackmailer. So I go back to deleting the messages and putting on a bright smile for my family and teachers until March arrives and the preparations for my university enrollment distract me.

In April, Colin and I submit our applications for the University of Cape Town. A lot depends on the marks we'll get in our final exams in October. The fight is far from over. My Dad drives us to the university and takes us on a tour of the buildings. It's a magical day in which I have him all to myself—well, if you don't count Colin—

but Colin is kind and wise enough to give my Dad and me some space.

My spirits lift a little in May. I haven't seen Roch in four months. There's a good chance he's no longer around and that I'm stressing about nothing. The more I think about it, the more I believe I'm right. My actions become carefree again, and I feel more like my old self. When a girl in my class invites me to her birthday party, I accept. It's time to live again and to have some fun.

May is a pretty girl with a great sense of humor. I don't tell my parents that hers are out of town on the weekend of her party. If Mom and Dad know the truth, they won't let me go. May invited the whole of our class as well as Colin's. The fact that Colin is going sways my parents to let me stay until midnight.

I pull on fishnet stockings and a black denim skirt with my Caterpillar boots, rounding off the outfit with one of Colin's shirts knotted in the front. I do my make-up dark and tie my hair into two high ponytails.

I'm painting my nails black when Mattie enters my room.

She stops behind me and studies my reflection in the mirror of my dressing table. "I don't know what look you're trying to pull off, but you're not quite cutting it."

I shrug. "It's *my* look."

She sighs. "That's why I'm not letting you wear whatever you want to my wedding. Thank goodness the bridesmaid dresses are designed in Cape Town." Reaching over me, she takes the bottle of nail polish. "You're smudging it. Let me."

I prop my left hand under my chin and give her my right hand, spreading my fingers. I'm wearing a ring on every finger like I often do when I dress to go out, but her gaze homes in on the ring on my thumb.

"I never noticed this ring," she says, frowning. "It looks like a signet ring."

I swallow. "It's just something I found at the antique flea market."

She grips the brush, dips it in the polish, and drags a neat line over my nail. "Has someone told you that you have weird taste?"

"You. All the time."

She sighs again as if there's no hope for me. "At least one of us was born with a good dress sense."

When my nails are dry, I grab my phone and a leather jacket, say goodbye to my parents, and meet Colin outside. Mattie is driving us. I can't wait to get my permanent license when I turn eighteen.

May's house is in a suburb of George. The beautifully renovated old stone building stands on the slope of a hill. The Porsches and vintage convertibles parked outside in the street give an indication of the status of the kids she invited. We all come from money. The private school we attend has an elitist reputation. Admission isn't easy, and not everyone can afford the extortionate fees.

"Looks like there are a lot of older kids here," Mattie says with a pleated brow as we pass the line of cars parked on the curb.

"Don't worry." Colin leans from the back and pats her shoulder. "I'll take care of Bella."

A car comes up too fast behind us, the headlights bouncing off the rearview mirror.

"Mm." Mattie squints and adjusts the mirror. "Maybe I should go inside with you."

"Maybe not," I say, rolling my eyes.

The car on our tail skips lanes. A midnight-blue Alpha Spider cruises past. The guy in the driver's seat has dark hair and a square jaw. He reminds me a little of Angelo.

My heart squeezes. The guy grins and overtakes us to park farther up the road.

"Asshole," Mattie mumbles.

I jump out before she's brought the car to a complete stop, worried she'll make good on her promise and escort us into the house. "Thanks, Mattie."

Colin parrots me, thanking her for the ride as he gets out of the back.

"I'll be here at midnight," she says through the open window on the passenger side. "Wait for me inside."

I wave, already running through the open gates.

"Let me know if you want me to fetch you earlier," she calls. "Or if there's a problem."

Before she can say more, I take the porch steps two by two and walk through the door. The music is pumping. A few people stand in the hallway, chatting and clutching paper cups. I make my way to the lounge, which is packed. Disco lights cut over the dancers who are gyrating to the beat of crunk rap.

"Wow," Colin says in my ear, his volume hurting my eardrum.

I spot May in the center of the floor and wave. When she sees me, she utters a shriek so sharp it's audible above the music and fights her way through the crowd toward us.

"Bella," she shouts when she reaches me, throwing her arms around my neck. "I'm so glad you could make it." She releases me and bats her eyelashes at Colin. "You look handsome. As always." Hooking one arm through mine and the other through Colin's, she drags us to the pool deck where a bowl of punch and paper cups are set out. "Let's get you a drink."

When we each have a cup in our hands, she introduces us to the people hanging out by the pool. The setup is pretty with tea candles floating on the water and colorful lights running along the edge of the awning. Chinese torches are planted in the lawn, their flames throwing a golden light over the garden. Thanks to an unexpected Indian summer, the evening isn't cold, but it's fresh enough for no one to be swimming.

I don't remember half of the names of the people after we've done the whole round. Some, I recognize from school. Many of them finished the year before and are first-years at uni. May has always been social and popular.

"Let's go dance," she says, pulling Colin and me into the lounge.

Dancing isn't one of my strengths, but Colin is great at it. One of Colin's classmates plays DJ. She goes up to him and says something in his ear. A moment later, the hip-hop beat changes to rock and roll. The crowd boos, but May only laughs, curling a finger at Colin and giving him a come-hither look.

The dancers clear a circle as Colin takes her hand and leads her into a spin. I forgot they both took dance classes in tenth grade. They're well-coordinated. They quickly attract a large group of spectators who whistle and cheer them on.

I watch for a bit until my cup is empty. Not enjoying the jostling on the dance floor, I go outside for a refill, and when I return, May and Colin are gone. The music is back to hip-hop, and people are grinding against each other on the floor.

My drink spills on my boots as I wrestle my way through the wiggling bodies. By the time I reach the hallway, the cup is already half-empty again. I don't mind. The punch is a disgusting mixture of something fizzy that tastes like orange, artificial sugar, and turpentine. Judging by the empty bottles lined up on the table, the turpentine is cheap tequila.

I empty the rest of the drink in a flowerpot, mumbling an apology to the plastic tree, and try to locate a trashcan. I follow a line of people to what I assume to be the bathroom, cut left to what must be the kitchen, and stop dead in the doorframe.

Only the spotlights under the high shelves are on. Thick white candles burn on the countertops. The corners of the room are dark, but you can't miss the couple entangled in each other in front of the open fridge. The light spilling from the refrigerator is like a spotlight on Colin and May. They're so busy snogging that they don't notice me. Or anything else for that matter.

Grinning, I leave them to it and go to the pool deck where the music isn't so loud. I find an unoccupied deck chair and stretch out on it. I'm supposed to have fun, but to be honest, I'm bored.

A guy steps out from the lounge. My attention is drawn to him because he's so much taller than the other kids who are emptying the punch bowl. He's wearing jeans, a striped shirt, and a denim jacket. When he turns his head and fixes his gaze on me, I recognize him from outside. He's the driver of the Alpha Spider.

His lips tilt as he scrunches up the cup in his hand and aims for the trashcan against the wall, throwing a perfect hit without taking his eyes off me.

I only return his stare because he looks so much like Angelo. No. No one can look like Angelo. He just reminds me a lot of Angelo. It's the hard cut of his jaw and the way his dark curls fall messily over his forehead, but that's where the resemblance ends.

He aims straight for my chair and stops in front of me. "Hey."

"Hey, yourself."

He smiles. "Having fun?"

I pull up my knees. I'm not worried he'll catch an eyeful of my underwear because I always wear shorts under my miniskirts.

"Are you?" I deadpan.

"Not yet." He spreads his legs and straddles the edge of my chair. "I have a feeling I'm about to."

Reflexively, I scoot back. "If you don't mind, you can get your own chair."

His grin is boyish. "What if I mind?"

"This is a terrible pick-up act." I make a face. "The worst I've seen."

"That's because you've never been picked up properly."

"Yeah?" His choice of words makes me laugh. "Exactly how is a person picked up properly?"

He edges closer. "For starters, you don't ask for her name."

I raise a brow. "No?"

"That's too boring, don't you think?"

"What do you ask for then?"

His attention fixes on my mouth. "A kiss."

I laugh again. "Just like that. And why would any girl give you a kiss if you're not interested in who she is?"

"I never said I'm not interested." His eyelashes dip, and when they lift again, he's looking into my eyes. "A name doesn't define a person. A kiss, however, says everything there's to know."

He's such a bullshitter, but at least he's entertaining. "Are you asking me for a kiss?"

"What if I am?"

I'm not remotely interested in him. He's attractive, but he seems shallow. Immature. Not sure of himself and a little dangerous like—

Shit.

Am I comparing him to Angelo now?

What the hell is wrong with me?

I glance toward the kitchen where Colin and May are probably still licking each other's tonsils. I've only had one kiss, and it was nothing but a peck on the lips. It was a kiss I saved for someone special, and I gave it to the wrong man. I'm seventeen. Most of my friends have already done a lot more than kissing. I'm lacking experience. I'm lacking fun. Hell, I'm lacking a life.

Facing him squarely, I say, "What if I say yes?"

His eyes narrow with satisfaction and a little surprise, maybe. Leaning forward, he grips the armrests and puts himself in my space. "You know what'll be even better?" He shifts his hands to my knees, tightening his fingers on my flesh as he drags me toward him. "Sitting on my lap while I kiss you."

Ew. My ass is not a wank cushion. I want to tell him to get off on the pillar if he's so desperate, but before I can utter a word, the guy is yanked off the chair and flung through the air. My jaw drops as he hits the pool on his back, causing a tsunami that washes out the candles.

The deck has gone quiet. It takes me a moment to process what's happening. I look up into Roch's face where he stands next to my chair, his fingers flexing at his sides.

The guy in the pool splutters and rows with his arms to keep himself afloat.

"What is wrong with you?" I ask Roch, shock and anger running through me. Shock, mostly. Because fuck. He's here.

Instead of replying, he grips my arm and drags me to my feet. People gape at us as he pulls me over the deck and through the garden to the front of the house.

"Let go," I say, straining in his hold.

His tone is hard. "Quiet."

He's here.

Even if Angelo isn't, his overbearing presence is everywhere, ruling my life with text messages and a muscle monkey set on ruining what's left of my freedom and my sanity.

I sag in Roch's hold as a terrible insight hits me.

There's no escape for me. Ever.

CHAPTER
TWENTY

Angelo

"**E**dwards is biding his time to kill you," my father says. "You know that, don't you?"

We're sitting in the library in front of the fireplace, sipping cognac after dinner. I register the color of his skin. These days, the evaluation is an automatic reaction for me. He has a healthy glow on his cheeks from the heat of the fire. The pallid complexion of a few months ago is gone. The surgeon is happy with his recovery. My father is still learning how to breathe with half of his lung capacity, but his life expectancy has been prolonged, a gift we don't take for granted. I'm only grateful he finally saw reason and agreed to the operation.

He makes an impatient sound. "Did you hear what I said?"

I wrap my hand around the glass to warm the digestif and to release its aromas. "He knows I've set measures in place for the bribe information to go public if anything happens to me. Besides, I'll be married to his daughter before he can try."

My mother enters with a tray of the Turkish coffee my father likes. She puts it on the low table and kneels to pour the strong brew from the cezve.

"Will the wedding take place there?" my father asks.

"We'll have a legal marriage before an officiant in South Africa." I swirl the glass and inhale the scent of bosc pear, caramel, and vanilla before taking a sip. The liquor is opulent and velvety. It's an excellent brand. "The ceremony and celebration will happen here."

A coarse rattle sounds in my father's chest. "When?"

"As soon as she turns eighteen."

"Angelo," my mother exclaims in a soft voice, quickly looking up from stirring sugar into the coffee. "Not in January." When I frown, she continues, "Not a winter wedding. The choice of flowers are so limited, not to mention that we won't be able to have it in the garden and profit from the view. At least let her wear a pretty dress without freezing to death."

I consider that as I enjoy my drink. What she says makes sense. Anyway, what do I know about what women want on their wedding day? However, I'm eager to close this deal. What prevents me from saying so is the rare excitement lighting up my mother's face. She's looking forward to this wedding, which will be the first of my generation in the family.

"Would you like to take care of the arrangements?" I ask.

Her expression brightens. "It will be an honor."

"Are you sure it won't be too much work?" I leave my empty tulip glass on the side table. "I can hire a company to oversee the planning."

"Nonsense." She straightens. "I'd love to do it. We can put a gazebo in the garden. We'll need plenty of flower arrangements to add color." Her eyes sparkle. "There will have to be a band. There will be enough young people to fill a dance floor. We can have it built on the side of the gazebo and put fairy lights in the trees. Oh, and the cocktails will have to be served at sunset. The view over the bay will be spectacular. It will make very beautiful wedding photos. Champagne. French of course. We don't want your bride to think we're used to nothing. And non-alcoholic cocktails for those who are driving."

"Slow down and give me my coffee before it gets cold," my father grumbles. "You're carrying on as if the wedding is happening next week."

A flush darkens my mother's cheeks. She hands first my father and then me a cup of coffee before taking the tray and walking to the door with an averted gaze, but I don't miss the smile that tugs at her lips.

"You did right to let her handle the wedding," my father says when she's gone. "When we got married, there wasn't money. She didn't have any of that."

My thoughts go to Sabella. What will she want? A small intimate gathering or all the bells and whistles my mother has in mind? Whatever the case, I'm not taking this joy away from my mother. Sabella will adapt. She'll see my mother's good intentions for what they are.

Speaking of weddings. "When are you going to get down to the business of choosing an appropriate match for Adeline?"

As the first-born, even if only by three seconds, it's my right to get married before my sister, but Adeline shouldn't wait too long. She's beautiful, kind, and generous. I'm not blind to how men stare after her in the street. The only reason our father allows her to study in the city is because she has a bodyguard who protects not only her life but also her virtue.

"There's time." The espresso cup looks like a toy from one of Adeline's childhood tea sets in my father's big hand. "We don't have to rush. Let's get yours over and done with, and then we'll deal with the rest."

My phone rings. I down the coffee and put the cup on the side table to take my phone from my pocket. It's Roch. My gut tightens. If he's calling at this hour, something must be wrong.

I push to my feet. "Excuse me. I need to take this." On my way to the study, I answer the call. "What's going on?"

"There's been an incident."

My muscles tense. "What happened?"

"I had to pull a guy off Sabella at a party."

I stop dead. My vision unravels. Fury bursts through my veins. "Did you break his bones?"

"I didn't have to. It didn't go that far."

I resume walking. "Where is she now? Let me speak to her."

"I already dropped her off at home. I don't think it would've been the right moment for a lecture. She was crying."

Fuck.

Clenching my jaw, I enter the study and slam the door. "Is anyone going to press assault charges?"

"No. The party was at a friend's house, a girl in Sabella's class." He chuckles. "There was a commotion after I threw the guy in the pool. May, the girl who hosted the party, wanted to know who I was. She was freaking out about me gatecrashing her party. Sabella told May that Edwards hired me as her bodyguard before I could say anything."

I sit down behind the desk. "Did this friend—May—

fall for it?"

"Sabella was very convincing. She's obviously not keen on her friends knowing I work for you. I get the idea she hasn't told anyone about me, not even her family, because she called her sister on the way with an excuse that the party was boring and that the chauffeur of her friend's father was driving her home."

I don't care if Edwards knows I'm having his daughter watched. He should be glad I'm taking my duties as her future husband so seriously. Sabella obviously feels differently.

"May was worried I'd tell Edwards there was no adult supervision. She said her parents didn't know she was throwing the party and that she'd get into trouble if they found out. She asked if we could keep what had happened quiet, so word of what transpired is unlikely to reach Edwards."

"Who took Sabella to the party?"

"Her sister drove her and her neighbor, Colin Taylor. Colin didn't want to let Sabella go home alone. He insisted on coming with us, but Sabella persuaded him to stay. I think she was embarrassed."

My grip tightens on the phone. I'm an embarrassment to her, am I? The inexplicable disappointment that had lodged into my heart when she broke her word to always like me hits me straight in the chest again. It's unfounded. I always knew there'd come a day she'd hate me. I have no scruples about who and what I am. I'm a devil. Scum. Despising me is unavoidable. But she said she'd always like me, and the sound of it was sweet. I didn't expect her to, but I wanted her to prove me wrong. She didn't, did she? No. She stopped looking at me like I was her hero just as I knew she would.

If not for her father's dishonorable deceit in misleading

us with his false promises, Sabella could've liked me still. Now, that's water under the bridge. All of it. That's okay. Once Sabella is living with me, I'll work on softening her toward me again. Like I told her, I did what I had to do to bring us together. I'll do whatever it takes to keep us together.

"What about Colin Taylor?" I ask, grinding my teeth.

"One of his friends from school offered to drive him home."

"I don't give a fuck how he's getting home." Jealousy erupts inside me. "Is he someone I need to worry about?"

"I've been watching them closely. They're more like brother and sister than what Sabella and Ryan are."

"How was she?" I ask, hoping, needing, wanting, and hating myself for it. I'm only setting the stage for more disappointment. "When you left her."

"Sabella? Upset. Mouthy."

Upset? "Does she seriously give a damn about that fucking prick who tried to touch her?" Because if she does, I'll kill him. With my own hands.

"Not about him. She said she was going to tell him to piss off. She was angry about *me*. Said my interference is ruining her life." He hesitates. "Do you want me to enlighten her family about me? Maybe you should let them know I'm keeping tabs on her. That way, we don't have to lie ourselves out of awkward situations. It can't hurt for them to know you have eyes on her. It'll motivate them to be more careful about where and with whom they let her go out."

"No. It's her family. She can tell them what she likes."

In a few months, it won't matter. Make that a year, seeing that I told my mother we can have a summer wedding. Sabella will be here, safely in my bed, not that she may consider that a safe place to be.

CHAPTER
TWENTY-ONE

Sabella

After the incident at May's party, I become more isolated. The girls in my class are as rich and entitled as kids in our school can be, but none of them has a bodyguard. The lie I told, that my dad hired Roch to protect me, puts me in a different bracket. My classmates are more guarded around me. Some are jealous.

I still meet them for brunch at the mall or at sport events on weekends, but there's a gap between us. No one is going to invite someone to a party if she has to drag a bodyguard along. They don't want what happens at these parties to get back to their parents. They're doing what many other kids of their age are doing, experimenting with booze and cigarettes and sometimes the occasional drug. A lot of heavy petting is also involved, which is why a bodyguard who throws the hottest boy at the party in the pool for chatting a girl up is unwelcome. That, and our community is conservative. These things aren't supposed to happen. As far as the adults are concerned, they don't. I'm not sure it's ignorance. I think it's more a matter of turning a blind eye. What the eye doesn't see, the heart doesn't grieve over, right?

Also, after the party, May and Colin become an item, which means I see Colin less. May is the only girl at school who is genuinely kind to me. She and Colin always invite me along to the movies or for weekends at her parents' beach condo in Hermanus, but I don't want to be a third wheel.

If it weren't for Pirate, my loneliness would've been complete. To fill the empty hours when I don't have homework to do, I swim out to sea and film the life under water. Every day, I push myself harder and farther. Roch swopped the suit for Bermuda shorts and sleeveless T-shirts. To my dismay, he *did* get a jet ski, and he's always hovering around, invading even this part of my life, the only place where I can find peace.

Mattie's wedding is in full preparation, and if I'm withdrawn, nobody notices. I try to be a better sister, involving myself in the arrangements. In October, when I finish my final exam, she has her dream wedding on a wine estate in Paarl. Jared has been promoted to junior executive in his father's law firm in Stellenbosch. I'm crying big, fat, ugly tears when my sister's room is emptied into a moving truck and she hugs me tightly and says goodbye.

The house feels horribly empty without her. It hits Mom even harder than me. She's always been closer to Mattie, seeing how much they're alike. At least Dad spends more time at home. He takes Mom out to dinner and to the opera in Cape Town. Now that the stress of organizing Mattie's wedding is over, they're snapping at each other less. When I walk into the kitchen for a snack after returning from the beach, I catch them in an embrace. They jump apart, looking guilty. Mom hurriedly continues to make a shopping list while Dad clears his throat and says he has to tidy the garage.

When the letter confirming my university admission arrives in November, Dad takes Mom and me to a game farm for the weekend to celebrate. On a warm Saturday, Colin, May, and I have a small party for a few friends at Colin's place. For a change, Colin's dad is home from his job that requires constant traveling. Mr. Taylor flips steaks on the barbecue, and Mrs. Taylor keeps the ice tubs filled with soft drinks and water.

While we're having appetizers on the pool deck, Mr. Taylor makes a toast to congratulate us on passing with distinction. Colin and I will start at the University of Cape Town in February. May is entering a college in George to study aesthetics. May and Colin have decided to break off their relationship before Colin leaves for Cape Town, and both of them seem surprisingly casual about it.

While May and I are making a salad in the kitchen, I use the opportunity to bring up the subject.

"Are you okay?" I ask, rinsing lettuce in salted water.

"Sure." She shoots me a smile from where she's dicing tomatoes on the chopping board. "Why wouldn't I be?"

"Colin told me."

She scrapes the cubes into a bowl. "That we broke up?"

I drain the water and transfer the lettuce to the salad spinner. "I didn't expect that. You're such a good fit." Turning the handle, I say, "You're perfect for each other."

She shrugs. "I love Colin, but we're young still. I don't want to inhibit him from going out or having fun at uni. That won't be fair."

"Wow." I grab a dishcloth and dry my hands. "That's very selfless of you."

"I want what's best for both of us."

"Aren't you a little sad though?"

"I'm sure I will be." She blows out a breath. "But not today. He's still here, and I intend on making the most of every minute before he leaves."

"Isn't there a way of staying together?" I carry the spinner to the table and implore gently, "Why don't you follow him to Cape Town? Can't you study there?"

She turns to face me. "I could, but Cape Town isn't for me. My life is here. My family is here. This is where I'm happy. I'm not going to sacrifice everything for a man. I don't want to end up resenting him for choices I made for all the wrong reasons." She opens the spinner and starts shredding the lettuce into the bowl. "We each have to follow our dreams."

I lean a hip on the counter. "Isn't being together part of the dream?"

"It's more complicated than that." She dusts her palms and studies me with a tilted head. "Have you never wanted to hit on him?"

"What?" I exclaim. "No. He's like my brother."

"I know the two of you are close. I just want you to know I'll understand if you take things further, seeing that both of you will be attending the same uni."

"We're not into each other like that."

"Just do me a favor." She drizzles dressing over the lettuce and tosses the salad with serving spoons. "Take care of him in Cape Town. I have every intention of living my life to the fullest, and I don't want him to lose out on the best years of his youth because he's waiting for me." She picks up the bowl. "He's chivalrous enough to do that."

"Wait. What do you mean?"

"There are a lot of cute frogs out there, Bella. I owe it to myself to kiss a few before I settle down with a prince." She wags her eyebrows. "Variety is the spice of life."

My hackles rise. "You're not playing with Colin's feelings, are you? He's a good guy, and he cares a lot about you."

She cocks an eyebrow. "Is that what he said? Is he discussing our relationship with you?"

"Of course not. Colin is too honorable to do that. It doesn't take a genius to figure it out. I've seen how he is with you. You're not just a fling to him. He's serious about your relationship. I hope you're being as honest with him as you're being with me. He's my best friend, and I'd hate for him to get hurt."

"Colin knew what he was getting into when we hooked up. We're at the verge of starting our lives. He can't expect me to tie myself to one man when I'm not even twenty."

"That's obviously not how he feels."

"You know how he is. He's always too serious." She heads for the door. "Bring the salt, will you?"

"What if he's the one? Aren't you worried you're throwing something special away?"

"How can I know he's the one if I haven't tried others?" She adds from over her shoulder, "You should follow my example. You're the only senior in school who hasn't gotten her v-card stamped."

Indignation burns on my cheeks. "You don't know that."

"Oh, come on. You have a bodyguard, for heaven's sake. Everyone knows you've never even kissed a boy."

"That's not true," I say, but my words are lost on her. She's already left the room.

Colin enters the kitchen and makes his way over to the fridge. "We need more ice." He takes a bag from the freezer compartment and throws it at me. "Here. Make yourself useful."

I catch the bag on autopilot. Do I tell him what May said? Surely, if they broke up, he already knows.

"Hey," I say. "You're all right, aren't you?"

He pops a carrot in his mouth and crunches down. "Yeah." Taking another bag of ice, he walks to the door. "Come on. Meat's done. Grab the napkins on your way out."

I gather the salt and the napkins, thinking about how our lives are changing. May will stay in town but date other guys, and Colin will move into the apartment his parents are renting for him in Cape Town. Their paths seem so certain. May knows exactly what she wants. So does Colin. I, on the other hand, am still battling to project myself in five years from now. Except for wanting a degree and to find a job, I have no idea where I'll settle.

What does the future have in store for me? I don't even know where I'm going to stay in Cape Town. Dad is tight-lipped about my accommodation.

As the days roll by and he makes no effort to contact rental agencies, I suggest moving into a student dorm, but he says it will be better if I stay with Ryan and Celeste. The prospect makes me very happy. I've seen too little of my nephew. Bradfield had colic when he was little, and he's a bad sleeper. My brother and his wife are always tired, therefore visiting us even less than before.

I'm not sleeping well either. I can't remember the last time I had eight hours of uninterrupted rest. It's not only the workload of school and the prospect of going to university that keep me up. It's the approach of my eighteenth birthday. The closer the day gets, the more apprehensive I become. I have no reason to believe Angelo will show up. His text and voice messages eventually dried up around June.

His silence can mean many things. Maybe he realized I was serious about ignoring his messages. Maybe he was just messing with my head and got tired of the game. Or maybe he met someone and lost interest in tormenting me.

I wish it was that easy for me to move on. I've never had the courage to show interest in another guy again. Every time I consider making advances, my throat closes up and I feel an anxiety attack coming on. Rather than making a fool of myself, I always turn away from potentially flirtatious situations. Things will go better in Cape Town. It's a big city. It's not Great Brak River where I'm constantly reminded of Angelo. Cape Town will be a new start. Everything will change there.

Yet I don't believe that one hundred percent. If I did, I would've long since chucked Angelo's ring in the trash. Instead, it's a permanent fixture on my thumb, a constant reminder of his promise. What it symbolizes dictates my behavior and shrouds my life in fear. I don't understand Angelo's motives. I don't know why he plays this sick game of possession. Only, deep down, I do know the answer. There can only be one reason why Angelo still wants to haunt me.

He wants all my firsts.

The thought is too disconcerting to entertain. Whenever it pops into my mind, I brush it away. The game is over. It has to be. I keep on telling myself that he's moved on and found himself another target, but there's only one way to know for sure.

I'll find out on my birthday.

All my classmates have already turned eighteen. My parents sent me to school one year early, hence, I'm the last one to celebrate the big milestone. The parents tried to outdo themselves with the coming-of-age parties they organized at fancy venues and on yachts in Mossel Bay. I begged my parents not to have another cocktail party at home. I won't be able to live through another night of oysters and champagne with the family while Colin entertains us on my underused piano.

It's Ryan's idea to throw a party at the casino nightclub in Mossel Bay. Isn't everyone eager to show their ID cards for the first time at a club? It's not what I would've chosen myself, but Ryan means well. He hasn't said anything, but after Bradfield's birth, he's started to notice my withdrawal from my friends and the world. My apathetic brother is more perceptive than what I give him credit for.

With some coaxing from Ryan, my parents agree. As the casino is a thirty-minute drive from home and the road is dark at night, their only condition is that we sleep over at the casino hotel. The fact that we're of legal age and, as per the tradition, some alcohol will be consumed, also plays a role in their decision. They're not taking risks with drinking and driving.

My mom says they're too old to accompany a group of youngsters to a nightclub and that she'll feel out of place. The lucky task of babysitting falls on Ryan and Celeste. Celeste will leave Bradfield with her parents for the weekend. Ryan and Celeste are calling him Brad now that he's reached the milestone of walking. My sister-in-law has strange rituals.

Mattie comes home to take me shopping for a dress. Too nervous to be excited about anything, I let her bully me into buying a slick golden dress with spaghetti straps that she pairs with matching heels. It's way too formal and smart for me, but Mattie swears the dress makes me look sophisticated and classy.

I invite Colin, May, and a few guys and girls from town.

May can't make it because she's visiting her grandparents in Port Elizabeth. When the big day arrives, Ryan and Celeste fetch me. Colin catches a ride with us. He's chatting to Ryan about his upcoming semester and subject choices at university while I'm staring through the window and biting my nails.

Celeste turns in her seat and slaps my hand. "Don't do that. You're ruining your polish."

I rest my palms in my lap. Celeste paid for my manicure and pedicure. The treat was her birthday gift to me.

Colin shoots me an inquisitive look.

At the casino, he pulls me aside when Ryan books us in. "You're not yourself. Is it him?"

I don't have to ask who he means. Not wanting to spoil the weekend, I say, "You know I haven't heard from him since June. What's he going to do? Show up here?"

"This is your party, Bella, and you're going to have fun."

"Damn right, I am." I don't sound as convincing as I'd like. "It's the stress about going to university and moving out of the house. Celeste isn't ecstatic about me boarding with them."

"She'll get over it." He grins. "Who can't love you?" His expression turns serious. "There's more to it. You're not telling me everything."

I just want to relax and enjoy the party. The burden I've been carrying for the past twelve months is dragging me down a little more with each passing day, and I feel close to hitting rock-bottom.

"You can tell me, Bella. We haven't spent that much time together, lately, but I'm always here for you."

He's right. We don't hang out as much as we used to, but he's still my bestie, the only person I can trust with my terrible secret. Maybe if I share the gnawing fear with someone, the load won't feel so heavy.

"This is going to sound stupid," I say.

His smile is encouraging. "Try me."

Glancing around, I lower my voice. "It's something Angelo said." I bite my lip, considering how to explain.

"About what?"

I take a deep breath before admitting, "About wanting all my firsts."

Colin frowns. "Your firsts? What's that supposed to mean?"

"You know…" I drill the tip of my sneaker into the carpet. "First kisses and everything that go with that."

He reels. "You kissed him?"

My tone turns defensive. "It was only a peck." At the shock and disapproval that pass through his eyes, I add, "It was before I knew he was using me."

"That's why he kissed you?" he asks with disbelief. "Because he wants all your firsts?"

"I don't know," I admit with a frustrated huff. "He told me that morning when he dropped off the gifts for Pirate. He brought it up again on my birthday last year."

"So what's supposed to be next? Your *virginity*?"

"He didn't say that in so many words. Maybe I'm seeing too much in his meaning. I really don't think he's going to show up this year, but I can't stop being paranoid." My laugh is uncomfortable. "I suppose I'm just nervous about losing my v-card, being eighteen and all. I'm the last virgin left in my class. I hate the teasing. There's all this peer pressure to get your cherry popped."

I can't tell him about the anxiety attacks that prevent me from hooking up with anyone. At this rate, I'm destined to become a nun. I take in the compassionate set of his handsome face. Colin is attractive, hot, and kind. We've known each other since forever. He's practically single, and next month, he'll be a bachelor again.

An idea takes root.

Before I can lose my nerve, I rush out the words. "Maybe we should just do it and lose our virginity together, you know, as friends, and then I won't have to stress about it."

He stares at me quietly.

"I don't mean now," I say, ploughing on. "I mean when we're in Cape Town and you're no longer with May. I know we're not into each other in that way, but—"

He interjects with a soft-spoken declaration. "I'm not a virgin, Bella."

The statement takes me aback. I'm at a loss for words. I thought Colin and I shared everything, but I guess we've grown more apart than I imagined. Why does that notion hit me so hard?

When I finally find my tongue again, I say, "Oh. I'm sorry. I just assumed—"

"There's nothing to be sorry about," Colin says good-naturedly.

Ryan turns and waves me over.

"Was it with May?" I ask.

"Does it matter?"

Of course Colin won't speak out of the bedroom. He's too much of a gentleman. It's so typical of him to protect a girl's honor.

"Um, no." I hook my hair behind my ear. "I didn't mean to pry."

He smiles, letting me know I'm forgiven. "I'm not going to sleep with a girl if there's nothing long-term for us in the cards." He deals the rejection gently. "That's not who I am. Do you understand?"

"Sure," I stammer.

"Our rooms are ready," Ryan calls.

"Come." Colin walks ahead, leading the way. "I'll carry your bag. I'm sure you'd like to hang out your dress."

I follow like a sleepwalker, feeling the gorge between Colin and me stretching. Feeling that I don't know him anymore. That I've fallen off the bus somewhere along the way. Feeling for the first time that we're not kids any longer. And for some strange reason, I'm lonelier than ever.

CHAPTER
TWENTY-TWO

Sabella

The queue for the nightclub stretches all the way to the bar next to the slot machines. We skip the line and head for the doorman. My heels sink into the plush red carpet with the casino logo, my calves already cramping from the unfamiliar height of the shoes. It takes all my concentration not to trip.

Ryan says something to the doorman. The man checks our ID cards and nods us in one by one.

When it's my turn, he looks up from my ID. "First time, huh?" He hands me back my card. "Happy birthday, darlin'. Have fun."

Colin takes my arm, allowing me to lean on him as we follow Ryan and Celeste into the club. Ryan has obviously been here before. Judging by how he cuts straight across the floor to a lounge area raised above the bar, he knows his way around.

The red, blue, and indigo lights that flash in a staccato pattern on the dance floor are blinding. It's not even ten, but the music is pumping. The risotto I had at the restaurant sits like a lump of clay in my stomach. Ryan insisted that I eat, making me finish every morsel on my plate. It's not that the food wasn't good. The on-site restaurant is renowned for its cuisine.

It's stress.

Clutching my evening bag under my arm, I pull on the hem of my dress, making sure my ass is covered. Why did I let Mattie talk me into buying this scrap of fabric? I glance down, checking that my boobs aren't popping out. They're not big, but the neckline gapes if I don't pull my shoulders back.

Colin leans closer and says above the music, "Have I told you how stunning you look?"

I scoff. "Only about ten times. I know what you're trying to do, and it's not working."

The hairstylist dried my hair in waves and arranged it over one shoulder. My make-up is light with a dusting of golden eyeshadow and a pearly lipstick to match the dress. It's not me. I look different. I feel different. It doesn't help to settle my nerves.

"You're a hottie, Bella." Colin grins. "Admit it."

I shove him playfully and immediately regret it when I have to maneuver the dangerous walk over the slippery marble floor alone.

Ryan leads Celeste deeper into the club with his hand on the small of her back. She's bouncing with excitement at being out for the first time after Brad's birth. She's gone to a lot of trouble with her appearance, looking gorgeous in a black fitted dress with dainty silver chains for straps and platinum heels.

I take a closer look at her. Why have I never realized

how beautiful she is? Her blond hair is ironed straight and tied in a high ponytail, exposing the fine bone structure of her face. The beautician did a great job with her make-up. The smoky eye shadow brings out the cobalt blue of her eyes, and the shimmery blush accentuates her high cheekbones. No wonder Ryan is holding onto her with so much possession, making a point of demonstrating to anyone looking that she's taken.

In a gray three-piece suit and a white shirt without a tie, my brother doesn't look too bad himself. Lighter than Mattie's and mine, his hair is dirty blond with natural highlights from the sun. Like his hair, he inherited his paler skin tone from Dad. Mattie and I got our olive complexions from Mom.

At the VIP section on the raised platform, Ryan shows his ID card again. The bouncer unclips the cord cordoning off the area and lets us through. A waitress who passes shoots Colin an appreciative look. His fitted white shirt and tailored beige slacks show off his muscles. The formal jacket he pairs with the otherwise casual attire as well as his signature loafers gives him that distinguished edge of wealthy people who underdress. He pulls the style off with ease.

Despite myself, I smile. "I'm not the one in danger of breaking hearts, tonight."

"No danger of that," he says.

He means it. Even though they've broken up, he's adamant about staying faithful to May until he moves to Cape Town.

Grateful to finally locate a seat, I sink into one of the transparent plastic chairs arranged around a Perspex table. The backrest is curved, and the seat is low. Getting up without flashing my underwear in the process will be difficult. The modern design of the furniture favors aesthetics instead of comfort. Now more than ever, I regret wearing a thong, but the dress is so tight that panty lines would've been visible.

Colin slides with considerably less difficulty onto the chair next to me. A waitress removes the reserved card on the table and asks what we'd like to drink. I open my mouth to say ginger ale, but Ryan orders champagne and sparkling water.

Celeste walks to the balustrade and leans over, swaying her ass to the beat of the music. Ryan goes to stand at her back, caging her between his arms with his palms planted on the rail. Unable to shake my unease, I look around, assessing the faces on the floor below before searching the bridge next to the DJ box.

Mistaking my motive, Colin says, "Don't worry. The others will be here soon. You know how long it takes them to get ready."

I give him a weak smile.

When the champagne arrives, the waitress uncorks the bottle and pours four glasses. I grab one and all but down it, needing the liquid courage. She tops up my glass before leaving.

"Thirsty?" Colin asks with a chuckle.

Ryan takes Celeste's hand and drags her back to us, preventing me from having to explain. My brother sits, pulls his wife onto his lap, and hands her a glass. Wrapping one arm around her waist, he rests his free hand on her stomach and says something in her ear. A flush darkens her cheeks. I don't often witness them in an environment outside of family. It's good to see them so happy.

By the time the rest of our group arrive, I'm on my third glass of champagne. Ryan waves the waitress over and tells her to keep the bubbly coming. I drink another glass while Ryan makes a toast, remembering too late to alternate with water. As if reading my thoughts, Colin hands me a crystal goblet of sparkling water.

"Let's dance." Celeste balances her empty glass in one hand while snaking her arms around Ryan's neck. She wiggles her ass on his lap. "I love this song."

He takes her glass and puts it on the table. "We're here to chaperone, remember?"

"Urgh." I make a face. "Don't let my friends hear that." Although, friends isn't the term I should use. We're not that close. Classmates or acquaintances would be a more fitting description. "Take your wife to dance, Ryan." My tone is teasing. "What kind of a husband are you?"

Ryan gives Celeste a panty-dropping smile and deposits her on her feet with a tap on her ass. The DJ hasn't opened the dance floor, but a few people are already warming up, shaking their bodies to the beat.

I watch the dancers until someone shoves a blue, fizzy drink into my hands. I look up.

"A blueberry gin and tonic," Veronica, the long-distance star athlete of our school, says with a wink. She clinks a glass with similar contents against mine.

The cocktail is sweet. I'm already buzzing from the champagne. Mixing isn't a good idea, but I need the alcohol to calm my anxiety. This is my party after all, and I'm still chasing the fun that seems set on eluding me.

The DJ opens the dance floor with a popular song. Everyone except me, Veronica, and Colin are dancing.

"Let's join the others," I say on impulse.

For the next hour, I try to get into the mood on the overfull dance floor, but the fragmented bursts of laser lights and the blaring music hurt my eyes and ears. A headache starts to build in my temples. The alcohol doesn't help. Neither does the paranoia that makes me see dark-haired and dangerous-looking men everywhere in the crowd.

The heat is insupportable. Or maybe it's just me. Perspiration covers my skin.

I touch Colin's arm to get his attention. "I'm going to the ladies."

"I'll come with you," he says, raising his voice above the music.

I'm glad for the hand he wraps around mine to steady me.

"Hey." He frowns when I almost lose my balance on the stairs. "Are you okay?"

I should be. I should be having the time of my life, but I'm not. I can pretend all I want to. The truth is that I'm hating this.

"I think you had a little too much to drink," he says with a laugh, opening the door to the VIP ladies' bathroom and holding it for me to enter. "I'll wait here. Shout if you need me."

"Thanks," I say, meaning it like never before.

Thankfully, the VIP bathrooms are less busy than the normal ones. I enter the nearest open stall and empty my full bladder. When I flush the toilet, the gold ring on my thumb catches my attention. Like a shiny piece of fool's gold, it mocks me, resembling everything that's been eating me since the day Angelo put that ring on my finger.

Vexation rises in a slow-burning path up inside me. The anger eradicates my self-control and reason. The point I'm at my lowest is the point I snap.

Enough.

Angelo ruled my thoughts and my life for the past two years. I won't allow him to take more than he already has. He won't destroy this night too.

Wiggling the hated ring from my thumb, I toss it in the

toilet. It hits the water with a plonk and lands with a clank on bottom of the bowl. I watch the jewel that glitters in the water with detached fascination as I push the button and flush it away.

Gone.

As easy as that.

It takes a moment for the fact to settle.

My hand feels strangely light.

My chest too.

I linger a moment like someone standing next to a grave. Only, I'm not mourning. I'm taking perverse satisfaction from the sight of the clear water.

The bathroom door opens and slams.

Taking a deep breath, I exit the toilet. An attractive woman gives me an absent smile as she goes into the stall next to the one I vacated.

I move on autopilot to the vanity. The world isn't spinning, but I'm off-kilter. A little drunk. I wash my hands and splash cold water on my face, not caring that I'm ruining my make-up.

Someone else walks in. I barely spare the woman a glance as I tear a paper towel from the dispenser and dry my face.

She stops next to me and takes a tube of lipstick from her bag. "You, um, have something here."

It takes me a moment to realize she's talking to me. I catch her gaze in the reflection of the mirror.

She points at the area underneath her eye. "Mascara. Do you need help cleaning that up, love?"

Shaking my head, I yank another paper towel from the dispenser, wet it under the tap, and scrub away the mascara smeared under my eyes. In the reflection staring back at me, my tanned skin is pale.

I straighten. I can do this. I can have fun.

As he promised, Colin waits outside the door. "Are you sure you're fine?"

"Yes," I say, my voice belonging to someone else.

"I think you had a little too much."

I head toward the dance floor. "You already said so."

"I'll get you a glass of water. If you're not feeling well, we can call it a night."

I rub my forefinger over my naked thumb. Backward and forward. It's hot in here. Suffocating. I want to go outside, strip my clothes, and swim for miles and miles into the ocean.

"Bella?" Colin stops me with a hand on my shoulder. "Do you want me to take you to your room?"

I'd rather go to the beach where I can breathe easier, but my finger is bare and it's my birthday. If that even makes sense. We're here to have fun. To be free.

I open my mouth to say no, but the word gets stuck in my throat as I lift my gaze to the bridge in front of us where everyone is dancing except for one man. He grips the rail in both hands, staring down at me with the darkest, most demonic eyes I've seen, looking like the devil in a black suit that molds to his tall form and broad shoulders. The lights dance over his face, illuminating the devastatingly handsome features I know better than my own.

Angelo Russo.

He stands there as if magically conjured by the act of flushing away his ring.

Adrenaline bursts through my veins. My heartbeat quickens. My mind can't decide if the reaction is from shock, fear, or excitement. It can't interpret the emotions rushing through me.

I pinch my eyes shut and open them.

The spot where he stood is empty.

There's no man, only dancing couples.

Am I seeing things now, things that aren't real? Is his hold on me so big that I'm hallucinating just because I finally scraped together enough courage to chuck away his damned ring?

I swallow.

"Bella," Colin says, giving me a gentle shake.

"Yes." My voice is surprising calm. "Please take me back to my room."

"Come."

He takes my hand and clears a path through the dancers until we reach Ryan and Celeste. Ryan has his hands on Celeste hips, rocking her to the rhythm of the music. He stares into her eyes with an intense expression.

Wow.

I've never seen my brother show that much emotion.

Colin taps him on the shoulder and says something. Ryan looks at me. Someone bumps into my back, making me stumble. Colin catches me.

Tilting his head toward the exit, Ryan takes Celeste's hand and moves in that direction. Once we've cleared the dance floor, he pauses.

"Bella had too much to drink," Colin says loud enough to be heard over the music. "I'm taking her to her room."

I wish he'd stop saying that. It's true, but I don't want the whole nightclub to hear him.

Ryan studies me with keen attention. "Are you all right?"

"Yes." It's a lie. I'm still shaking from what happened, from what I thought I saw. "I'm tired. I just need to rest."

My brother nods. "We'll come with you. Give me a moment to tell the others."

"Aw." Celeste pouts, taking Ryan's hand in both of hers and holding him back. "I'm having so much fun, baby." She makes a puppy face. "We haven't been out in a year."

My sister-in-law is tipsy. If the situation wasn't so stressful, it would've been funny.

"We're here for Bella, remember?" Ryan says.

"No." I clutch my bag under my arm so that I can grip the rail in my free hand to better keep my balance. "You should stay. Colin can walk me to my room. The party doesn't have to end because I had one glass of champagne too many. I don't want to spoil everyone else's fun. Besides, it's better if you stay to keep an eye on the others."

"See?" Celeste bats her eyelashes. "Bella wants us to stay. Colin is big enough to protect her." She giggles. "Right, Colin?"

"No problem," Colin says. "It's not as if we have to cross town or something. The room is right upstairs."

Ryan searches my eyes.

"I'll be fine. Really." I give him what I hope is a bright smile. "It's only midnight. After all the trouble you went to with the arrangements, it will be a waste if you leave so early."

"Fine," Ryan says in his usual unreadable demeanor. "Call me if you need us. Otherwise, we'll see you at brunch tomorrow."

"Maybe. With the way I feel, I'm not sure I'll make brunch. Thanks for tonight." I wave at Celeste before Colin steers me toward the door. "Have fun."

Ryan stares after us. He's a head taller than the people around him, which makes him stand out in the crowd. I easily keep a visual on him. He stays in the same spot until the door closes behind us, shutting out his image.

The dinging of the slot machines is loud. The floor is packed. I glance around, looking for Angelo in the sea of faces as Colin pulls me to the elevator. Of course he's not there. It's only been my imagination. Throwing away his ring was a symbolic act that had such an impact on my psyche it triggered the vision.

We get into the elevator and ride to the top floor. There are only two levels, but I'm glad for Colin's consideration not to make me navigate the stairs in my heels.

"Where's your keycard?" Colin asks when we stop in front of my door.

I remove the card from my bag and hand it to him.

"I can stay if you like," he says. "We can watch a movie or eat all the snacks in the bar fridge."

"That's kind, but no." I need to be alone, and I can't even tell him why. "I'm going to crawl into bed and sleep forever."

"Don't forget Ryan booked the brunch for eleven."

"Don't count on me to be up by then."

"Checking out is at twelve. Do you want me to call you to make sure you're awake?"

"I'll set my alarm."

He inserts the keycard in the slot and opens the door before handing me the card. "Drink a glass of water before you go to bed."

"Thanks for walking me." A shiver ripples through me. I glance over my shoulder, but the hallway is empty. "Go back to the party and have fun. It's not every day that the drinks are on Ryan."

He smiles. "Night, Bella. Call if you need anything. I'll keep my phone on me."

"I appreciate that."

"Happy birthday. You're officially inaugurated. Welcome to the tipsy club."

I finger-wave from over my shoulder as I go inside and shut the door. Darkness and silence wash over me. At last. No more cutting lights and banging music. I utter a sigh of relief, my shoulders sagging when I toe off my shoes.

The headache has grown to an uncomfortable pressure in my skull. I need paracetamol.

I dump my bag on the bench in the entrance and flick on the light switch. The overhead dim lights wash over the room, basking the modern furnishings in a soft golden glow. They dispel the darkness in the corners and illuminates the man who sits in the armchair with an ankle resting on his knee, the shadow he makes on the wall looking larger than life.

CHAPTER
TWENTY-THREE

Sabella

M y breath catches in my throat. My heart starts pounding, my pulse keeping time in my temples. The beat is like a hammer in my brain.

I stare at the sight in front of me, battling to process that it's real. That he's real. That he's truly here and not just in my head.

"Hello, Sabella," Angelo says, his voice suave like velvet.

I swallow away the dryness of my mouth. Anger masks my fear. "What are you doing here?"

"You didn't think I'd forget your birthday?"

The words are like déjà vu. Their meaning chokes me. "How did you get into my room?"

His lips curve. "With a keycard of course."

If the receptionist gave him one, he must have bribed

her. I return his smile, mine wry. "Money always buys you what you want, doesn't it?"

He gets up, the movement lithe like a panther's.

I glance at the door.

"Don't even think about it," he says, rounding the bed. "You don't want me to chase you through the casino with everyone bearing witness."

I back up, hitting a barrier of bricks as Angelo pauses a step away from me.

Faking calm, I fold my hands behind me and lean on the wall. "It was you." My accusation is sharp and bitter. "In the club. You were there." Then it hits me. "You wanted me to see you."

He cuts a path over me with his gaze. "You look beautiful. It was hard to let you have your fun in that sinfully sexy dress. The only thing that prevented me from dragging you out of the club is that you've been a very good girl." He closes the last step between us, stopping too close. "You didn't dance with another man. That made me very happy."

My pulse is all over the place, the rhythm of my heartbeat erratic now. He allowed me to see him because he chose to. He let it happen when he wanted to. "How long have you been watching me like a creep?"

The insult doesn't faze him. "Since the beginning."

"Why didn't you show yourself earlier?"

He considers the question for a couple of beats. "I enjoyed watching you. I liked seeing the men drool after you even though they couldn't touch you."

"How do you know they weren't going to touch me? Who said I wouldn't let them?"

"I'd never let that happen."

"You're crazy."

He leans closer, pressing the length of his body against mine. Fixing a heated gaze on my mouth, he asks in a husky voice, "Did you save your first dance for me?"

His proximity does things to me, things I can't control. My body tightens, and a flame licks my belly.

"Why, Angelo." My tone is sarcastic. "Are you here to claim another first?"

He presses closer still, letting me feel his weight. His heat. The threat of his mere presence. The hardness growing against my stomach.

"Why, Sabella?" he parrots, studying me with a mocking light in his darker-than-night eyes. "Is that what you're hoping? That I'm here to take?"

It's difficult to breathe when he occupies all my space. It's impossible to think with the silent nuance of that taunt trapped between us and with the truth that spills like liquid heat between my legs.

My weakness angers me. That I still want him after everything he's done infuriates me. His power over me terrifies me.

It's the anger and the fear that make me lash out, needling him in turn. It's the alcohol in my blood that makes me brave. Irresponsible. "Don't hold your breath." My laugh is cold. "That first is no longer up for grabs."

The change in him is instant and terrifying. Fury contorts his features. Calculation hardens the lines of his face. "Do not lie to me. Not about that."

The thread stretches thinly between us. I sense the snap, but I don't shut my mouth. "What? Did you really think Roch could be everywhere? In a dirty toilet stall in the mall? On the backseat of a car? In a dark parking lot? Behind the—"

The muscles of his jaw bunch as he strikes faster than I

can anticipate, fisting his hand in my hair and tugging my face up. "You don't want to go there. Not with me."

"Oh." I blink, making an innocent face. "I thought you might want the juicy details. Where it happened. How many times we did it." I'm pushing, not caring that I'm taking us over the edge. "How big his cock was."

He spits out the words. "You're lying."

"Really?" I hold his gaze with a brazen challenge. "Am I?"

He tightens his fingers in my hair. My scalp stings where he's pulling the roots, but I doubt the discomfort he inflicts is conscious. He's too consumed with fury to register the strength of his grip.

"Last chance to be honest, *bella*."

I hate the invisible chains he put on me. I want to break them so badly I'll do anything, even let him believe the lie. "It was amazing. Best fuck of my life. There. I've confessed. That first wasn't yours. Do you know what the best part was? It was knowing you wouldn't get what you wanted. That alone made every second enjoyable."

The look in his eyes shifts. The chilling expression on his face almost makes me want to retract the untruth I told, but the impulse only lasts for a second before a buildup of frustration and resentment that stretched over months steels my heart again.

"My, you look disappointed. I bet you're dying to know what you missed out on. Are you sure you don't want the details, Angelo?"

"There's only one thing I'm interested in," he says measuredly, his nostrils flaring. "His name."

I purse my lips.

"Who?" He shakes me. "Give me his name."

I meet his cold rage and blazing jealousy head on, taking satisfaction from hitting him where he's most vulnerable—his ego. "So that you can do what?" I laugh. "Get Roch to throw him in the pool? Beat him up?"

The corners of his eyes crinkle. "Never mind." His smile is cruel. "I'll find out." Wrapping his free hand around my neck, he applies slight pressure. "When I kill him, it won't matter that he's been inside you." He watches me, letting me see the intention in his eyes. "You know why?" He swoops in, inhaling deeply as he drags his nose over my temple before pressing a whisper on my ear. "I'm going to fuck him out of you."

That's when I get scared, when the promise turns me on instead of disgusting me. He lifts my hair to his nose and, like he did with my skin, breathes me in like a male animal sniffing a female. Like a predator deciding if the flesh in his claws is prey.

When he's had his fill, he gently drapes my hair over one shoulder exactly like the hairstylist arranged it. For some reason, this frightens me the most—that I didn't notice for how long he'd been watching me. Stalking me. That I didn't see him sooner. But I felt him. My instinct wasn't wrong.

At the same time as his weight lifts off me, the iron vise of his fingers around my neck tightens. He uses the leverage to hold me in place while reaching between us with his free hand. It takes me a moment to realize what he's doing. I don't fully believe it until I hear the clank of his buckle. The grate of his zipper.

I bring my hands from behind my back and splay my palms over his chest. Instead of pushing him away, I bury my fingers beneath the fabric of his jacket. The push and pull is like being caught in a current, but it's not the gentle lapping of the sea on the shore at low tide. It's the rough and violent lashing of spring tide.

He grips my wrist, squeezing with too much force. I

look down. His fly is open, and his cock is freed. He's hard, his thick length jutting out from the dark fabric of his pants. It's the only part of him that's undressed, the most intimate part. The sight is erotic, more than I expected. He's big, the crown large. I home in on the veins running under the velvety skin along his shaft, on how the skin around the head is darker, and on the moisture leaking from the tip.

"You shouldn't have done that," he says, lifting my hand to his lips and sucking my thumb into his mouth. His tongue is warm and wet, the tip curling around my digit. He pulls my thumb from his lips and drops my hand. "You're going to regret it."

I don't know if he means taking off his ring or allegedly giving my v-card to someone else. Both, probably.

I almost do regret it when he bunches the hem of my dress in his hand and yanks it up to my waist. I'm watching him watching me, his gaze fixed on the triangle of silk that's damp with my arousal.

He fastens his hold on my neck, giving me just enough air to breathe. Not enough. "You're ungrateful and disobedient. Behaving like a slut doesn't become you." He eases his grip a little, letting me drag in a lungful of oxygen. "What did you do with my ring?"

I don't know what comes over me. Maybe I just want him to take this too, to break the magic spell he's cast on me so that this can be over. To take my last first and let me live in peace.

Another untruth tumbles from my lips, its cruelness sparked by a desperate need to even the score between us. "I gave it to him. He took it as payment for popping my cherry." The nasty fabrication is vile, but he's the one who taught me to lie.

He closes his hand so hard around my neck that my vision goes blurry. His face is a fuzzy picture behind a veil of fog as he dips his fingers under the elastic of my thong and tugs. A rip tears through the space. The thong slides down my thighs and brushes my ankles. My sight fades around the edges as I feel him between my legs, a hot, hard, velvet fist that wedges between my folds. We're both slick. When he brushes the tip over my clit, pleasure hits my core.

"You're such a slut, Sabella," he says, his words coming to me through a gushing noise in my ears.

As if to validate the statement, I curl my fingers around the lapels of his jacket, instinctively holding on.

He taps my clit two, three times with the head of his cock, a light reprimand. A sweet punishment. "But you're *my* slut."

Proving the point, he tears into me.

I think I may pass out, and not from a lack of air. The way it hurts is excruciating. My lips part, but no sound escapes. It's the worst torture, being torn in two.

He stills, pulls back to look at me, and eases up the pressure on my neck. His face comes back into focus. Somehow, I feel everything more intensely, as if my nerve endings have been starved for oxygen like my lungs, and the sudden rush brought on an onslaught of sensations.

"No," he says, sounding angry. Concerned. "No, no, no." He looks down at where we're joined. "Sabella, you're a wicked liar."

The vengeance isn't as satisfying as I thought it would be. The buzz of the alcohol isn't enough to dull the discomfort when he starts moving. I bite off a cry of pain.

"Shh," he says, his jaw muscles flexing. "The damage is done. We have to finish this now."

And he does. He pushes deeper, stretching me further.

Going all the way. He doesn't stop until I've taken every inch of him.

Breathing hard, he leans his forehead against mine and locks his hands around my hips. Then he pulls out until only the head is lodged inside and impales me again. His movements are rough and uncoordinated. He seems to battle to control himself. Like me, he appears to be struggling with the torrent of stimulation. He jostles me between his palms until he finds a rhythm that works for him.

Unable to keep up or to follow, I burrow my face in his neck and simply let it happen, embracing the pain, but just as I do, the stretch turns to pleasure. My inner muscles submit to the intrusion. I inhale his scent. He smells like citrus and cedar and sex. His skin tastes like salt where I'm pressing my lips on the pulse that beats in his throat.

He tenses, his neck muscles straining.

He comes.

It's over.

Yet he continues to pump himself dry. He thrusts until he softens inside me, waiting and watching.

He braces a hand on the wall next to my face, his arm a rigid, solid mass of muscle under his jacket. "Did you come?"

Biting my lip, I shake my head.

He nods. Pulls out. Looks down.

I follow his gaze. We're a mess, covered in my blood and his cum.

"Sabella." He grips my chin and tilts my face, forcing me to meet his eyes. "Why would you lie about this?" His voice is pained. "Is this what you wanted? How you wanted it to happen?"

I look away, sagging a little as I let the wall carry my weight. My legs aren't up for the task. My limbs are heavy, my arms like lead. I barely manage to pull down my dress and cover myself. "I'm drunk."

His voice is level. "I know."

Lifting me into his arms, he carries me to the bathroom. It's a big bathroom with a spa tub. My parents didn't spare any expenses. He deposits me on the closed lid of the toilet and strips. I watch as his clothes come off, first the jacket, then his shoes and socks, and finally his shirt. He's lean but strong, his muscles a portrait of perfect masculinity.

The ink on his chest holds my attention. Two salivating wolves with vicious teeth are in a stare-off. The artwork is exquisite. It's the first time I get a good look at it, and I itch to trace the ornate outlines framing the black picture with my fingertips. A single word is inked over the deep lines that cut with a V into his waistband.

Resilience.

It's fitting. The word sums up everything he represents and is.

He pops the button of his pants and shoves them with his briefs down his thighs. He's big and toned everywhere, his powerful legs well-proportioned. His cock is semi-hard again, tinted with the color of our lust.

Our sin.

A mistake.

He leaves his clothes in a heap on the floor and, fastening his hands around my upper arms, drags me up. I sway as he finds the zipper on the side of my dress and pulls it down. He pushes the thin straps over my shoulders and brushes the fabric over my hips. Wrapping his arms around me, he unclasps the strapless bra at my back. For a fleeting moment, I thought he was hugging me. I'm glad he wasn't. It was too tempting to lean into the embrace and soak up his heat.

When I'm naked, my automatic reaction is to cover myself with my hands, but he takes my wrists and arranges my arms at my sides.

"No." He cups my cheeks between his palms. "Let me look at you."

The gentleness of the act catches me off guard. He traces my jaw with a finger before brushing his knuckles over the curve of my neck. He takes his time to study me, following up each look with a touch by weighing my breast in his palm and feeling the shape of my nipple between his fingers. He measures the dip of my navel and the swell of my stomach before trailing a path down my thighs. Then he reverses his direction to sample how the globes of my ass fill his hands.

I'm too mesmerized by the reverence in his eyes to stop him. He's looking at me like he's never seen a naked woman. The fascination and sensual awe that are written in his features give me power I've never had.

When he's finally satisfied, he turns on the tap in the shower. After testing the water, he pulls me by the hand into the stall with him. He's unrushed and meticulous, cleaning every inch of my body and massaging my scalp when he shampoos my hair. He's gentle when he washes away the blood between my legs.

He takes less time for himself, his movements efficient and economic. I'm absorbed in studying his actions, in having this intimate glimpse of a man's grooming routine, so when he pushes me down onto the bench and kneels in front of me, I'm taken by surprise.

Holding my gaze, he cups my knees and pushes my thighs apart. The water runs over his head and down his back, making his dark hair look blacker and slicker than oil.

"What are you doing?" I ask, gripping his shoulders.

He observes me from hooded eyes as he lowers his head and buries his face between my legs. The soft press of his lips on my clit makes my eyelids flutter closed. When he parts me with his tongue and traces the seam of my opening, my hips lift off the bench of their own accord.

"Does it feel good?" he asks.

I open my eyes. Angelo kneeling between my legs is one of the hottest sights I've seen. Despite the fact that he's the one on his knees, he looks powerful. Scary. As if he holds my future in his hands. As if he can either give me pleasure or break me at his will.

"This?" He licks my clit, making my toes curl. "Or this?" He gives my opening the same treatment.

I moan. "Both."

"You didn't come when I was inside you." There's vulnerability in his words. A tinge of uncertainty. "Did I not last long enough?"

"I don't know."

"How do you normally come?"

Frowning, I try to pull away, but he holds fast, keeping my legs spread.

"Why do you want to know?" I ask.

"We're not done. I didn't get you off."

"Are you pretending to care about my pleasure?"

His smile is chastising. "I don't do things in half-measures."

"So, it's about your ego and not—"

He clamps his lips down on my clit before I can finish my sentence. What I was going to say flies through the window as he nips before sucking.

It only takes a few seconds. I come so hard it feels as if an electric current is running through my body, convulsing my muscles. In the back of my mind, I'm worried that he won't like my taste, but I'm too zoned out with the aftershocks racking my body to give it another thought.

Sitting back on his haunches, he wipes his mouth with the back of his hand and sets my mind at ease with, "You're a real treat. I can get addicted to eating your pussy. How hard did you come?"

I'm too lethargic to answer, which is an answer in itself.

Satisfaction sparks in his eyes. "Next time, *bella*, we'll come together."

I want to say there won't be a next time, but he's already scooping me up in his arms and putting me on my feet. He turns off the water and grabs a towel from the rail that he drapes around my shoulders. After drying me and squeezing most of the water out of my hair, he leaves me on the rug outside the stall to dry himself off.

This is the version of Angelo I got to know during the first year after we'd met, the broody and Byronic man who's kind and gentle with me. Only, deceiving and using someone isn't kindness.

I make to turn for the door, but his words stop me.

"Don't move."

He drops the towel and picks me up.

"Put me down," I say.

"Are you going to make fighting me a habit?" He walks to the bed and dumps me on the mattress. "There. Happy?"

Pulling the duvet over me, I try to cover my body, but he yanks it away, climbs onto the bed, and crawls over me. His heat is intoxicating. The touch of his skin against mine is soothing and soft. Warm. I want to curl up in the safety of his strong arms, but I can't forget that we're enemies. I can't forget what happened, not when I turned seventeen and not what we just did.

He hovers over me, studying my face.

"We're done," I say. "You got me off. Why aren't you leaving?"

An unfriendly smile plucks at his lips. "We're not done by a long shot, *cara*."

"What do you still want?" I ask, tired—no, exhausted—and in no shape to fight clever or with words.

"Plenty. Starting with making sure you understand that if you ever lie to me like that again, I'll take my belt to you, and I won't be playing. The welts I'll leave on your pretty ass will be the proof."

"Anything else?" I ask with sarcasm.

"If you do manage to evade Roch and fuck another man in a dirty alley, in a public toilet, on the backseat of a car, or any-fucking-where else, I'll kill Roch for failing in his job. Then I'll go after every man who laid a finger on you."

He can't be serious. "You're out of your mind."

"I'll be very clear. If that happens, *bella*, you'll be signing those men's death warrants. Their murder will be on your conscience."

No, he's not joking. The statement is enormous. I don't want to believe it, but I do. Angelo is the kind of man who means what he says.

I don't understand his possessiveness. "You got what you wanted. Now, go. Leave me in peace."

His reply is calm, almost soothing. "No."

The unreasonable stubbornness only confuses me more. "I'm tired. I just want to sleep."

"I know, *cara*." His voice is soft. "You can sleep soon but not yet."

"Why?" I ask with frustration. "There can't be anything to add after all that you've said."

He rests his weight on one elbow and brushes the wet hair from my forehead. "I saved myself for you, Sabella.

I waited a long time for you. A *very* long time. That's why."

I saved myself for you.

He can't mean what I think he does. Not Angelo. Not the handsome, darkly alluring, virile man with the body of a god and a cock that presses against my stomach like a steel rod. Not a man of twenty-two who seems so much older than his age, a wealthy man from a powerful family who must have plenty of female admirers. Yet his voice held vulnerability and uncertainty. His fucking was rough and clumsy, almost violent.

A realization stabs into my brain.

Oh my God.

He wasn't battling to control himself.

He's inexperienced.

"Was I—Was this your first time?" I ask, dumbfounded. "I thought…" Wait. The way he looked at me in the bathroom… "You've never seen a naked woman before?"

His smile isn't insecure or embarrassed. It's proud. "You're my first."

"Why?" I whisper.

"You're mine, and I'm yours."

My head swims with his words, my brain struggling to process their meaning. I want to ask for an explanation, but he lowers his head and presses his lips on mine. The kiss isn't like our first. It's not a dry peck that's over too soon. It's wet and dirty and untamed, filled with longing and passion, and it stirs something in my body again, something Angelo satiated not minutes ago.

I don't know why I don't tell him to stop. Maybe it's his confession that softened me. That he waited. For me. Maybe it's being drunk on champagne and lust, but when he strokes his tongue over mine, I forget about everything else. No, that's not true. I don't forget. I simply choose not to remember. Just for a short while, I ignore all the reasons why this is wrong.

Wrapping my arms around his neck, I thread my fingers through his hair and pull him closer. I kiss him with all the anger I've locked inside me, punishing him for all the suffering he's caused. My teeth do damage, but he doesn't fight me. He gives me an outlet for my vengeance, letting me use him savagely and primitively.

Arousal sparks in my belly when he parts my legs with his knee and settles between my thighs. His cock nudges my entrance, hot and hard and slick. My inner muscles give when he parts me with the broad head, my body already welcoming the possession.

This time, he enters me slowly. Painlessly. The stretch still burns, but the pleasure that wakes my nerve endings is instantaneous. The anticipation that runs through me contracts my nipples. The sounds falling from my lips should make me cringe, but I'm too lost in the moment to care, too lost in the haze of pleasure, too lost in the endless darkness of his eyes.

He's gentler than earlier, rocking inside me with a lazy pace. He lifts my leg and bends my knee to find a different angle. The penetration is deeper.

I cry out.

"Like this?" he asks, concentration etched on his face.

He's trying to make it feel good for me. Moaning, I nod. I quickly find his rhythm, moving my hips with his.

"Fuck, *bella*." A trickle of sweat runs down his temple. "Slow down a little, *cara*."

I brush a hand over the hard muscles of his chest, closing my fingers over the black ink. Taunting, again. "Are you close?"

"Too close." He bites out the words. "What you do to me."

"Then do it." I arch my body, rubbing my clit against his groin. "Make us come."

Uttering a growl, he lets go of my leg and slips a hand between our bodies. He takes care not to crush me, supporting his weight on the arm he puts next to my face. I turn my head, my gaze drawn by the flex of his powerful muscles. His bicep bunches as he picks up his pace while rubbing circles over my clit. I can't look away from the perfect cut of those muscles, but then the sparks between my legs vanish and he's digging his fingers into my cheeks, forcing me to face him.

Our gazes lock. The truth is naked and messy. How can something so beautiful be so ugly? The smell of sex and us clings to his fingers. He's not asking me to tell him. He's finding the answer for himself in my eyes. Fisting his hair in one hand, I slide the other between our bodies and finish what he started. A little pressure on my clit is enough. When my body bows and my vision blurs, he crashes his mouth on mine and lets go.

Our thrusts are like the tangling of our tongues, savage and desperate. We're each chasing our release so that we can go over together. Even in this, in our shared physical goal, we're at war, punishing each other with pleasure.

He comes while kissing me as aftershocks convulse my body. In the aftermath, he holds me. The storm has wreaked its havoc, and it leaves me like a shipwreck washed up on the shore. The headache that built in my temples flares.

I push on his chest, trying to get up. "My head. I need a pill."

"Stay." He kisses my forehead and detangles himself from me, making me feel cold when he pulls out.

I should tell him where to find my toilet bag, which I left in the bathroom cupboard, but sleep is already stealing over me. I'm dozing off by the time he returns with a glass of water and paracetamol.

"Here." He cups my nape and helps me to sit up before bringing the glass to my lips. "Drink everything. You'll feel better for it in the morning."

I let him slip the pill onto my tongue and drink the water like he instructed. When the glass is empty, he puts it aside.

"One more thing and then I promise to let you sleep." He sits down on the edge of the bed, brushing his fingers over my nape. "Where is my ring?"

For a moment, I consider not telling him just to be spiteful, but I'm so tired. I'm tired of looking over my shoulder. Of feeling guilty for what I did to my dad. Of all the lies. "I flushed it down the toilet."

He raises a brow. "When?"

"Tonight. But if you're thinking about going hunting for it, you'll probably need a plumber to dig up the pipes."

"Don't worry," he says, picking something up from the nightstand and holding it in front of my face. "I have another one."

The insignia on the gold ring comes into focus, the image of the wolves facing off that's burned into my mind.

"How many of these damn things do you have?" I ask.

His tone is laced with humor. "Apparently, not enough."

Why doesn't he sound angry? And why, when he says, "Sweet dreams, *cara*. Now you can sleep," is there a note of regret in his tone?

He increases the pressure of his fingers on my neck. He's squeezing those sensitive points like he did when he held me in a similar grip on the day I took off his ring in the hotel room in George. That was the day he threatened to *put me out*. Now, he's pinching harder. I fight to free myself as his hold becomes painful, almost unbearably so, but I'm no match for his strength.

The last thing I hear before the light fades is, "I'm sorry, *cara la mia bella*."

Angelo

Enough pressure for long enough on the carotid arteries on both sides of the neck can render a person unconscious. I learned the trick in a martial arts class. I practiced the skill on the kids in my school until the principal sent my father a letter to complain about my violent and invasive behavior.

That night, my father gave me a hundred-euro bill and a gun. I already knew how to shoot. Owning a weapon of my own was just a formality. I was eleven years old. I've shot many bullets since then, but none of them was aimed at killing. Up to now, my father has always been pulling the trigger, a task that has now fallen on me.

But I don't want to think about the business, tonight, not when I've claimed my woman with a strange need to both consume and protect her. Not when she's naked and the night has too few hours.

Sabella sleeps peacefully. Her dark hair is splayed over the pillow, the silky waves and neat curls from earlier tangled. Her long lashes brush her cheeks. I take in her features—the fine set of her cheekbones, the straight line of her nose, the plumpness of her lips, and the beauty spot just above the corner of her mouth.

I take my exploration lower, noting the faint bruises my fingers left on her neck. I don't regret the roughness because that's part of me. I can change it as little as I can stop wanting her. The marks, however, I do regret. I caress the arch of her neck and trace the delicate line of her collarbone. She's like a bird, her bones as frail as a dove's. Her breasts are small and pert, her nipples a beautiful shade of peach.

Not resisting the urge to touch, I let my hands get to know her too. I've felt her up in the bathroom, but I can touch her until sunrise, and it won't be enough. Her skin is soft and warm. The muscles underneath are toned. She doesn't stir when I brush my hand over her abdomen. Only her stomach quivers under my palm.

I cup the triangle between her thighs and thread my fingers through the dark curls. That inexplicable urge to be rough overcomes me again. The desire isn't born from violence. It comes from an urge to caress something so fiercely that a touch can't be a gentle brush of fingertips. It has to be a hug that cuts off air, a kiss that bites, a grip that possesses. I close my fingers harshly, pulling hair and digging my nails into warm, damp skin. I want this part of her so much that if I don't check myself, I'll crush her like I'll burst a juicy ripe orange in my fist, mashing it into a delicious, sticky mess and covering my face in it as I fall on the feast like a starving beast.

Wiping away the sting of my touch, I stroke lower. Between her legs. She's warmer there. Wetter. Her hips are beautifully curved. Her ass fits perfectly in my palms. Her slender legs will look so pretty when she wraps them around my waist. How flexible is she? Will I be able to arrange her thighs over my shoulders and fold her double as I surge inside her, going deeper and harder until I've found all her secret spots? No doubt she'll look stunning, no matter in which way I bend her. Over my lap. On her hands and knees. Riding me. She'll be a picture that makes me hard from any angle.

She's perfect.

All mine.

Every inch of her, inside and out.

Moving down her body, I rub her feet. She has a dancer's feet—narrow with a high bridge. The arches are pronounced. She was made for wearing heels or walking on her toes. With the pink polish on her toenails, her small foot in my big hand is overwhelmingly feminine. I pull away the covers and push her legs wide apart. Just as a precaution, in case she wakes too soon, I use the belts of the twin robes in the bathroom to tie her wrists to the bedpost. I don't want her to hurt herself in a panic.

Lying spreadeagled, she's a sight to behold. I can look at her all night, but my work isn't done. I get my razor and shaving gel from the bathroom, set a towel underneath her ass, and get busy.

First, I trim the curls with hair scissors, and then I shave her pussy clean. I don't mind body hair. I don't have a particular preference, but the view is as hot as hell. She's exposed for my observation, presented for no other purpose but my looking pleasure.

And I do look. She's swollen from our fucking, red and plump, ripe for the picking. After wiping the shaving cream away, I pat her skin dry and learn her shape by tracing the outline of her pussy lips with my thumb. I part her with no more than the tip of my finger, revealing the button at the top of her slit that triggered her orgasm.

But feeling and looking aren't enough. Burying my head between her legs, I inhale deeply. She smells like soap and musk. Like woman. *My* woman. Unable to resist tasting her again, I lick her from top to bottom. This time, I'm unrushed. You taste more when you swallow slower.

I like that no one but me has had his tongue inside her. I like the way that little button swells in my mouth when I suck. I like how her inner muscles grip my finger when I sink it up to the knuckle inside her. I love to touch every inch of her, love how she feels all over her body, but I'm fucking addicted to how she feels inside. The wetness that coats my tongue makes me delirious. I growl around her, biting down as the knowledge that I turn her on, even in her sleep, drives me insane. I'm like an animal with her. I want everything.

If she could come in her sleep, I'd bring her to a climax right now, using my fingers, teeth, and tongue. Does she feel pleasure in her unconscious state? She's slicker, her arousal like nectar on my lips. The way her body reacts to my touch pleases me beyond measure. I was made to coax orgasms from her, and I'll do so by honorable or unscrupulous means. By any means necessary. She was made to give me her pleasure.

I haven't had my fill, not by a long shot, but I force myself to stop. To sit back. To look at her. Naked, like this. Naked everywhere. Fuck, she's beautiful. So pretty. So stunning. No longer innocent because I took that. I'll take everything. All of her.

Mine.

I'll prove it too. To her. To me. To the world.

Getting up from the bed, I go to the bathroom and light the decorative candle. The light is softer, kinder. I leave it on the nightstand and flick off the overhead lights. The wax smells like vanilla. It's romantic. She'll sleep better like this.

I pick up the ring and study it in the gentle light of the flame. The emblem is fitting. It suits our family and what we stand for. The gold is twenty-four carats, the purest you can buy. Its melting point isn't as high as iron's. Gold is a soft metal. It needs to reach two hundred and sixty degrees Celsius to inflict a third degree burn that will leave a permanent scar. The temperature in the center of the flame is one thousand four hundred degrees. I hold the head just long enough over the flame, still burning my fingers.

The band of the ring scorches my fingertips when I kneel between Sabella's legs. Carefully, I press the flat side that's glowing red on the mound of her pussy, just above her slit. Ten seconds are enough. When I pull away, she's wearing a circle with two wolves facing each other, their intertwined bodies eternally locked together on her skin.

Branded with my mark on her pussy, she's not only ethereally beautiful. She's utterly perfect.

TWENTY-FIVE

Angelo

For the rest of the night, I don't sleep. I untie Sabella's wrists and make sure she's comfortable before retrieving a first-aid kit from my bag. I never travel without one. In my line of business, I never know when I'll need it. Using a sterile saline solution, I disinfect the brand mark. Then I simply watch her.

I'm fast getting addicted to the sight of her naked. I never want to see another woman without her clothes. I don't want to spoil the perfect picture seared into my brain.

The burn is a little swollen. It will hurt for a few days, but it's a lesson she needed to learn. I'll have to take care that the wound doesn't get infected. It needs to heal properly. The picture I branded into her skin needs to be as flawless as she is. She's too beautiful to carry anything ugly on her body.

When the sun comes up, I blow out the candle and put

the do-not-disturb sign on the door. Her family and friends are not going to look for her before eleven. I'm aware of the brunch her brother organized. Sadly, she's not going to make it.

At a reasonable hour, I call reception and instruct them to leave a message from Sabella for her brother, saying she's sleeping off a hangover. Going through her clutch bag and taking out her phones, both hers and the one I gave her, is another shameless act of invading her privacy. My objective is to make sure the phones are charged, but I'm not going to miss out on an opportunity to steal a glimpse at her content.

Using her thumb print to unlock the phone, I open her photos. Most are of the beach, Pirate, or her family. She's not a big fan of selfies, it seems. What surprises me are the videos. There must be a hundred or more, all of underwater sea life. Some of those videos are downright astounding.

From our chats during that first year, I know her dream is to become a marine biologist. Now I understand how passionate she is about the subject. I was going to tell her she needn't attend university. Enrolling in February only to drop out in June is pointless. However, I didn't consider the depth of her interest. If this is truly her ambition, I should look into a degree she can complete at home. *My* home. Which will soon be ours. For now, maybe it's better that she keeps busy. It's best to keep up the front until the time is right.

I leave the phones to charge, go back to bed, turn her on her stomach, and push a pillow under her hips. I arrange her with her elbows bent at her sides and her hands next to her head. Face to the side. Feet wide. Legs spread. Then I crawl over her and wet the tip of my hard dick in the slickness of her slit.

Catching my weight on my palms, I brush my lips over the shell of her ear. "Sabella." My voice is hoarse with desire, rough from holding back. "Wake up, *cara*."

Her folds stretch around me. I rock my hips, sinking the head of my cock into the sweet heat of her pussy.

I kiss her temple. "Open your eyes, *bella*." A devil's promise now. "I don't want to fuck you while you're unconscious."

She moans, her lips parting and a frown pleating her brow.

"That's it, my good girl." I press my lips on her neck. "It's time to wake up, gorgeous."

She battles to surface from her dreams. Her eyelashes flutter. She utters another soft protest.

Her inner muscles clench around my cock, sucking me deeper into velvet wetness. Fuck. She's so tight, it's like shoving my shaft into a clenched fist. A lubricated, slick fist.

My restraint is already weak as it is. Now? It snaps. I surge all the way in, burying my groin against her ass.

That wakes her up.

She strains her neck, eyes flaring, looking at me from over her shoulder. "Angelo."

Yeah, that sounds perfect. I pull out and thrust again. Gasping, she hollows her back. We're both slick now. I slide in and out with ease, working her gently, coaxing her muscles into relaxing and letting me in however I want, whatever I choose to give her. Shallow. Hard. Soft. Deep.

I'm breathing fast already, my head as drunk as my body, but I pay attention to the signs. She scrunches the sheets in her fists, lifts her ass to meet my thrusts, and moans as she sets the pace. Faster. Harder. Deeper. These are her choices.

I give her what she wants, all of it, rocking when she does

and slamming into her when she pushes back. We're not messy and disjointed like last night. We're quickly getting the hang of this, getting to know each other's bodies and trigger points. Hers is when I slide a hand between the mattress and her stomach to massage the little bud I sucked all night.

She hisses when I accidentally rub my wrist over the mark on her skin. I change my angle, making sure I don't irritate the spot, and when I pinch, her body arches like a string on a bow. My climax hits me like an arrow. I've come in my fist plenty, but shooting my load in her pussy is different. Incomparable. A ton and then some more satisfying.

Leaning on one elbow, I kiss her shoulder and withdraw my hand from between her legs. Our chests move rapidly. Our skins are covered with a layer of perspiration. I only pull out so that I can watch my cum drip down her thighs. She tries to close her legs and roll over, but I pin her in place with a palm on the small of her back, only easing up when I'm satisfied.

She twists around, her pretty brown eyes shooting sparks. "You like that, don't you?"

I sit back on my heels, letting her watch. "What?"

Her gaze is drawn to my cock. "Watching."

"So do you."

She flushes. "You know what I mean."

"My cum dripping from your cunt? Yeah, that's one hot and juicy sight."

Her face turns scarlet. "You're crude."

"But you like that too."

She flinches, looks down, and then she pales. She all but falls back on her ass as she scurries away from me, shifting up to the headboard.

"What have you done?" she exclaims.

Many things. Too much to answer. I only observe her as the truth settles on her pretty features.

"You fucking prick." She sounds breathless, as if she's battling to draw air into her lungs. "You fucking branded me. Like a cow."

It's obvious. No answer is necessary except for, "Not like a cow."

She scoots to the edge of the bed and tries to jump off, but I catch her wrist. "I warned you, Sabella. That's something you'll learn about me. I never bluff, and I always keep my promises."

Her bones are fragile beneath the vise of my fingers. So small. Her slender arm trembles in my hold. "You shaved me!"

"I could only apply the mark on smooth skin."

"While I was sleeping." She yanks, trying to free herself. "Wait. It was more than sleeping. You did something to me. You pressed on my neck. It hurt. And then it's all a blank. What did you do to me?"

I rub a thumb over her pulse. "I put you out so you wouldn't feel pain."

"Wouldn't feel pain?" She scoffs. "It's hurting like a bitch."

"Now, yes. I tried to minimize the friction by turning you onto your stomach, but you must've rubbed against the pillow."

"Me?" She covers her breasts with one arm. "You were the one fucking me from behind."

I can't help but smile. "If I remember well, you fucked me right back. Came real hard too." I dip two fingers between her legs and catch some of the slickness. Holding my hand in front of her face, I say, "This is more than just mine. Smell it if you don't believe me."

Her eyes blaze. She slaps my hand away. "Go fuck yourself."

"That's no longer necessary. We're doing such a good job of it together."

She utters a cry. "I hate you."

"You don't have to. You'll make it a whole lot easier on yourself if you like me. You know you want to."

She grits her teeth. "Let me go. My head is killing me and that burn you inflicted on my skin is hurting like hell. I need painkillers."

"Are you going to behave?" I ask, squeezing her wrist with a gentle warning.

"Yes," she says through thin lips. "Do I have a choice?"

"Good girl." I let her go and get to my feet. "Stay put. I'll get you what you need."

Her tone is angry, but there's something else to her words when she says, "I need more than painkillers."

"I'll order breakfast. Coffee. We can both do with some."

She covers herself with a sheet. "Food isn't what I had in mind."

"You need to eat, and you will, but what else would you like?"

"The morning-after pill," she says in a quieter voice.

The request catches me off guard. Of course she'd think about it. I should've expected it. That doesn't mean I have to like it.

"We didn't use protection," she says. "I mean, I know we're both clean, seeing that it was our first time." She clears her throat. "First *times*. But we didn't talk about birth control. I'm not on the pill."

I can't help how the sound of that pisses me off—not that she's not on the pill but that she wants to use protection with me. I narrow my eyes. "It didn't bother you last night."

"Don't be a dick, Angelo." She gives me a hard look. "I was drunk."

"Yes, you had too much to drink, but you don't get to play that card. You knew perfectly well what you were doing."

"All I'm saying is that I would've probably reacted differently if I were sober."

I take a step closer, stopping right at the edge of the bed, towering over her. "Sober or not, I don't regret what we did. I own my actions, and so will you. Whatever happens, we'll deal with it."

She stares at me with parted lips, looking disheveled and wild and so fucking beautiful. "I'm eighteen, Angelo. You're twenty-two. You can't seriously imply that if I fall pregnant, we'll simply go with the flow, and everything will be all right."

"If you *fell* pregnant."

She blanches. "What kind of parents do you think we'll make? With everything that's happened?" Tears well up in her eyes, making them glitter. "I can't cope with something like that too. Not now."

I ball my hands to prevent myself from touching her, from soothing her. From feeling sorry for her. "You didn't think about it when you came in my mouth and on my cock. You didn't tell me to stop when you screamed in pleasure."

"I didn't scream," she says with a sharp intake of her breath.

My grin is savage. "Our neighbors will disagree."

"Shit." She drags her hands over her eyes and pushes her hair out of her face. "If Ryan finds out…"

"So what if he does?" I say harsher than I intended.

She looks at me. "My parents are religiously conservative. You don't know my mother. The shame I'll bring over my family will kill her."

I don't care about any of those things—shame and religion and right and wrong. I was raised Catholic, but I've never practiced as an adult. I can imagine how a baby conceived out of wedlock will bother my mother though. That much I can understand.

I curl my fingers, fisting my hands hard. Harder still. Until my knuckles make a cracking sound. "Fine. I'll go to a pharmacy. But you'll stay put until I get back. Is that clear?"

She gives a small nod, biting her lip as she looks at me. I can see she's on the verge of tears and that she's in pain. Both bother me—her pain and her tears.

"We'll shower when I get back," I say, going through my bag where I left it on the sofa and pulling out clean clothes.

"Your stuff is here," she says as if it surprises her.

I glance at her from over my shoulder. "Who do you think pays for your room?"

"But..." She glances at the door as if she'll find the answers beyond it. "But my parents..."

She doesn't know. They didn't tell her this whole party is on me, that it was her brother's idea but that I'm paying.

I pull on briefs and a clean pair of jeans. There's a lot Sabella doesn't know. She doesn't know what kind of business her father is involved in. I won't disillusion her. She clearly adores him. I won't be *that* brutal.

After yanking a T-shirt over my head, I grab my wallet and the car key and walk to the door.

"The hyper pharmacy in town should be open," she says in a small voice to my back. "Do you know where it is?"

My reply is gruff. "I'll find it."

"I can pay—"

I jerk the door open. "That won't be necessary." I stop and face her again, taking in her pale cheeks and the sweat that beads on her forehead as well as the way she rocks herself as if she's trying to manage the pain. "Shall I get birth control pills while I'm there, or are we going to use condoms until falling pregnant is no longer an issue?"

She stares at me with wide eyes for a moment, opens her mouth, closes it again, and then shakes her head and looks away. "This was a mistake. I know having been drunk wasn't an excuse, but it won't happen again."

I laugh. "There are so many wrongs in those two sentences. This wasn't a mistake. I'll fuck you drunk or sober because I'm not a gentleman or a good enough man to care about morally gray areas. And most importantly, it will happen again. So I'll decide for you. Seeing that the pill will fuck with your hormones, condoms it'll be." I fix her with a look. "Just know one thing. This is the last time we're killing something we could've created. The fact that I'm even doing this should tell you how much I fucking care about your wishes."

Leaving her with that statement, I slam the door behind me. Everything she said made sense, but I don't like how easily she thinks she can walk away from this, how little she wants my baby in her belly. Because I sure as hell don't feel the same. Exactly the opposite, in fact. I'd love to plant my seed inside her and see her grow big with my child. I'd love to see my baby in her arms and my ring on her finger, and I can't give a damn in which order that happens.

But she's only eighteen. She's only been legal since a few hours, and I've already taken my due. I've already claimed everything I've waited two long years for.

The hotel lobby is quiet this early. It reminds me of the morning I left to kidnap that junior accountant, the one who jumped out of the window.

I get into my car and easily locate the hyper pharmacy Sabella mentioned. After buying an emergency contraceptive pill and several boxes of condoms as well as painkillers and ointments for burn wounds, I drive back to the hotel.

Sabella is waiting obediently naked in bed. The sight somewhat calms my turbulent thoughts. Her submission pacifies some of my anger. I make her drink another glass of water with two painkillers and the morning-after pill, and then I strip and wash both of us in the shower, a task I already love. I enjoy taking care of her.

When I've patted her dry, I mix a few drops of lavender oil in aloe vera jelly and apply the homemade ointment on her mark. The lavender has antibacterial properties, and the aloe vera soothes burns. The scar will look pretty when the angry red has faded and only the embossed lines are left.

She lets me administer the treatment, for once saying nothing. I blow a kiss over the wound and cover it with a non-stick bandage.

Cupping her cheek, I ask, "Better?"

She turns her face to the side, away from my touch. I let her escape. I've put her through a lot in a few short hours.

While we're dressing, I order room service. I pull on my discarded clothes with clean underwear while she shimmies into skinny jeans and a light summer sweater. She leaves the button of the jeans undone, hiding it under the sweater.

A waiter knocks on the door just as she's dried her hair. When I answer the door, he wheels a trolley into the room.

He lifts the silver dome covers to reveal scrambled eggs, bacon, and baked beans on toast.

I tip him and lock the door when he's gone.

"Come here," I say, dragging a chair closer.

She walks over without arguing.

I seat her in front of the trolley and spread a napkin over her lap. Unable to resist, I kiss the top of her head. She smells like the hotel shampoo, a scent that reminds me of luxury spas. Using the bench as a seat, I sit down opposite her. After serving her a big helping of everything, I pour coffee and add one sugar and milk like she prefers. I watch her from under my lashes as I help myself to the food. She must be hungry, hungover, or both, because she eats everything on her plate and takes a portion of fruit salad and yoghurt.

By the time we're done eating, the color is back on her cheeks.

"Don't worry about your parents," I say, finishing my coffee. "I'll handle them."

She pushes back the chair and jumps to her feet. "What does that mean?"

"I'm not going to be your dirty little secret, Sabella." At the flare of her eyes, I add, "They'll be more understanding than what you think."

"No," she says quickly. "They don't have to know. Nobody does."

I get up. "Why? Are you're worried about what your family will think because you had sex or because you had sex with me?"

"Both," she admits with a bluntness I didn't expect.

I gnash my teeth. The insult stings, provoking cruel humor. "I'm afraid your virginity is non-returnable, so you'll just have to bite the bullet."

She gasps, shock and hurt flashing in her eyes.

Not caring for that expression on her, I stalk to the bathroom and gather our belongings. She studies me as I shove clothes and toiletries into our bags. I want to come clean and tell the world about us. I want everyone to know what we've done. While I want to shout from the rooftops that she's mine, she'd rather hide the fact that she gave her first time to me.

It doesn't matter. Her first time *was* mine, and no amount of denial can ever change that. Her innocence always belonged to me. Her virtue was always mine to take. It's been my rightful claim to stake. In a few months' time, when I put a ring on her finger, there'll be no question about what happens in our marital bed. The people from whom she wants to hide her improper secret will know. They'll all know.

Taking her bag in one hand and mine in the other, I carry them downstairs and leave them with a bellboy while I check out. Sabella says nothing. She stands aside, looking shellshocked in the cold light of day.

Just before twelve, we exit the lobby. Ryan, his wife, and Colin, that pretty boy with the soft, white, piano hands whom Sabella calls her best friend, are outside. Ryan and Colin are loading bags into the trunk of Ryan's BMW. Ryan's wife, Celeste, looks the worst for wear with a pair of oversized sunglasses shielding her eyes. She's sitting on a bench next to the entrance, her face whiter than porcelain, sipping green slush that must be some miracle hangover remedy in a takeout cup.

At the sight of her family, Sabella stops dead. She takes three wide steps to the side, putting a stretch of space between us. Celeste spots her first. She gives a weak wave and makes a puking face.

The action catches the men's attention. Ryan and Colin look up simultaneously. When they notice me, they still. Ryan's expression gives nothing away. Neither does his relaxed stance. Colin fists his hands and takes a step forward, but Ryan stops him with an outstretched arm across his chest.

Not taking his eyes off me, Ryan asks in a calm, almost curious tone, "What are you doing here?"

I look at Sabella, my smile mocking. "Will you tell them, or shall I?"

Panic streaks across her face. Her pretty eyes plead with me. I'm not immune to her feelings. Far from it. But when she begs, I can't deny her.

I address her brother. "It looks like I'll be breaking the news."

Sabella hovers on the balls of her feet like a rabbit about to run. To me. To stop me.

Before she gives herself away, I say, "I brought Sabella's birthday gift of course."

Ryan regards me with a narrowed gaze and a half-smile on his lips, no doubt questioning my explanation.

To prove my statement, I take the key from my pocket and press on the button to unlock the doors. The alarm of the red Ferrari in the parking lot beeps, and the signal lights flash.

Colin stares at me with a slack jaw. Celeste sucks in a loud breath and sits up straighter. Ryan's smile grows, but it's not a friendly gesture. However, it's not their reactions I'm interested in. I search my girl's face. And I don't like what I see there. Shock. Embarrassment. Anger.

"I had the car delivered here because I thought you may like to drive it home," I say to her. "The papers are in the glove compartment."

She turns to me, standing tall with squared shoulders. "I don't want it."

"Aren't you going to say thank you first?" I taunt. "At least before telling me what model you prefer."

She bites off every word. "I don't want a car."

I raise a brow. "Isn't that an appropriate gift for an eighteenth birthday?"

"From my parents, maybe." She lifts her chin in an unspoken challenge. "Not a Ferrari." She omits the *from you.*

"Come on, Sabella." I laugh. "Don't pretend in your circles it's not common." I throw her the key. "Take her for a spin. I know you're dying to."

She catches the key more out of reflex than free will.

Her reluctance to accept my gift angers me. I close the distance between us, stopping short of her. "I thought you'd like it." More mocking. "Is red not your color?"

Colin widens his stance, but Ryan lays a hand on his arm.

"It's inappropriate," she says through clenched teeth, her words meant only for my ears. "Too much."

I don't know why I don't tell her that as my future fiancée a car is the least of her rights. Why don't I tell her we're getting married? Why didn't I last night when I had the chance? Or a year ago, or the year before that, or on the very day we met? Because I know she won't like the idea. I know she'll resist. I know she'll put up a fight. She told me so in not so many words when she threw my ring back at me. Nothing can spell it out clearer than pretending in front of the world last night didn't happen. But hey, why prolong the war? I'll deal with it when the time comes to walk her down the aisle. I'll tie her up and drag her to the altar if I must.

She holds the key out to me on her open palm. "I can't accept it."

I lean closer, saying softly enough for her family not to

hear, "Nothing about my gift or last night is inappropriate. You have no idea just how *appropriate* it is." Closing my hand around hers, I lock her fingers on the key. "Enjoy the ride, Sabella." I cup her nape, drag her closer, and take the kiss that's my right. My due. My goodbye until I put a ring on her finger. I press my parting words in a whisper against her ear. "Take care of my mark. Let me know if it gets infected. I'll send a doctor to have a look."

She leans back, straining in my hold while staring up at me with big, wild eyes. If she's scared I'll give away her secret, she doesn't need to worry. I may not like being the dirt she sweeps under the carpet, but I never break my word.

"Happy birthday," I say, the normal volume intended for everyone.

The bellboy comes out with our bags. "Are these yours, sir?"

Sabella turns red, but she doesn't break our eye contact. She lets me shadow her, concealing the truth that's written on her face from her family.

Probably sensing the tenseness in the atmosphere, the bellboy leaves the bags on the pavement and slips back into the hotel.

I hold her gaze as I pick up my bag. Letting her go takes every ounce of willpower I possess.

Five months.

That's what I tell myself. Five months, and she'll have a pretty summer wedding.

Me, I'll have everything.

Not sparing her family another glance, I walk away before I do something she'll regret, something like stealing her last five months of freedom.

CHAPTER
TWENTY-SIX

Sabella

Angelo walks away with long, powerful strides, *angry* strides, and gets into a car. We stare after the sleek Jaguar as he takes off with screeching tires and turns onto the road that leads to the airport.

I take a deep breath, mentally preparing myself to face up to the people who turn their gazes on me like one man.

Ryan's voice is quiet. "Did he bother you?"

Bother is a light way of putting it. Shame heats my cheeks. They can never know what happened, that I slept with the man who betrayed me and stole a part of my dad's company. That's not only weak but also despicable. I wounded my dad when I let Angelo into our house. I don't want to hurt him again. I'll never live down the humiliation if anyone finds out Angelo and I had sex—repeatedly—and that I'm branded like property. Like an animal or a slave.

"Sabella?" Ryan says, taking a step toward me.

Celeste shifts to the edge of the bench, all eyes and ears.

"No," I say, heaping on the lies.

"What the fuck did he want?" Colin asks.

Celeste dumps the plastic cup with the Starbucks logo she clutches in the trash. "Language, Colin, please. I think we've had enough unpleasantness this morning."

"Sorry," he mumbles. "Seriously, what did he want, Bella?"

"You heard him." I wave at the ridiculously expensive car. "He brought me a birthday gift."

"He came all the way from Corsica to give you the key for a car he had delivered?" Colin asks, clearly not buying it.

"That's what it looks like," I say.

Colin flexes his jaw. "That's it?"

"Look, I ran into him on my way out," I say. "Just like you. What else do you want me to say?" I'm going straight to hell.

"Why would he give you a car?" Colin glances at Ryan. "Don't you think that's fucking weird?"

"Language," Celeste sing-songs.

Ryan grabs a suitcase and loads it into the trunk. "Who the hell knows? The guy is the personification of weird."

"But don't you think—" Colin starts.

"Let it go, Colin," Ryan says, slamming the trunk shut.

The harshness of his voice startles not only me but also Celeste and Colin. Colin stares at him with parted lips, looking as if he'd like to say more, but when he takes a breath to speak, Ryan cuts him short.

"What do you want to do with the car, Bella?"

I watch my brother, trying to read him. His face is blank. Why do I get the impression he's hiding something?

He doesn't want Colin to ask those questions. Shouldn't Ryan be asking the same questions? Not that I'm complaining about being let off the hook.

"I'll drive it," I say.

"Are you sure?" Ryan asks. "Sports cars can be tricky until you get used to them."

"It's a Ferrari." I pick up my bag. "They're all automatic. I'll manage."

"I'll go with her," Colin says.

Ryan nods. "We'll follow you."

Colin takes my bag from me and loads it in the trunk while I adjust the mirrors and the seat. When he's buckled up, I pull out of the parking lot and head toward the highway.

"You missed the brunch," Colin says.

"I said I would."

"How's your hangover?"

"Not too bad. I had to take pills."

He shoots me a sidelong glance. "The others were asking about you at the restaurant."

I check in the rearview mirror to make sure that Ryan is keeping up. "What did you tell them?"

"That you enjoyed your party a little too much and needed to sleep it off."

"Thanks."

"It won't hurt to make an effort, you know."

I brake too hard, the momentum jerking our bodies forward. I take my foot off the pedal and try again, getting the force of stepping down right on the third try. "Sorry. Ryan was right. Damn, the brakes are sensitive. This is a very different drive compared to my mom's Audi." At the exit, I turn toward George. "An effort with what?"

"To make friends with the other girls in your class. They're trying."

I scoff. "They're not. You don't know how things are. And you're supposed to be on my side."

"I am. That's why I'm telling you, Bella. Why are you isolating yourself like this?"

Keeping within the speed limit, I accelerate. "I'm not."

"You never hang out with anyone but me."

I grin, going for humor. "Because I like you. I thought you'd be glad."

"You're not even attempting to meet someone. How many guys in my class have hit on you? You pretend not to notice. It's your birthday, but you don't dance with the single dudes. You don't give any of the guys a chance to get near you. You have this air of being unobtainable that puts men off before they can make a move. It's like you're keeping everyone at a distance. If you only behaved that way with guys because you're not interested in dating, I'd understand, but like I said, you're not going to the trouble of getting to know the other girls. Friendship takes investment, Bella. It's as if you just don't give a damn. You don't even make it to your own fucking birthday brunch."

I slam a hand on the wheel. "Why are you giving me such a hard time about this? So what if I'm not a social person? Everyone isn't like you."

His voice rises in volume. "The fuck how like me?"

"Perfect," I shout, regretting it the minute the word left my mouth.

"Jeez." He turns away from me, staring out of his window. "Fucking thanks a lot."

"For crying out loud, Colin. What's gotten into you? Can you just give it a rest?"

"Maybe what's gotten into me is Angelo," he grumbles under his breath.

I utter a sound of frustration. "I have enough to deal with as it is. Do you mind not adding to it?"

"He's got a hold on you." He twists in his seat, continuing with renewed anger. "He told you he wouldn't miss one of your birthdays. You said he wasn't going to show, and he did. The guy gave you a fucking Ferrari for your birthday. He flew all the way from Corsica to be here, happening to know where you were throwing your party. Don't you find that strange?"

"He's doing business with my dad. My dad could've mentioned something to someone." I shrug. "George is small. You know how people talk. It's not difficult to find out details like that here."

"Fine. Say he picked up something via the grapevine. It's still nuts. The guy is clearly obsessed with you. Do you now see why you need a restraining order?"

My driving is almost aggressive in the way I take the bends. From the way the car grips the road, it's clear that it was made for speed. Ryan has fallen behind. His BMW is no longer visible in the rearview mirror. I slow down and take a few deep breaths, trying to calm myself.

I can't confess why going to the police isn't an option. My dad's business is still on the line. Besides, a restraining order will make no difference to a man like Angelo. I don't know how to explain that to Colin who lives his life by the letter of the law. I don't know how to convey the darkness in Angelo in words. I can't tell Colin about the mark of shame I carry on my body or that I can't ask my brother or my dad for money to have it removed. I'll have to get surgery when I can work and save up the cash. I can't tell him that the car is nothing but payment for last night. Why else would Angelo give me a car?

I'm losing my enthusiasm for birthdays. Angelo gave me defiance for my sixteenth birthday, allowing me to keep Pirate. The betrayal for my seventeenth was sealed with a sweet kiss. He paid for my v-card on my eighteenth with a Ferrari.

In George, I head toward the east side of town and turn into the car park of the church where a bazaar is being held in the adjoining hall every weekend to raise money for the homeless shelter.

For a while, we're quiet.

Closing my eyes, I lean my forehead on the wheel.

"I'm not trying to be hard on you, Bella. I'm only looking out for you."

I sigh and sit up. "I know."

When I spot Ryan pulling up behind me in the rearview mirror, I cut the engine. "I won't be long."

Colin gets out when I do, a question burning in his eyes. I take the steps to the hall two by two and slow down when my underwear brushes over the burn, chafing the inflamed skin.

The lady who sits behind the cash register in the foyer looks up with a smile. "The stalls with the second-hand items are on the left, and the home-baked and crafts goods are on the right."

I push the key over the counter. "I'd like to donate a Ferrari. It's parked in the lot. The papers are in the glove compartment." Picking up the pen that lies on the book in which she scribbles down the sales, I write down my name and telephone number. "Here are my details. Just call me when I need to come down and sign whatever documents are necessary."

She stares at me as if I'm an alien, still gaping when I turn and walk out.

Outside, Colin leans on the car with crossed arms.

"Come on," I say, getting my bag from the trunk. "We'll have to catch a ride with Ryan."

"What did you do?" Ryan asks when I shift into the back of his car.

"You did not," Celeste says, twisting in her seat.

Colin gets in beside me, only shaking his head.

"What?" I raise my palms. "You didn't think I'd keep it?"

"Fuck." Ryan laughs as he turns the car around and pulls into the road. "I can't wait to tell this story at the office."

We're quiet the rest of the way home. Colin jumps out with a muffled goodbye when Ryan parks in the cul-de-sac in front of our house. My best friend makes his way to their gate without looking back.

The gap between Colin and me is growing. I understand that he's worried, but behaving in such an overbearing manner makes it difficult to be open with him. He won't be able to handle the truth. Just as well I have no intention of anyone ever finding out what really happened at my party.

Celeste blows me a kiss when I get out. I'm not surprised that she's not coming inside. My mom isn't crazy about Celeste. She's never approved of Ryan's choice of a wife. Needless to say, Celeste isn't overly fond of my parents either.

"Give Brad a hug from me," I say, shutting the door.

Ryan is already getting my bag. He stands quietly, observing me with a too perceptive gaze as I come around the car. We face each other for a couple of beats before he hands me the bag.

"Mom and Dad know. I called them from the car." The corner of his mouth lifts. "Expect some drama."

I arrange the strap of my bag over my shoulder. "Thanks for the warning."

He gives me a piercing look. "I had to warn Dad."

Kicking at a tuft of grass, I avert my eyes. "I know."

"Good luck, Bella." He squeezes my shoulder. "You know where to find me if you need anything."

He's halfway around the car before I say, "Ryan?"

He stops.

"How did Angelo know where to find me?"

The habitual mask drops back in place. "It can't be too hard to get your hands on information like that." He continues with a stoic expression, "Do you feel unsafe?"

"No," I say quickly, not wanting him to dig deeper and pose questions I can't answer.

He offers a semblance of a smile and opens his door.

"Thanks again for the party," I say.

He nods and gets behind the wheel.

When he drives off, I glance around me. Roch is out there, somewhere, always watching. A shiver races down my spine. It's most probably him who told Angelo about the party.

Finally alone, my composure slips. I lied to Ryan. I do feel unsafe, but not in the way he suggested. I feel mostly unsafe from myself, from how I feel when Angelo presses his lips on mine and says despicable things in my ear. I can't trust myself when he strips me naked under the bright lights of a hotel bathroom and studies my body with unabashed fascination.

I'm the first woman he saw naked, but that unexpected tidbit of information isn't what hit me the hardest or what made me the weakest. It was *how* he looked at me—as if I'm the last woman he'll ever see naked. Then he branded me, reminding me all too vividly why I should hate him. Why I *do* hate him.

Shit. I'm a traitor, and I betrayed my family in the worst way. Angelo was right about one thing. I can't blame my moment of weakness on the alcohol. I did what I did, and now I have to live with it.

Taking a deep breath, I push away everything and prepare myself to face my parents as I enter the house. My chest constricts when their heated voices reach me from the front garden. They're fighting again. Things have been going so well, lately.

"You have to tell her," Mom says. "For crying out loud, Ben. Can't you own up to your actions for once?"

I cross the lounge and stop in the open sliding door. My parents are standing on the veranda, facing the sea. They each have a drink in the hand. Dad's prized bottle of Scotch stands on the table. Considering that it's not even lunchtime, whatever they're discussing is bad enough to warrant a strong drink.

Mom's words have an edge to them. "Is it so hard to admit you made a stupid mistake because you were driven by your greed?"

"Enough," Dad says, his voice hard. "Telling her won't serve her any good."

I drop my bag on the floor. "Tell me what?"

My mom spins around, regarding me through slitted eyes. "Are you eavesdropping? In my house? Don't you know how—"

"Margaret," Dad says, his tone shutting her up. "This house belongs to everyone in this family, not only to you."

"I see nothing ever changes around here." Mom slams her glass down on the table. "My opinion clearly doesn't matter."

My dad tilts his face to the sky. "For heaven's sake. Can we not do this now?"

"Sure." Mom smiles sweetly. "Whatever you want. You're the breadwinner. That earns you all the say."

I look between them. "Tell me what?"

"It's not about you," Dad says. "It's business-related."

Mom pulls her lips into a thin smile and looks away.

"More importantly, we want to talk to you about what happened this morning," Dad says.

I don't want to discuss it anymore. "Ryan said he already told you."

Mom crosses her arms. "Where's the car?"

"I donated it to charity."

"What?" She laughs like she does when she's upset. "Which charity?"

"The homeless shelter."

"You did the right thing," Dad says, shooting my mom a look. "Is that all?"

"I told them to call me when I have to sign the transfer of ownership papers."

"I meant with regard to Angelo Russo." He clenches his jaw when he says the name.

"Yes," I say, crossing my fingers behind my back. I still hate lying to my dad even though I can do it now without blushing. "Why don't you stop doing business with his family?"

My dad frowns. He gives a soft, uncomfortable chuckle. "What?"

"Why are you still in business with them?"

Mom lifts her chin and glares at him in a way that says, *I told you so.*

"It's complicated," Dad says. "Unfortunately, it's one of those necessary evils."

Mom snorts. "That's putting it mildly."

"Margaret," he says again, harsher this time. "Shouldn't you check on the lunch?"

"Of course." She untangles her arms and squares her shoulders. "Whatever you say."

Dad groans as she walks with a stiff back to the lounge. "Margaret, come on. I didn't mean it like that."

Ignoring him, she makes her way to the kitchen.

My heart beats a little faster when I face my dad. "What's really going on, Dad? You're scaring me when you and Mom fight like this."

"Nothing." He crosses the veranda and rubs my arm like he used to do when I was little and he wanted to soothe me. "Would you like a glass of wine before lunch? You're eighteen now after all."

"No, thanks."

He chuckles. "Ryan said you had a little too much champagne last night. I'm glad you had fun."

I don't correct him about the fun part.

He clears his throat. "You know how much you and your siblings mean to me, don't you?"

"Of course."

"You've always been the apple of my eye." He smiles as if to himself. "I'd always get into trouble with your mother for that."

"For having a favorite?" I ask, my throat tightening. Mattie is Mom's favorite, and I know how much that used to hurt before I was old enough to understand. I'd hate for Mattie to have felt the same about Dad and me.

"For spoiling you." He takes a sip of his drink. "Yet you're not a spoiled child." He chuckles. "Sorry. You're not a spoiled *adult*. Where does time go? My little girl is a grown woman now. You're a good person."

"Um, thanks," I say, not quite meeting his gaze, because I'm not a good person.

"Your happiness is important to me. Very."

"Dad?" I search his eyes. "What are you saying?"

"If you and Colin ever decide to get married, it'll make me very happy."

I blow out a sigh. "Mom put you up to this, didn't she?"

He shrugs. "Colin is a good young man. I know you like him."

"Like a brother," I exclaim. "Please don't start with the matchmaking too. It's bad enough that Mom has been on my back about it since high school."

"I'm only saying if you should ever develop romantic feelings for him, I'll go to my grave peacefully, knowing you're in good hands and taken care of."

I hook my arm around his. "First of all, I can take care of myself. Secondly, you're not going to your grave any time soon, so let's drop the subject of finding me a husband."

"I'm just saying." He pats my hand. "I know you're capable of doing perfectly fine without my—or your mother's—meddling."

"Thank you," I say, kissing his cheek. "Shall we go see if Mom needs help? I don't want her to think we're excluding her from our conversations."

"You go ahead. I'll be there in a minute."

Mom is banging spices on the counter when I enter the kitchen. The fragrant smell of bobotie rises from the stove. Although the sweet Malaysian curry is one of my favorite dishes, my stomach turns at the odor of the garlic, turmeric, cinnamon, and ginger that hangs in the air. It's going to take a while before I find my appetite. The painkillers are working out. I'm raw and sore, not only where my skin is burned but also inside.

"Can I help?" I ask.

I give a start when my mom turns abruptly and puts her arms around me. She holds me close, hugging me like she's never done. I wrap my arms around her shoulders and give her an awkward pat on the back.

Tears shimmer in her eyes when she pulls away.

"Are you all right?" I ask, tensing in alarm.

She wipes a finger under one eye, catching a tear. "Oh, it's just the idea of you also leaving the house so soon. I'm not looking forward to being an empty nester."

"I won't be far. Cape Town is only a four-hour drive away."

She sniffs. "I know, but you're moving in with Ryan and Celeste, and I'm not welcome there."

"Oh, Mom. You know you're always welcome at their place. Celeste just feels bruised about how you criticize her."

She waves a hand. "I'm not going to turn my own heart into a cesspool of sin by lying about my feelings."

I laugh. "That's a bit dramatic, don't you think?"

"You and your father would think so. When the two of you side together, it doesn't matter what I say."

"That's not true." I lean against the counter, dipping my head to catch her gaze. "Your opinion does matter. We may not always agree, but that's a different issue."

She scoops raisins from a jar and adds them to the spiced minced meat browning in the pan.

Biting my lip, I study her. I always turn to my dad with questions because he gives me straight-forward and honest answers. His truth isn't as tainted with manipulation as my mom's.

However, there's something he's not telling me. I didn't buy the story about discussing work when I caught them fighting. This time, my mom may be the one to ask.

"You know something?" I start carefully. "We never talked about the night I let Angelo into the house. I know I disappointed and hurt you."

Startled, she looks at me. "You said you were sorry. There was nothing more to say."

"I still regret that I did it. Sometimes, I think the guilt will never go away."

"Nonsense." Grabbing a cloth, she wipes down the counter with jerky movements. "We moved past that. Angelo Russo manipulated you in a scandalous way."

"And because of that, Dad lost a part of his business."

She stills, clenching her fingers around the cloth.

"I'll never forgive myself for that," I say honestly.

"Is that how you feel after all this time? Guilty?"

"Yes," I admit in a whisper. For so much more than I'm telling her.

"Well, you shouldn't. It's over. We can't change what happened. We just have to move forward." She adds after a beat, "Without guilt."

"Earlier, outside…" I hesitate. "What were you and Dad really arguing about? What doesn't Dad want to tell me? Does it have something to do with the money he lost?"

She dumps the cloth in the sink and brushes her hands over her apron before facing me. "It sounds as if you've suffered more than enough guilt. Why don't we let this go, hmm? You'll see. Things will be better once you're in Cape Town."

I want to believe that. At some stage, I did. Didn't I say the same to myself? After last night, I no longer do. Nothing will be different. Angelo will always be a part of me, ingrained in my soul. He did a too good job during that first year. He's part of my dreams and my nightmares. He's imbedded in my guilt and burned into my skin. He'll continue to show up on every day I turn a year older. I know it with a deep-seated certainty.

The situation won't change in Cape Town.

It won't change anywhere.

The question is why.

Is it some sick game? Does he get off on tormenting me? Does he ruin other people's lives for fun?

The only way to stop a game is to no longer play it. It sounds easy, but it's not as simple as that. How can I end or win the game if I don't even know the rules?

CHAPTER
TWENTY-SEVEN

Angelo

When I arrive home, my mother is kneeling on the library floor with hundreds of brochures spread out in front of her.

"Oh, hi," she says, shuffling the glossy pamphlets. "You're home early."

"I made good time with the boat. The wind was behind me."

She smiles up at me. "How was the birthday party?"

The memories that flood me makes me work my jaw. "Good." And bad. But mostly memorable. Inarguably satisfying.

"Did she like the car?"

"Apparently not." My tone is wry. "She donated it to charity."

My mother's brow pleats. "I told you it was too flashy."

"Don't worry about it. I instructed her brother to buy

her a more *average* car." I peer over her shoulder. "What are you doing?"

"Organizing the wedding leaflets by themes and color. I was thinking of apricot as the principal color and palettes of orange as accent colors. How does that sound?"

It takes effort to smile. The way in which I left South Africa put me in a foul mood. "Like you have everything under control."

"Does Sabella like roses? I thought we could make flower arrangements with white, brown, beige, and burnt-orange roses. Brown roses are all the rage. Will that please her? I'm making theme boards that we can share with her to get her input."

"We don't need her input. Whatever you like will be fine."

"But Angelo—"

"Trust me, Maman. Sabella has other things on her mind."

"Like what?" she asks, incredulous. As if the colors and flowers of a wedding aren't the most important things in the world.

"Like university."

She sits back on her heels. "What? She's going to university? To study what?"

"Marine biology."

"Where? There isn't a marine science faculty in Corte."

"It'll have to be in Marseille, but I haven't looked into that yet. She's joining the university in Cape Town for the moment."

"The applications would've closed already." She tilts her head, studying me. "You should've done that for her last year. Don't you want her to study?"

Shoving my hands in my pockets, I ride on the balls of

my feet. "I don't have a problem with letting her attend university. Adeline does, doesn't she? Although, the logistics will be a challenge. We'll have to stay there in the week and come home on weekends."

"What about the application?"

"I can submit a late application until April. Besides, with our connections, getting her in won't be a problem."

"Good." Her shoulders sag as she blows out a breath. "You shouldn't prevent her from getting a good education." Her voice is wistful as she adds, "I didn't have that opportunity."

She never says anything, but I know she's ashamed of not having finished school. I notice how she withdraws from conversations about academics and how she clams up in the company of women she considers to be learned.

My father married her when she was sixteen. The year after, Adeline and I were born. Although her face is youthful, she seems twenty years older in spirit. All those miscarriages after my sister and me took their toll. Her other pregnancies always ended in the same way—with grief and tears. My parents only stopped trying for another baby two years ago when the obstetrician said her body couldn't sustain another pregnancy.

"Or from getting a job for that matter," she adds.

"I'm not opposed to that either."

"Good," she says again, nodding as if the matter is settled.

I glance toward the stairs. "Papa?"

"He's doing much better. He even went to the city yesterday to meet your uncles. You'll find him in the study, going over the books." She picks up a brochure and shows me a three-tier cake with a plastic bride and groom on top. "Shall we order a classically traditional cake or something more French like a pièce montée?"

My phone vibrates in my pocket. "Whatever you decide will be perfect," I say as I take the phone out. It's Edwards. I've been expecting his call. "Excuse me." I press the phone against my ear and walk to the door. "I have to take this."

Grateful to escape the talk of weddings and cakes, I go outside into the garden. The winter sun is bright in the sky, shimmering on the ocean below.

I answer with, "Mr. Edwards."

Since the day I stole his book, our interaction has been minimal and only via email. For understandable reasons, he's been avoiding me. I've mostly dealt with Ryan, but the instructions I sent yesterday concerns the father, not the son.

"What is the meaning of this?" he splutters, sounding incoherent and distressed.

"I assume you're referring to the arrangements for the wedding I emailed yesterday," I drawl.

"You got what you wanted," he grits out. "There doesn't have to be a wedding."

"If you think running your business is what I wanted, you don't have a clue."

"You have the money," he says, turning to pleading. "The power. Leave my daughter out of it."

"See, here's the thing you don't understand. I didn't do what I did for the money or the power." I chuckle. "Well, not only. I did it for Sabella. I did it for what you always owed me."

"Do you honestly think she'll pack her bags, leave her studies, and follow you to a country she's never set foot in and where she doesn't know a soul? If you think my daughter will put on a white dress for you and say yes, you're the one who doesn't have a clue."

"I'm not worried about Sabella. She'll do as I say. Just

make sure her things are packed. Or don't. I don't really care. She can buy new clothes here. Whether you attend the wedding is up to you. Out of courtesy for Sabella, I'll save places for your family at the bride and groom's table. You decide if you fill those seats."

With that, I end the call.

CHAPTER
TWENTY-EIGHT

Sabella

Life is hectic when Pirate and I move in with Ryan and Celeste and my university course starts in February. I embrace the strenuous pace with open arms. Being busy helps me to forget about birthdays and the unexpected gifts—or rather, curses—they bring.

As I need my own wheels to commute from Bloubergstrand to the campus, Dad buys me an entry-level Mini Cooper. The car is still expensive, but it's a far cry from a Ferrari.

Colin and I spend our free time together studying in the library. The separation from May left him heartbroken. We're not as close as we used to be, but he's still my only friend.

Moments of leisure are scarce at the beginning. I have classes back-to-back from eight in the morning to six in the evening. On weekends, I either have lunch at Colin's apartment or he dines at Ryan and Celeste's place. On the odd occasion, we squeeze in a swim at one of the many beautiful beaches. If Celeste is busy, we take Brad to the rock pool. I adore spending time with my nephew. The older he gets, the more he looks like Ryan.

Celeste took up her old job as a volunteer at the Green Earth Association, which means I get to babysit in the evenings when she's running late. Ryan always fetches her from the office at night. He prohibited her from driving alone after dark. Living with them revealed my brother's overprotective streak, another side of his character I didn't know existed.

Mattie falls pregnant in April. We all go to visit them in Stellenbosch for the weekend. Mom has been staying over with them frequently, at least a couple of weeks every month, which makes me wonder about her and Dad's relationship. Dad has always been busy with work, often traveling to visit his clients across the country, but these days, Mom is absent from home more frequently. If she's not at Mattie's, she's at a spa retreat. And what about Jared? Doesn't he mind that his mother-in-law is living more with them than at her own house? When I tell Mattie about my concern, Mattie says Mom is only enjoying her newfound freedom now that there are no more kids in the house.

May flies past. My skin has long since healed where Angelo left his stamp. The seal is drawn in embossed lines that, once the angry red has faded, are lighter than my olive tone. The hair Angelo had shaved grew back, covering the mark. I don't have time for a part-time job in the week, but when my course hours decrease in my second year, I can take up waitressing to save money for plastic surgery, which isn't covered by my medical aid. A skin graft costs an arm and a leg.

I'll have to undergo the procedure on the sly, maybe during a winter holiday when I can make up an excuse of going away for a couple of weeks. I can always say I'm joining a class expedition. Senior students sometimes join film crews or researchers on boats, offering their services for free in exchange for experience. Job opportunities in my field are few and far between, and every little extra you can add to your CV helps.

I become a frequent participator in the campus social life. I even join a fundraiser to save endangered sharks. My dad's company donates a substantial amount, which earns me the title of secretary of our association. When I'm not submitting funding proposals to high-end companies in the city, I'm delivering weekend lectures at tourist information centers about conservation and false shark perceptions.

I'm no stranger to the on and off-campus parties either. I attend every concert and beer festival. I'd be lying if I say I enjoy the smell of stale lager in sweaty tents, the tabletops that are covered in sticky alcohol, the stench of vomit in the trashcans, and trudging through a muddy sports field through a mass of drunken people. The only reason I'm doing it is to prove to my family and Colin that I'm not anti-social. That I'm not a prisoner of Angelo's sinister promises. That he doesn't have an invisible hold on me.

Whenever I consider accepting an invitation for a glass of cheap wine or sharing a pizza, I think about what happens after wine and pizza. A relationship? Sex? I'm not up for either. As I don't have a minute to waste, I always end up declining. It has nothing to do with the memory of the sex I had with Angelo and the fear that no other man will compare. Neither is it related to the fear that Roch is watching me. At least, that's what I like to believe. From time to time, I think I spot Roch's shaved head in a crowd or outside my class, but if he's there, he's good at hiding.

Angelo's phone remains charged and on my person, but he's not sending text or voice messages any longer. He's eerily quiet after I rejected his gift and donated it to charity. Is it the quiet before the storm? Will he show up next year in January? What will he claim this time? I gave him my innocence and my virtue. I gave him my love and my hate. Is there anything left to give?

When we break for the winter holiday in June, Colin goes to a game farm in the north with his family. Instead of going home to Great Brak River, I stay in Cape Town. I promised the association I'd present talks at the aquarium, and I need to brush up on studies in which I've fallen behind.

My parents come over for lunch on a Sunday. They're staying at Mattie and Jared's house for the weekend, but it's Ryan's birthday and Celeste invited the family for an intimate gathering. Her parents, Vida and Oliver, arrive windblown and bone-thin from the shack on the West Coast they moved into a few months ago. The relocation from their comfortable home in Constantia is meant as a spiritual retreat to reconnect with nature.

Oliver proudly tells us how they live on barnacles they pry from the rocks and the kelp the sea gifts them, shaking his head when Celeste offers him a duck a l'orange appetizer. My mom huffs something under her breath and makes herself scarce to play with her grandson.

"I'll take that," I say, grabbing the tray with caviar and olive ciabatta toast from Celeste.

"Thank you." She offers me a grateful smile. "You're a star."

I exit onto the veranda with the tray. My mom lounges on the bench swing with Brad, reading his favorite book about a blue butterfly that leaves his cocoon to go on a trip around the world. Vida and Oliver are sipping lemon juice diluted with water while explaining the benefits of fasting to Ryan, who looks bored. My dad sits at the garden table, nursing a tumbler with amber liquid.

It's only eleven. I hope the early drinking isn't becoming a habit.

Going over, I make my voice bright. "Caviar?"

He looks at the tray and then at my face, seeming miles away. "Oh. No, thank you, darling."

Leaving the tray in a shady spot on the table, I take a seat next to him. "I miss you."

He smiles. "I miss you too. The house is empty."

"Is that why Mom is away so much of late?"

His smile turns knowing. "Stop worrying about your mother and me. We're not planning on leaving each other."

"That's not what I meant. I just want both of you to be happy."

"We are." He winks. "Relationships are dynamic. They have a way of evolving with time and situations." Looking toward the sea, he continues, "It means constantly adapting to accommodate yourself and the person you love. It's just something we have to figure out as we go along. Right now, your mother and my relationship has changed. We went from being alone in the world to having you kids and back to being alone, again. It requires some adjustments. Do you understand what I'm saying?"

"Yes." I lean my head on his shoulder. "Are *you* happy?"

"Very," he says. "I couldn't ask for a more beautiful family."

"Good." I straighten to look at him. "How about work?"

"Work is work." He sips his drink. "You know my philosophy. I don't mix work and my personal life. It's a good motto for happiness, Bella."

"I'll remember that."

We sit in an amiable silence, enjoying the winter sun on our faces, until his phone pings.

"Sorry," he mumbles, fishing the phone from his pocket.

His expression changes when he checks the screen. Taking his handkerchief from his other pocket, he wipes his nape and his brow. I don't miss the fleeting glance he exchanges with Ryan or how my brother's stance tenses. Oliver is still talking up a storm, but Ryan's attention is fixed on my dad. They're isolated in the moment, sharing something that makes the rest of us vanish. I'm not sure why that scares me.

"Dad?" I say, touching his hand.

He puts away the phone and wraps his fingers around mine. "Love you, Bella, darling. Never forget that."

A lump lodges in my throat. I miss spending time with him. I miss falling asleep in his study and waking up to the sound of his pencil scratching over paper and a soft blanket covering me. I miss falling asleep in the back of the car when we return from a late night at friends only to wake when Dad carries me up to bed.

My dad has never been stingy with his compliments or in showing Mattie or me affection. Yet for some reason, this moment feels major. He picked up more weight, and the dark rings under his eyes say he's losing sleep, but he's healthy and still in good shape. He's strong and dependable. He's not going to have a heart attack or a stroke.

I tell myself this as I wrap my fingers around the sea turtle pendant on the gold chain around my neck and huddle closer. "I love you too, Dad."

The piece of jewelry is my most precious materialistic possession. The bracelet Angelo's family gifted me is now lying in the bottom of my drawer. After my seventeenth birthday, I never wore it again.

Celeste exits and claps her hands. "Everyone at the table, please." On her way back into the house, she calls, "Ryan, you're at the head. Everybody else can sit wherever they please."

Knowing what's to come, I don't offer to help. I stay next to my dad while the others take their places. Mom leads Brad by the hand to his highchair, which is placed between Ryan and Celeste. Mom sits down on the other side of Dad. When he takes her hand and cups it on his thigh, my heart warms.

A moment later, Celeste walks out with a giant cake smothered in chocolate frosting. Twenty-eight candles burn on top.

"Happy birthday, Ryan," she says, glowing more brightly than the combined flames of the birthday candles.

Ryan gives her a private smile as she puts the cake in front of him and takes her hand when she straightens next to his chair. His parents start singing happy birthday. Mom rolls her eyes but joins in as everyone takes the cue. Ryan looks mildly embarrassed.

Brad claps his hands and laughs from his belly, which makes everyone chuckle in turn.

"You know what to do," Celeste says, kissing Ryan's cheek.

He turns to Brad. "Ready, champ?"

Brad makes big eyes.

"Wait." Vida takes a phone from her pocket. "I have to film this. Oh, shoot. It's not working. No. It's fine. I've got it. Go ahead."

My mom rolls her eyes again.

Ryan takes a big breath and blows out the candles, much to Brad's delight.

Celeste hands Ryan a knife. "The honor is yours."

"No cake for us," Oliver says. "It'll upset our diet. If it didn't come straight from the sea, I'm afraid we can't touch it."

"Does caviar count?" Mom asks with a bite in her tone.

Oliver looks genuinely puzzled. "That's a very good question. No, I guess it doesn't. The sea didn't offer it, did it?"

"Didn't it offer the fish?" she asks.

Dad kicks her under the table.

Celeste hands out the slices of cake, starting with Brad who digs his little fists into the frosting and makes a huge mess of stuffing his face.

"You'd think we'd eat before dessert is served," Mom says under her breath.

"There's nothing wrong with doing things out of order every now and again," Dad replies.

Mattie cups her stomach. "This baby does not like chocolate."

"Do you need the bathroom?" Jared asks, jumping to his feet.

Mattie waves him away. "I can make it there just fine."

"First trimester," Mom announces with an air of expertise to Vida and Oliver.

"Oh." Vida takes a sip of her lemon juice. "We've all been there."

Mom pins me with a look. "Almost all of us."

"Don't start," I say around a mouthful of cake. "This is delicious, Celeste."

"Thank you." She plonks down in a chair next to Ryan. "Who's hungry for food? Someone other than Ryan has to man the barbecue. He's not allowed to work on his birthday."

"Oh, dear." Mom takes a gulp of wine. "If it's your father, we're eating burnt chicken."

"Chargrilled chicken," he says with a wink.

Everyone laughs.

I sit back and observe the people around the table. They all speak at once. The conversation is chaotic and loud. Mom is throwing jabs and Celeste is ignoring her. Brad has dumped a lump of frosting in Vida's lap. Oliver is trying to clean it with a napkin he dunked in his glass of water, making an even bigger mess. The gathering is disjointed, but it's us. It's not the cocktail party Mom would've liked, but somehow, it seems normal.

Like family.

For once, despite our problems, everyone seems happy.

CHAPTER
TWENTY-NINE

Angelo

The improvement in my father is remarkable. In the sunlight filtering through the big windows in the dining room, his countenance is radiant. His cheeks have a healthy color, and his eyes are clear. They've lost their cloudiness of the last few months. The surgeon did, however, tell him he wasn't operating if my father didn't quit smoking. My father gave up his cigarillos, which makes him cranky.

He regards the fruit salad and yoghurt that Heidi puts in front of him with a downturned mouth. "What happened to having a croissant for breakfast like all normal people do?"

"Spreading an inch of butter on a croissant that already contains a pound in the dough and adding fifty grams of jam on top are what happened to it," I say with a smile. "And not everyone has croissants for breakfast."

"This diet will kill me," he says, glaring at Heidi.

"Quite the opposite." I motion for Heidi to remove the basket of pastries from the table. "You know what the doctor said about your cholesterol."

He scoffs. "I'm going to die anyway. Why can't I at least enjoy the food I like?"

Heidi leaves quickly. She's taken more than enough verbal abuse from my father since the cardiologist changed his diet.

I'm not fond of fruit and yoghurt for breakfast either, but I serve a helping of each in a bowl as a way of showing empathic support. "The older you get, the more you complain like a child." I add with good humor, "It's a wonder Maman still puts up with you."

Stabbing a grape with his fork, he shoots me a look from across the length of the table. "Talking about your mother, how do you think she's going to feel about having her family on the property when she finds out?"

I contemplate that as I dribble honey over my yoghurt. I should've considered it before I made statements and decisions. Like always, I feel that I'm failing my mother, that we're all failing her for not asking her opinion. It's too late now. The ball has already been set rolling.

My tone is blasé, masking the mistake I may have made. "She'll be happy."

"Don't be so sure." He shoves the grape into his mouth and chews. "Why do you think they don't have contact? That bastard was never a father to her. He sure as hell won't be a grandfather to anyone."

"I'm not expecting him to be. He can do whatever he wants, but those kids need to be fed, clothed, and sent to school."

"Those mongrels?" He waves his fork in a general

direction. "They won't hesitate to bite the hand that feeds them."

"Then they can do it with a proper roof over their heads."

He abandons the fork and grabs a spoon. "Does it have to be on our property?"

"On the edge of our property. You don't have to see them if you don't want to. None of us has to."

Digging the spoon into his bowl, he stirs the content. "You had to take up the reins early. Managing the company and taking responsibility for everyone are tough." He brings a spoonful of fruit and yoghurt to his mouth. Pulling up his nose at the runny, low-fat yoghurt coating dices of apple and kiwi, he sighs and drops the spoon back in his bowl. "You're doing a good job. I admire you for that. Not everyone can pull that off at your age. Just remember, I'm not dead yet. You should've consulted me."

"You're right." I add muesli to my bowl. I won't admit it to my father, but I'd choose a croissant ten times over the watery yoghurt. "I made an impulsive decision on the spur of the moment."

He pats the space next to his place setting, a habitual reaction in groping a packet of cigarillos that's no longer there. Instead, he takes his mug of herbal tea. "I wish you hadn't gone there to start with."

I get up and fetch orange juice on the buffet table to fill his glass because the green mint tea will be criticized next. My mother is following the doctor's orders to the tee, cutting down on caffeine too.

"I was curious," I say, omitting the part about taking my mother to the village and witnessing the inhabitants' disrespect. If he finds out, the village will be a bloodbath by noon.

He mumbles a thank you but ignores the juice I place at his elbow.

"Any news from Edwards?" he asks.

"Not yet."

I pour juice for myself and walk to the windows. The garden was transformed in preparation for the wedding. A space was cleared on the front lawn for the gazebo. Plants were removed from their beds in the soil and temporarily transplanted into pots. A wrought-iron pergola was constructed at the farthest point to benefit from the view of the sea. Pots with creeper roses were placed at the pillars and the roses twisted over the frame of the structure. In a month's time, the blooms and leaves will form a canopy, providing not only shade but also the roof that the law requires for a bride and groom to say their vows.

"He won't comply," my father says. "He'll do nothing to make anything easy for you. You saw his reaction, saw for yourself how he treated us. He despises our name."

My temper flares at the memory. I turn to my father. "It doesn't matter. I'll be flying to South Africa to fetch Sabella myself."

He studies me with a sly expression. "Why haven't you told her about the deal or our business? If she's going to be your wife, she needs to know."

For her to *despise* me more than she already does? I've been living with judgment and the curse of a bad name my whole life. I'm used to people's scorn. What difference does hers make? The problem is that I got used to her kindness, love, and admiration. I always knew I was going to destroy those sentiments—*had* to destroy them if I were to take my promised cut of the business and make her mine—but I never could've guessed how much I'd like all that sweetness she lavished on me.

"I'll tell her when the time is right," I say.

"You better be sure you can trust her. If she runs to the media or the authorities—"

"I'll handle her."

"I damn well hope so." He catches my gaze with a dark look. "Because you know what you'll have to do if she becomes a threat to our family."

Kill her. I don't think so. I'd rather chain her up in the basement.

"And that will be a shame," my father continues. "Seeing that this wedding is costing a damn fortune."

My smile is grim. "It's not like we can't afford it."

He pushes the bowl away. "Having plenty doesn't mean you have to waste it."

"Don't worry." Fuck, I need a cup of coffee. "I'll make sure it's not wasted."

"Oh, Ang," Adeline exclaims, running into the room and slamming her palms over her mouth. "I just saw it." Her eyes sparkle. "The wedding dress. Oh my God. It's amazing. She's going to look so beautiful."

My mother follows on my sister's heels, wearing an off-white designer suit with black stitching on the collar and a thin black belt. Paired with a black patent leather handbag and shoes, she looks classy and wealthy, exactly the way my father likes her to dress.

"Don't give your brother any descriptions," my mother says with alarm. "He's not allowed to know anything about the dress before the big day." She frowns as she addresses me. "I wish you'd let Sabella try the dress on before. What if she doesn't like it?"

"Maman." Adeline clasps her hands together. "It's perfect. There's nothing not to like."

My mother adjusts her silk scarf. "All women have different tastes, not to mention that the dress may not fit properly."

"It'll be fine," I say. "She'll be here at least a couple of days before the wedding. If alterations are necessary, there'll be time."

"Well," my mother says, pushing the handle of the handbag over her forearm. "The dressmaker will be on standby just in case. He offered to come for the wedding and help her dress."

That last bit catches my attention. "He?"

"Don't worry." My mother pats my arm. "It's his job. It's like a doctor seeing patients."

"No." My tone leaves no room for argument. "No man will help my bride get dressed."

Adeline laughs. "You're so jealous, Ang, and you're not even married yet."

I clench my jaw. "Married or not, it makes no difference."

"We have bigger problems than Angelo's jealousy." Addressing me, my mother continues, "I have an appointment with the baker in Bastia to sample the cake, and it looks like my car has a flat tire. I'm already late as it is."

I leave my glass on the table. "I'll have a look."

"Thank you," she says, blowing out a sigh.

My father pushes to his feet. "Couldn't he bring the cake here?"

"There are so many options," my mother says, looking flustered. "It's easier to do it in the shop. There's frosting to consider, and colors, and decorations—"

"You know what?" Adeline hooks her arm through my mother's. "Why don't I come with you? It'll be fun, no?"

"But..." My mother works her lip between her teeth. "What about your classes?"

"I can miss my classes for one day. We're closing for the holiday next week anyway."

"No," I say. "Eating cake is not a valid reason for missing your course."

"Guess what, brother?" Adeline bats her eyelashes. "The three seconds difference in our age doesn't make you my boss."

"The three-second argument is getting old, sister."

"Please, Papa?" She pouts. "I haven't been involved in any of the wedding arrangements because I always have class."

My father looks at my mother.

My mother gives him a soft smile. "A wedding is a once-in-a-lifetime event. Men may not think much of it, but it's one of the most important days in a woman's life."

My father swallows. For a second, guilt flashes across his face, but he quickly hides it with a curt reply. "Fine. Go then. But you will catch up with the work you'll be missing."

"Thank you, Papa." Adeline scoots over and kisses his cheek. "My grades are always good. Are they not? You don't have to worry."

If only my bride will be so excited about our wedding day. One thing is for sure. It won't be the happiest day of her life. Yet I have a suspicion it wasn't the best day of my mother's life either, and look how she and my father turned out. They're making it work. They respect and care for each other. My mother loves my father in her own way. As for him, he'll never say it, but he can't live without her.

"I better have a look at that tire then," I say, leading the way outside. "Why didn't Cusso pick up that the car has a flat tire?"

"I left the car in front of the house," my mother says, following on my heels. "I came home late from shopping yesterday, and I knew I needed to leave early today." She adds quickly, "I didn't ask him to park my car in the garage."

She's always covering for the staff, making sure they don't get into trouble for not doing their jobs. Cusso should've parked her car in the garage without being told to do so. That's what we pay him for. But my mother has a soft spot for the ex-mechanic who was retrenched from his previous job and who needs the money to feed his six kids.

Adeline exits with my father leaning on her arm for support.

"I would've offered to take my scooter," my sister says with humor, "but I guess you're not up for a ride on the back, Maman. Anyway, you're not exactly dressed for it."

"Another reason why you should drive a car and not a toy on wheels," my father says.

"Come on." Adeline nudges my father. "My scooter is vintage. It has style." She grins. "Plus, it's pink."

"We can always buy you a pink car if that's the tipping point of your purchase decision," I say.

My father huffs. "Over my dead body."

"Hey." Adeline props a hand on her hip. "At least my favorite color isn't black like the rest of my family's, judging by their cars. I can't help it if you're all boring." She tests my father's balance before heading for the front door. "Give me a minute to grab my bag. I'll be right back."

Cusso has already brought my father's car to the front of the house. He pauses in polishing it and takes off his cap when we approach.

The front left tire of my mother's car is flat. I crouch down to inspect the wheel. The problem is a thorn lodged in the rim. The gardeners trimmed the date palm trees because my mother wants to decorate the trunks with fairy lights for the wedding. They removed the branches and raked the driveway, but my mother must've been unlucky enough to drive over one of the thorny parts that was left behind.

"Slow puncture," I say, straightening. "Cusso, get that fixed as soon as possible."

"Yes, sir," he says, keeping his head bowed.

"Next time, make sure you notice it before my mother does," I add.

He twists the cap in his hands. "Yes, sir."

My mother trains a panicked look on me. "I can't cancel the appointment. The baker is the best in the country. He's booked up for months."

"He'll move the appointment to whenever I tell him to," my father says in a heated voice.

"No, Santino." My mother replies, startled. "Don't work yourself up over this. It's not good for your heart. Besides, we don't want to arrange the wedding like that. No threats or violence. It's supposed to be a day of love."

"Ah, hell," he says with a grumble, taking his key from his pocket. "Take my car."

Relief floods her expression. "Didn't you say you were going to meet your brothers at the club?"

Adeline returns with a tote bag slung over her shoulder. The man who's on bodyguard duty today approaches from the direction of the barracks. He'll follow the women in his own car. My father always gives my mother and sister the illusion of privacy. Some will call that illusion of privacy the illusion of freedom.

"I'll drive Papa there," I say. "I haven't seen Uncle Enzo and Nico for a while. It'll be a good opportunity to catch up on some business before the wedding."

"That's a good idea," my mother says, already pressing the remote to unlock the doors. "Especially as you'll be away on honeymoon after the wedding."

I raise a brow. "Who said anything about a honeymoon?"

"Angelo Russo." My mother pulls herself to her full height. "You will take your wife on a proper honeymoon to a romantic location. It's the least you can do."

Getting into the car, she slams the door on that statement. Adeline winks as she hops into the passenger side, clearly enjoying how our mother put me back in my place.

My sister winds down the window, sticks out her arm, and waves as my mother pulls off.

"Look at them," my father says, shaking his head. "Women. You'd swear they're going to a funfair."

I don't miss the note of pride in his voice.

Staring after the car, he muses, "Arranging this wedding made your mother more certain of herself. Assertive almost."

"It's good for her," I agree, watching the car as my mother turns at the gates and follows the road that snakes along the cliff. "Maybe we should give her a job in the business, something that'll keep her busy and that she'll enjoy." Something that'll get her out of the goddamn isolation of the kitchen.

The bodyguard nods in greeting as he drives past us.

"A job?" my father asks. "Like what?"

I shrug. "Event organizer. She can make travel arrangements and plan dinner parties. She seems to be enjoying the running of the wedding, and she's good at it."

He makes a non-committal sound.

The more I think about it, the more I know it's a good idea. My mother spends some time working at charities, but that only occupies her for a few hours every month.

I follow the path of the car with my gaze as I ponder the possibility that part of my mother's low self-esteem may come from not having a purpose other than taking care of us, not that taking care of a family isn't important. Part of her insecurity comes from the fact that she feels inferior because she's uneducated. Another part stems from her roots. The wedding gave her a goal and a challenge. It makes her feel needed and useful.

The sun rays bounce off the shiny bodywork of the Mercedes sports model, reflecting back to me like from a mirror and temporarily blinding me. I squint. The sparkling turquoise sea at the bottom of the cliff makes a pretty contrast with the azure blue of the sky. The summer heat is already stifling. A trickle of sweat runs down my back.

The car is moving too fast, speeding toward the bend. My father says something and turns toward the house. My mother is a good driver. She should be braking.

But she doesn't.

I take it all in like an out-of-body experience—the warm weather, the glorious view, and the racing car. It feels like a dream. Unreal.

The tires lose traction on the tar. The car skids toward the hairpin turn. My mother overcorrects, pulling too sharply to the left.

Someone says, "No." Me.

The car hits the barrier and goes into a spin. The back wheels go over the cliff first. The car dives, flips, and falls. It falls and falls while horror rips through my chest and I grope through the air as if I can stop it. And then it slams onto the rocks on its roof with the sickening thud of crushing metal.

CHAPTER THIRTY

Angelo

I have no recollection of how I got there. All I know is that I'm half-falling, half-sliding down the bottom of the cliff and clawing my way over rocks to the car wreck. The voice screaming my mother's and sister's names belongs to a mad man, a wild person, not to me.

Sirens sound somewhere above me. I have no idea who called an ambulance. My only notion is getting them out of there.

I reach the driver's side first.

"Maman!"

I yank on the door. It's smashed in, the metal bent. The window exploded. The airbag too. It's already deflated. My mother hangs upside down, strapped in by her safety belt. Her hair falls down like a neat curtain, hiding her face. It's still smooth and brushed out from how she styled it this morning. Not disheveled and unkept. Not full of blood.

"Maman. I've got you." I reach inside and feel for the clasp of her belt next to the door. "You're going to be all right. Hold on, Adeline. I'm coming. Hold on."

I brace my mother with an arm as I free the clip. Her weight sags against me, her mere forty-five kilos weighing me down.

She could've injured her neck or her spine. The logical human in me knows I should wait for the paramedics, but the being inside me that's ruled by instinct only knows how to break her fall to not hit her head on the roof. It only knows how to drag her, shoulders first, through the narrow space of the condensed window.

My father's car is sturdy. It has a strong framework. It was made to withstand any impact. It could've been worse. The car hasn't been flattened.

It's not that bad.

It's not that bad.

Her pelvis gets stuck. Someone grips my biceps and pulls me away. I'm swinging my arms, letting my fists go feral. I land a sucker punch on a man's jaw.

More hands hold me back as others spread my mother out on the rocks. She's whole and clean except for the trickle of blood running from a cut on her forehead, but I don't need the medic to tell me she's broken. I see it in her eyes, the brown eyes I inherited, in how the light has gone out of them.

Christ.

She's not even forty.

"Adeline."

I shove off the people holding me, faking calm.

It works. They let me go.

I climb over the rocks. Fall. Carry on.

But I already feel it, the hollowness under my breastbone, as if a part of me has been torn out.

"Adeline."

She's covered with a space blanket that hides her face.

A man shakes his head when I grab the corner, but I push him off too.

I have to see.

My sister is blood and devastation, her beautiful features crushed into the hole where her face used to be, pulped by the rock that penetrated the windshield on the passenger side.

Death burns cold in me, but life burns hotter.

A part of me dies.

Another part wakens.

The devil born from the flames inside me is nothing compared to the monster who rises from the cold ashes.

Whoever did this will pay.

They're about to suffer the wrath of hell.

~ TO BE CONTINUED ~

ALSO BY CHARMAINE PAULS

White Nights Duet

(Contemporary Russian Billionaire Romance)

White Nights

Midnight Days

The Loan Shark Duet

(Dark Mafia Romance)

Dubious

Consent

The Age Between Us Duet

(Reverse Age Gap Stalker Romance)

Old Enough

Young Enough

Standalone Novels

(Enemies-to-Lovers Dark Romance)

Darker Than Love

(Second Chance Cheating Romance)

Catch Me Twice

Krinar World Novels

(Futuristic Romance)

The Krinar Experiment

The Krinar's Informant

---

7 Forbidden Arts Series

(Fated Mates Paranormal Romance)

Pyromancist (Fire)

Aeromancist, The Beginning (Prequel)

Aeromancist (Air)

Hydromancist (Water)

Geomancist (Earth)

Necromancist (Spirit)

Scapulimancist (Animal)

Chiromancist (Time)

Man (The Boss)

ABOUT THE AUTHOR

Charmaine loves to write dark and edgy romance that will melt both your e-reader and your heart. She's a mom of two teenagers, an adorable dog, and a dominant cat. Her country of birth is South Africa where many of her stories play off. Her French husband kidnapped her to the south of France where she currently lives with her family. When she's not writing, you'll find her in the kitchen baking cakes or in the gym lifting weights (because ... all those cakes!).

Join Charmaine's mailing list
https://charmainepauls.com/subscribe/

Join Charmaine's readers' group on Facebook
http://bit.ly/CPaulsFBGroup

Read more about Charmaine's novels and short stories on
https://charmainepauls.com

Connect with Charmaine

Facebook
http://bit.ly/Charmaine-Pauls-Facebook

Amazon
http://bit.ly/Charmaine-Pauls-Amazon

Goodreads
http://bit.ly/Charmaine-Pauls-Goodreads

Twitter
https://twitter.com/CharmainePauls

Instagram
https://instagram.com/charmainepaulsbooks

BookBub
http://bit.ly/CPaulsBB

TikTok
https://www.tiktok.com/@charmainepauls

www.ingramcontent.com/pod-product-compliance
Lightning Source LLC
LaVergne TN
LVHW031322190726
843493LV00013B/3015